# Don't Shoot.
# We come in peace.

# Don't Shoot.
# We come in peace.

Dennis Ganahl

Grey Matter, LLC
St. Louis, Missouri

## Other books written by Dennis Ganahl

Two-part American coming-of-age adventure series

*Heroes & Hooligans*
*Growing Up in the City of Saints*, 2017

*Scouts & Scalawags*
*Growing Up in the City of Saints*, 2020

ISBN: 979-8-9864705-0-4 Paperback
ISBN: 979-8-9864705-1-1 Ebook

References to historical events, real people, or real places are used fictitiously. Names, characters, and places are products of the author's imagination and storytelling.

Cover artwork illustrator Gary Varvel
Interior graphic designer Peggy Nehmen
First Edition printing, 2022
Published by Grey Matter, LLC
St. Louis, MO

# Contents

# Dedication

I dedicate this book to all hillbillies—past, present and future. My childhood memories of hillbillies are as lovable people and characters. My dear grandmother, Ruth Marie Carmichael-Strub, and our Carmichael clan in Indiana were the first Hoosiers I ever met. Do you remember the hillbilly holding a moonshine jug on the green Mountain Dew soda bottle saying, "It'll tickle yore innards!"?

Sundays we'd lay on the living room floor reading *Snuffy Smith* and *L'il Abner's* color comic strips wondering how to get a job testing mattresses or what Kickapoo joy juice tasted like. Rainy Sunday afternoons, we'd watch black and white *Ma and Pa Kettle* movies. Our family rarely missed the *Beverly Hillbillies*. Ellie Mae, Donna Douglas, was hot and so were the guitar and banjo licks on *Hee Haw* in Kornfield, Kounty. Hillbilly men were typically cast as poor, shiftless, slow-talkers, who were oddly self-reliant and distrustful of the government. The women did all of the work and had all of the brains. After college, I started my newspaper publishing career in the Missouri Ozarks—hillbilly country. Most of the stereotypes were wrong.

City folk use the word "hillbilly" as a perennial pejorative term for their dumb country cousin. I don't. I admire hillbillies. They're the heroes of my book. They're the only group of people you can mistreat in commercials and TV shows without getting fired. Insult any other group or call them a name and you're canceled and sued. Elitists see hillbillies as the unwashed masses, the ignorant lower class. Hillbillies see city folk as conceited, needy and unable to take care of themselves. I agree. The country western industry and comedians like Jeff Foxworthy, Larry the Cable Guy and the *Duck Dynasty* family understand how underappreciated hillbillies are. Hillbillies don't give a tinker's damn what people think of them.

Hillbillies think elitists, who are endlessly lecturing them on global warming and every other socio-nonsense, are dead weight. When I lived with Ozark hillbillies, they taught me to listen more, talk less, and focus on family and faith. They had common sense. Is it even possible for elitists to talk less, let alone scream quieter? If only they'd laugh.

I also dedicate this book to one of my favorite journalism professors, Tom Ladwig. Tom taught me not to take myself too seriously. He didn't abide elitists. His book "Grandpa Had a Word for It," is sold on Amazon. It was my source for many of the hillbilly sayings I use in this book.

Finally, I dedicate this book to my best fans, my dear wife, editor and partner, Gina Ganahl, PhD and my sons,

Denny and Kevin. My mother, Doris Irene Strub-Ganahl taught me to laugh at it all. It was a lot more fun than crying.

I hope my story makes you laugh, maybe even at yourself.

Grateful for my readers,
—Dennis

# Acknowledgments

I want to acknowledge and directly thank the people who help me publish my books and are always there for me. Ryan Morris is back for his third encore. Ryan is a very patient and talented graphic artist. David Peters, author, artist, and scholar is always generous with his ideas and support.

I want to also introduce a new member into my publishing family, Gary Varvel. Gary is a nationally-prominent, award-winning political cartoonist. I was blessed to get him to design and draw the covers for this book. Please check out Gary's website and page in the back of this book. Peggy Nehmen is a very patient collaborator and gifted book designer.

I also want to thank my dear friends Mark Lang and Larry Conrads for their encouragement and inspiration while writing this book.

Also, a big thank you to my Launch Team. They're the engine that is helps me promote my books.

# Listen to my *Moonshine* playlist while you read this book.

Everyone uses their favorite songs to create personal music soundtracks throughout their lives. I create Spotify music stations while I write my books to put me in the mood of the setting and my characters. Playlists for all of my books are available under Dennis Ganahl on Spotify.

My *Moonshine* playlist was selected to imitate the best country western and bluegrass music I could identify. I wanted to listen to true classics from the best of the best. My goal was to give a wide sampling of the various music being played over the past 70 years or so. Afterall, hillbillies have been around a long time.

I've also thrown in a few surprise songs from artists and groups mentioned in the book.

# Author's notes about how hillbillies speak

We all talk funny, but no one thinks 'they' speak or sound funny. It's always the other person from somewhere else that sounds funny. We identify where people grew up simply by listening to how they speak and sound. We've all made fun of the nasally sounds from people who live in 'New Yark.' They talk way too fast to be understood. Hillbillies talk nice and slow in case you don't hear so good. Hillbillies have been accused of taking naps in the middle of their sentences, and love to end their sentences with 'Don'chya know,' which is a statement, not a question.

I wrote hillbilly dialog in stereotypical hillbilly diction during my first draft. Since it was too mind-numbing to write and read, I changed it back to everyday English, which nobody speaks, but we all read. Hillbillies don't pronounce the letter 'g' at the end of a word. They say 'sumptin,' and 'walkin.' A hillbilly says, "My dogs are barkin," for my feet hurt, or, "It's spittin' distance," for it's close enough to spit.

Sometimes, hillbillies throw away the whole darn 'ing' like when they say 'gonna.' It sounds more purty.

A hillbilly's tongue can't pronounce the letter 'O' unless someone drops something heavy on their toe. Otherwise, their mouth can't be shaped like an O. They don't say forty. They say, 'farty,' and 'fart' for fort, which can be confusing depending on what you had for dinner. It's also a challenge when the road forks. A confused hillbilly will spend half an hour lookin' for a fark 'cause it's time for vittles.

The letter 'R' is particularly nettlesome to hillbillies. Rs have their own minds. They only like being where they want to be. For example, hillbillies don't wash their clothes or bodies. Hillbillies 'warsh,' and they wouldn't give a 'quater fer a politishun in Warshinton.'

When a hillbilly, ridge-runner, cracker, Hoosier, MoJack, redneck, or hick ain't got no money, 'they're piss po', an y'er whistlin' Dixie if you'n think they're gonna pay.'

Since it was so blasted complicated writing dialog the way hillbillies speak, I decided to use their colorful language and phrases throughout my book instead. When you butcher the whole prime hog, you can use it all but the grunt and the squeal. Of course, that doesn't hold true when you butcher your character's dialog.

## CHAPTER 1
# Trucker and the U.F.O.

It was an outer-worldly celestial phenomenon. Mac, the elected sheriff of Lincoln County and Iraq war veteran, was under assault. At first blink, he thought it was the moonlight, but the stark white light kept getting brighter until it was as bright as an explosion. Mac was working like a miner to keep his monster-truck Bronco, named Buster, from flipping. Whenever Mac sped up, the bright light sped up. If he turned left or right, the light followed. He couldn't shake it. Mac turned off Buster's headlights and raced off on a network of winding gravel and dirt logging roads only ridge-runners knew. He was driving too fast, but he was able to keep Buster on the road. He prayed he wouldn't hit any wildlife. After driving miles in darkness, Mac thought he'd lost the UFO. He hadn't. It was sitting at the upcoming intersection of two gravel roads.

He veered sharply off the narrow road into Shawnee Creek. Mac's Bloodhound, Elvis, flipped off the back seat onto the floor and thought, 'What the heck are you doing? Settle down, son.' He moaned and growled to show his displeasure.

"Sorry, ol' buddy," blurted Mac as he kept both hands on the steering wheel. "I didn't realize the creek was so deep. Damn." The Bronco stalled, and Mac briefly wondered if the UFO had killed its engine. It started right back up and was soon hurling rooster comb sprays of water from its oversized tires churning the creek's water. The shimmering light reflecting in the mist made it hard to see much less steer. Mac was as nervous as a cat in a room full of rocking chairs. He didn't want to smash Buster into a boulder or one of the giant Sycamores standing sentinel along the banks.

Mac's gushing adrenaline from the chase brought back memories of driving armored Humvees in Afghanistan and Iraq while avoiding land mines and rocket launchers. He prayed the UFO couldn't follow him under the canopy of gigantic trees. The UFO's light was so penetratingly bright, the creek's trees didn't hide them. Mac was between a rock and a hard place, so he hurdled the creek's bank and raced across Roy Haskell's neighboring pasture, throwing dirt clods in every direction. The UFO persisted. Its light lit up the field like high noon making it easier for Mac to avoid the spooked cows whose eyes were round as dinner plates. The cows were bouncing off of each like pinballs.

Usually, not much kept Elvis awake, but he was all shook and one step ahead of a fit when he started howling like a fox was raiding the chicken coop.

"Shut the hell up, Elvis. I'm trying to concentrate. We need to haul ass," said Mac as he steered the Bronco towards the wooded hillside.

Elvis didn't shut up. 'Why are you telling me to shut up? Don't you know a dog draws its emotions from its owner? You need to settle down, soldier boy, if you want me to relax,' thought Elvis.

The UFO anticipated Mac's move and cut him off like a quarter horse. It stopped abruptly hovering about 20 feet off the ground blocking the Bronco's path. Mac felt like it was staring him down. Testing his mettle. Then quicker than a pecker's head, the UFO launched straight up like a rocket. It was gone taking the bright light with it. Mac and Elvis sighed in relief.

"I'll be gone to cornbread hell. What was that, Elvis? A UFO?" Elvis groaned and tried to settle down as they drove home. Elvis knew Mac rarely got upset. So, when he saw his best friend get riled up, it made him nervous.

'UFO?' thought Elvis, 'What the heck's a UFO?'

Rob 'Mac' MacGregor wasn't given to drama, and he wasn't born to be a house cat. He was an outdoorsman and self-reliant. Mac grew up working on the family farm helping his dad run their cow-calf operation. He was still a rancher today. His mom and dad lived on the other side of the farm in a home Mac helped build. His dad taught Mac what it meant to be a man. Mac had the confidence, skills, tools, and knowledge to build or fix anything around the farm. Growing up, he hunted and camped all over the hills and valleys with his dad and his friends. At 18 years of age, Mac joined the Navy. He became a member of SEAL Team Six and was asked to serve in Operation Neptune Spear. Locally and nationally, he was considered a hero when his team killed Osama bin Laden in Pakistan. After he mustered out of the Navy, Mac took over the family farm, Ironwood.

Mac was a plain-speaking guy you couldn't help but notice. He stood six-foot-four and looked like Conan, his favorite comic book character. He drove nails into lumber using the same two-pound blacksmith hammer he used to shoe horses. His favorite horse was a buckskin mare. He called her Honey. Curiously, his confidence with horses, cattle, and other animals didn't transfer to women. He wasn't a braggart or full of himself. He was a much-sought bashful bachelor and a little awkward around women. Mac rarely dated and preferred the quiet company of animals, who were treated like pets.

If being Sheriff didn't prove his courage, Mac also taught 'Shop' to smart-alecky high school kids who usually had their heads in their cell phones, and their minds on shooter video games. A lot of students didn't even hunt or fish anymore. He taught students discipline by teaching them how to rebuild and 'soup-up' gas-combustion engines, straighten frames, re-wire electric harnesses, weld all kinds of metals, and spray paint unique finishes on hot rods. Mac was so ruggedly handsome female cheerleaders took his class to make him blush at their intimate innuendos and hang out with the boys.

Mac was churning his memory to recall the night's events as he drove home. It was Friday night. Everyone had stayed late working on the once-rusty 1965 Pontiac GTO Mac found in a farmer's barn. His students had been giddy. They were getting ready for graduation, and it was hard keeping them on task.

After the kids left, he locked up the garage and loaded up Elvis to drive home. That's when Mac noticed the bright white light. He shuddered after replaying the startling events and parked Buster in the barn. They jumped out of Buster and headed to the house. Mac locked the front door, which he rarely did, knowing it wouldn't stop an alien.

He realized he'd forgotten to eat dinner as he dropped off to sleep, thinking about the types of lures he should use in the morning. His last thoughts were, 'Did it happen? Did I really see a UFO?' He and Elvis slept restlessly.

## CHAPTER 2
# Ring of Fire

Sunrise was glorious. The Lake wasn't crowded with tourists fishing. Only hillbillies, known as 'locals,' knew which coves to fish. Hillbillies had been living in the hills and hollers long before there was even a Lake. Many of the original hillbilly towns and farms were drowned when the government confiscated their land to build the Lake to generate electricity for large corporations and cities.

As the sun slowly rose over the hardwood forest, Mac caught five Largemouth Bass, but only kept two. The two smaller ones and the large pregnant female were released back into the Lake. Mac was smiling, and thinking about his catch, as he and Elvis strolled from the dock into Sizzerbill's Bar & Grill. The good ol' boys' fishing boats were already docked. Sizzerbill's was the locals' and wannabes' favorite hangout at the Lake. They went to drink coffee, eat home-made pie, listen to gossip and tell their best stories. Happily,

Mac noticed Abner's bass boat. Abner was Faith's dad, and Mac hoped Faith had gone fishing with him today.

"Morning, boys," said Mac as the rusty spring slammed the screen door behind him, almost catching Elvis's tail. Johnny Cash's deep baritone voice was singing 'Ring of Fire' on the local radio station, KORN.

Mac's cobalt eyes immediately found Faith sitting at her dad's table. She was a few years younger and had a peaches-and-cream complexion to complement her soft brown eyes and curly, raven-colored hair. Faith was as pretty as a spotted pup in the sunshine, and she had a body that made everyone take a second look. Her overprotective dad made her wear his camouflage hunting jacket in public whenever she went fishing with him. He was exhausted by all of the guys ogling his only child. Faith was his pride and joy. Abner had taught her how to out-wrestle, out-shoot, and out-run most of the boys, and later the men, she dated. Her challenge was going on a date without her dad clandestinely following them with his double-barrel 12-gauge shotgun loaded with salt. Faith's mother, Hope, would've never stood for it. Tragically, Hope passed and went to heaven during Faith's birth.

Abner suggested, read that as insisted, Faith only teach kindergarteners because boys and men alike became spell-bound when she walked into a classroom or anywhere else for that matter. All the stores wanted Faith to model their fashions, but Abner didn't want everybody gawping at her on TV or the Internet. He insisted she only model shoes because even her feet were attractive and a perfect size 5. She relented on the hunting jacket, but today she was wearing lipstick red stiletto heels with it. On Faith, nothing looked out of place even in Sizzerbill's. She never noticed all of the attention, and it never affected her honey-sweet disposition.

Faith sweetly smiled at Mac while the men said, "Morning, Sheriff," and returned to their coffee and fish stories about the ones that got away.

Seeing Faith's beguiling smile, Mac said, "Good morning, Faith," as he tipped his sheriff's camouflage cap and blushed.

"Hello, Mac! It's great to see you," she said in an excited tone that sounded almost like a song while fluttering her eyelashes.

Elvis grated, padded over, and curled up on the floor next to Mac's chair. 'Look, sister,' groaned Elvis, 'Go find your own best friend. Mac's mine. Shoo fly.'

"What can I get you, Hero?" asked Harry Cobb, the proud proprietor of Sizzerbill's, as he poured a steaming mug of black coffee. Harry had moved to the Lake when he returned from Viet Nam. He had been a Marine helicopter pilot. He found the Lake in 1973 when he was looking for a warmer place to fish than Saint Ignace, Michigan. He wasn't considered a 'local,' but he was considered a skinflint. He was the kind of guy who'd sell you a dozen eggs and borrow one back for breakfast. He was amiable and always had a ready laugh. Although his hair was grey and thinning, he could still fit into his Marine uniform. His wife, Dottie, was born a Hatfield and had a heart as big as the outdoors. The locals thought she had taken pity on Harry when she married him. Dottie, like Abner, was a sixth-generation hillbilly and proud of it.

"Semper Fi, Harry, but please don't call me hero anymore."

"Hell, you got the bad guy, Hero. Of course, I will respect you," said Harry as he stood at attention and saluted.

Mac sighed as he picked up the white ceramic mug of black coffee and blew across the top. The coffee was so robust you could smell it on the Lake or in the parking lot. Sizzerbill's didn't waste time making lattes and mochas nobody would drink. You could stand in a barrel of any other place's coffee and still see your toes. Not at Sizzerbill's. Harry and Dottie served fox-hunting coffee.

"Here you are, Elvis," cooed Dottie as she set down a bowl of coffee with a meaty soup bone next to Elvis' extra-large head.

Grateful, Elvis looked up at her through his saggy eyes, blinked his thanks, and thought, 'If you weren't with Harry, we'd be running the fields together, sweetie.' Then Dottie rubbed his head and scratched his floppy ears while he took the bone into his saggy jowls and cracked it in half with one bite.

"Why'd you name your puppy Elvis?" asked Faith, trying to start a conversation.

"Well, Faith, Elvis ain't nothing but a hound dog. What else would I name him?" said Mac trying to make a joke as his longing eyes met hers.

Abner irritably noticed Faith snicker at Mac's dumb joke. "Well, there are lots of better names for a dog besides one from a broken-down, dead singer," said Abner crossly giving Mac the stink eye. Mac politely smiled, and Elvis rudely skreiched as he slurped his coffee and chewed his bone.

'At least I'm not named after a cartoon character, Li'l Abner. Touché,' thought Elvis. 'Tell the truth, Mac. It's because I'm the king. If you're going to tell a dumb joke, tell the one about the big-mouthed bass,' thought Elvis as he taunted Abner by baring his teeth.

"I've always wondered why you named this place Sizzerbill's, Harry?" asked Mac, trying to shift everyone's attention. "What the heck is a Sizzerbill?"

"Well, have you ever heard of a jack-a-lope?" asked Harry.

"Nope. Not before coming in here."

"Neither had I, but there's one hanging over there on the wall. Obie shot it about 20 years ago somewhere in Montana. He claims they're fiddly to hunt."

"Oh, come on, Harry, that's a prank. There's no such thing as a jack-a-lope," laughed Mac. "Obie Blevens is lovable, but he's a practical joker. He wouldn't know the truth if it hit him in the face with a pie and sat on his head. There's no such thing as a jack-a-lope."

"You're a skeptic, Hero," said Harry acting mock-serious. "Some people don't believe in Bigfoot either, but I've got its footprint right in front of Sizzerbill's door. Bigfoot's real, and so is the jack-a-lope," said Harry nodding toward Faith with a wink. "I'm surprised you don't know what a Sizzerbill is. You've been hunting and fishing your whole life."

"I've never heard of a Sizzerbill or seen one hanging on your wall," smiled Mac pointing around the room.

"Sizzerbills live north along the US-Canadian border. They like it real cold, so you only see them in the northern states and Canada. They're part bird, part animal, and the size of an Atlantic Puffin. They fly like birds and swim like penguins, so they're almost impossible to trap or hunt. And boy, they're as wily as a coyote. I've only glimpsed one right after it cut my fishing line when I was hauling in a huge Lake Sturgeon on Lake Michigan. They have a twisted bill they use like scissors to bite through your fishing line, which leaves you with an empty net. They're a true aggravation to fishermen."

Everyone in Sizzerbill's, especially Fleagle, nodded their heads in unison to Harry's story. They'd heard it a million times and believed it to be true, even though they'd never seen a Sizzerbill.

Sizzerbill's had become the hot spot at the Lake when an extra-extra-large Bigfoot footprint was found near the front entrance in the early '80s. The mammoth footprint made Harry a national celebrity, and Sizzerbill's was a major tourist attraction for years. Truth be told, Harry missed all of the media and attention. His photo had even been on the cover of *People* magazine. There were still faded gigantic life-size Bigfoot silhouette signs on posts planted along the highway and shoreline. The signs pointed the direction to

Sizzerbill's, but tourists had lost interest. Bigfoot's magic was gone. Nobody had claimed to see a Bigfoot at the Lake in almost thirty years.

Since then, the Lake had grown from a quaint family-fishing destination to a four-star tourism Shangri-La. Some called it the 'Redneck Riviera.' There was even a *Margaritaville Resort*. It was the plushest hotel at the Lake with a continuous reunion for aging Parrotheads. Today's tourists were more interested in cruising the Lake in big-ass boats rather than bass boats.

They preferred ogling and taking photos of itty-bitty bikinis or, better yet, no bikinis at Party Cove to taking a picture of a concrete cast of a Bigfoot footprint. Tourists fancied glitzy boat docks with loud rock music and attractive bikini-clad bar wenches chasing drinks and filling their gas tanks. Dottie didn't blame them. She and Harry were getting older, and although she was sweeter than a honeycomb, she wouldn't be caught dead wearing a bikini. Dottie preferred the locals who ate and drank at Sizzerbill's. Sizzerbill's fans listened to bluegrass and country and western music rather than rap or heavy metal.

"You look exhausted, sweetie. Aren't you sleeping well? You must have something, or somebody, on your mind, Mac," said Dottie nodding knowingly toward Faith while Abner and Elvis groaned.

"I didn't sleep well last night. That's for sure," said Mac.

"Why not?" said a smiling Dottie as she gently nudged him to learn more.

"I'm not sure I want to talk about it, Dottie," said Mac as he shook his head back and forth and leaned away from her in his creaking wooden chair. Everybody in the place went quiet. You could've heard a mouse fart. Like a bushel basket of strawberries, gossip was an actual currency at the Lake. Dottie collected more gossip than anybody, but she didn't spread it. She knew how to get a person relaxed until they would spill their heart out. Everybody in Sizzerbill's knew Dottie would get every last smidgeon of information from Mac if they waited quietly. It was hopeless to resist. Dottie was a snake charmer. It was just a matter of time before Mac spilled the beans, so everyone got up and refilled their coffee mug.

Mac shouldn't have uttered a syllable. He was tired and got caught off-guard. He knew he better tell what happened or he'd never be allowed to leave, and he had work to do. He decided to tell his story as an understatement of the facts. That was Mac's style. Everybody, especially Harry, wanted to hear about Operation Neptune Spear. Still, Mac never said a word, not even a humble brag about it. Heck, they wouldn't have ever known about his involvement if the local newspaper hadn't written a front-page story about the 'Local Hero' before Mac got home.

"Oh, it's not much of anything, Dottie. I might've seen a UFO last night on my way home from the high school," said Mac trying to sound nonchalant.

"A flying saucer? You saw a flying saucer last night, Mac. Where?" asked Dottie.

"I was over by Shawnee Creek near Dogwood Valley. It wasn't a big deal."

"Not a big deal? How many flying saucers have you seen?" asked Dottie.

"Well, I've never seen one before, Dottie," said Mac.

"Well then, it's a big deal. Ain't it, Mac?" said Dottie.

"Aw hell, Dottie, I've seen lots of flying disks before," said Virgil, who had the fastest bass boat on the Lake. Virgil had more money than a porcupine had quills.

"When?" asked Dottie, amused by the interest Mac's UFO story was inciting. She wasn't sure she believed in UFOs, or Bigfoot either for that matter.

"Back in '56 with Pappy. We were off the point at 'Possum Cove, letting the hounds tree raccoons. There were so many flying disks, they looked like lightning bugs on a summer night in the meadow." A couple of other guys nodded in agreement as if they'd seen oodles of UFOs before too.

"I've seen plenty of them too, along with haunts and spirits of all kinds," said Fleagle as he grappled for credibility. Fleagle was so poor he could hardly pay attention ever since his worm farm went broke. Dottie never charged Fleagle for coffee, but he always left her a quarter tip.

Mac was pleased with the momentary reprieve while the other guys talked over each other to tell their flying saucer tales. Dottie patiently brought the conversation back around to Mac. Mac was trusted and well-liked by almost everybody. The locals knew his family and had watched him grow up. He'd been an all-star on the high school's sports teams, and everyone prayed for him when he went into the Navy. Mac was elected Sheriff without even putting his name on the ballot. His neighbors put their heads together, wrote his name on their ballots, and he was elected. He reluctantly accepted and had been the Sheriff of Lincoln County ever since.

Lincoln County didn't have much crime. Seeing Mac with his determined look discouraged even the most confident cock on the walk. All Mac had to do was smile in his knowing way and point the way out of the door.

"What did your UFO look like, Mac?" pried Dottie hoping to get more information.

"I can't say exactly. I'm not sure it was a real UFO. All I saw was a blinding bright light coming from the sky. Then, Elvis started howling like his tail was caught in the door."

'Hey, wait a minute, ol' buddy,' grumbled Elvis raising his red and droopy eyelids but not his head. 'I didn't bark one syllable until you screamed so loud it made my ears ring. Hero, my eye. More like, Barbie doll.'

"What happened after you saw it, Mac?" asked Dottie. Locals viewed Dottie as the hostess of Sizzerbill's daily talk show. She was Oprah-like and considered to be the house shrink. It was her job to mend marriages, help others make friends, and in Mac's and many others, be a marriage broker. Her strategy was to expose others' vulnerabilities so they would open up and share their feelings. No one got angry because Dottie made them feel like the most important person in the room.

"Not much; it chased us a little while. That's all." He forgot to tell her when the wild chase was over, he was in a cold sweat and worried.

"Did it hurt you?" asked Faith as Abner's neck turned scarlet red, and Elvis moaned. Both thought Faith was prancing like a wild mare going to stud.

"No, nothing like that happened," said a shy Mac who felt uncomfortable talking about himself. Faith was an itch Mac didn't know how to scratch.

"How fast was the bogey?" asked Harry, talking like a combat pilot with rapid-fire questions. "How many did you see? Were there any aliens? Were your evasive maneuvers effective?"

"It was super-fast, and I only saw one. I didn't see any aliens. No, I couldn't get away. It just took off. I guess it got bored following me. Well folks, I better get going," said Mac as he finished his coffee, put his money on the table, and stood up. "I've got sheriff's business to do and fences to mend over at Roy Haskell's. Goodbye, Faith," said Mac tipping his cap. Elvis groaned and followed Mac out the door, careful not to get his tail caught. Everybody said and waved goodbye.

Faith rushed out to the dock, and called back over her shoulder, "I've got to get something from the boat, Daddy." She felt bold and impatient and planned to take control of her relationship with Mac.

"Hey, big fella, when are you asking me out on a romantic date? You're not scared of me, are you, Hero?"

"Oh no, Faith. You don't scare me or anything. It just seems like I'm always busy, that's all."

"You make me feel so unimportant compared to your big important job, Mac. I thought you liked me," she smiled.

"I do," gulped Mac feeling totally awkward around the stunning Faith.

"You do?" asked Faith as she mocked Mac, making him feel even more uncomfortable. She enjoyed putting him on pins and needles and watching him squirm like a worm. "I'll make sure to remind you, Mac. Okay, then, it's settled. We'll go out next Saturday for dinner to a nice restaurant anywhere but at the Lake. I don't want my Sheriff distracted when he's with me. I want all of his attention. Please pick me up at six," said a smiling Faith as she batted her eyes, turned, and slowly swayed away towards Sizzerbill's. She had the bottom of a forty-dollar mule, and it couldn't be hidden even under a man's camouflage jacket.

"Yes, ma'am," gulped Mac as he stared at her backside, swaying away. Impatient, Elvis clambered onto the boat while Mac stood dumbstruck.

When Faith got back inside, everyone was still bragging about UFO sightings they'd seen. Nobody wanted to seem surprised by Mac's experience. They were surprised it was the first UFO Mac had ever seen. Heck, he was a local. Hillbillies had been watching flying saucers for as long as anyone could remember.

CHAPTER 3

# Whiskey River

The Hokums had two multi-generation traditions, which made them the envy of many hillbillies. Hooch and hounds. Bubba Hokum, his daddy, and his grand-pappies had a rich, high-octane, centuries-old history of distilling and bootlegging amber-colored moonshine. They also bred blue-blood foxhounds in the hillbilly hollows they called home.

Tonight, Bubba's foxhounds were baying at the Full Flower Moon. His invited neighbors stood around the large bonfire sipping his newest batch of moonshine. The moon was more prominent than any full moon of the year, and the hounds howled at every shadow dancing around in the trees. Moonshine is the slang term for high-proof distilled spirits produced without government authorization. The roaring bonfire was reflected off the copper pot still sitting behind everyone in its own barn. Everyone was chatting about anything that came to mind as the moonshine loosened their tongues. Bubba's moonshine was a truth serum. People freely admitted what they liked, hated, and believed. Politics was always a popular topic since hillbillies don't think much of politicians and the government.

The Hokum farm was blessed with a spring-fed limestone aquifer which removed iron from the sparkling aquamarine spring water. Their mineral enhanced water was perfect for distilling their mountain dew which was aged in charred oak barrels. Nobody ever went blind drinking Hokum moonshine, they got as happy as a clam in high tide. Hokums only popped the cork on their properly aged casks when the moon was shining full, and they always invited their best friends to join the celebration. It was an honor to be invited.

Everyone gathered had a thirst to quench and were eager to taste Bubba's new batch, even the womenfolk.

Obie Blevens and his band, the Practical Jokers, were plucking and strumming *Mountain Dew* as the crowd relaxed and settled into the spring celebration. Obie and the Jokers were the regular house band at the *Hillbilly Opry*. Obie's personality was big as his girth. He was always dressed in some outlandish costume he'd put together at Margie's Re-Sell-It Shop. He had a house full of different instruments and costumes. He played and wore all of them for various occasions and songs. Tonight, Obie was dressed like a Russian aristocrat. He completed his ensemble with an accented dialect. It made him sound like he was from someplace ending in 'Sylvania.' Some of his instruments, like his washtub bass, which he was playing now, were homemade. His favorite instrument was his battered brass Sousaphone which was lit up with a blinking Christmas wreath.

Obie had trimmed his Van Dyke beard to a fine point that matched his splendid red coat and tails. His ornate wide black belt set off his knee-high patent leather black boots, which had spurs that whistled when he paraded around his band. Either Obie's costume or Bubba's moonshine had him sweating like a sinner in church as he played and sang for all of his worth. The only thing louder than Obie's clothes was his laugh. Everyone thought his tongue was loose on both ends because of his fantastic imitation of various dialects and corny off-color jokes. Obie was everybody's best friend, and everybody was going to be the butt-end of one of his practical jokes when he got around to them. It was a sign of respect when Obie kissed you with his fake-rotted teeth, put a plastic spider on your shoulder, or got you to kiss his ringed hand because you really thought he was a Russian aristocrat. Everyone loved to listen to Obie's legendary ballads about renowned hillbilly moonshiners.

Many of the original moonshiners, like the Hokums, still lived around the Lake. The rural radicals defied government 'Revenuers' trying to collect taxes on their unlicensed moonshine. During prohibition, moonshiners were the rebels being chased by troopers and the FBI on the backroads. They delivered moonshine into the cities. The original NASCAR race drivers were moonshiners being chased by government agents shooting at them.

Nowadays, moonshining was tame. Most law enforcement agents, including Mac, didn't care if someone made a little moonshine, beer, or wine without a license. They didn't even get too obsessed with someone growing a little pot for personal use. They were fighting hillbilly heroin, fentanyl, and the methamphetamine cartels. Bubba's family and many of his friends were old-school. They had a long history of being rogues sipping aged, cask-strength moonshine under a full moon with their friends. It was a hillbilly tradition, and Harry Cobb was proud to be accepted and happy to be sipping moonshine with his good friend, Bubba.

Harry took a long pull of moonshine from the glazed Hokum stoneware jug and smiled up at the night sky through his moonshine haze. He couldn't get Mac's story about seeing the UFO out of his mind. He'd never actually seen a UFO, but he did remember seeing strange lights from a bogey in Viet Nam one night when he was returning from a mission. It shook him up. Lately, he'd been reading and hearing many stories about UFOs in the news. The media had really whipped up public interest and panic in UFOs. There were lots of movies, dozens of video clips, special cable TV shows, podcasts, and network news stories reporting UFO and alien sightings. You couldn't escape the news. You had to believe, or you were a science-denier.

"What do you think of it, Harry? Do you like it?" asked a smiling Bubba, who stood head and shoulders above Harry. Bubba was seven feet tall in his stocking feet, which were over 15 inches long. He wore size 23 shoes and towered over everybody. He was as big as a skinned ox, weighing around 300 pounds. Bubba was the youngest in a family of five boys. His mom and dad lamented not having daughters who would've eaten half as much and worked twice as hard.

After Bigfoot's footprint was found near Sizzerbill's, Bubba got a gig at the Hillbilly Opry's Christmas show. As a teenager, he dressed up like Santa-Bigfoot and sang, in his falsetto yodel, 'Santa-Bigfoot is Coming to Town.' The crowds, especially the young kids who believed in Santa and came to sit on Santa-Bigfoot's lap, loved Bubba. Alas, Santa-Bigfoot was a shooting star who gradually fell back to Earth as interest in Bigfoot waned without any new sightings. Bubba was a self-sufficient hillbilly. He ran a few head of cattle, farmed a big garden, cut and sold firewood, and used his D9 Caterpillar bulldozer to grade building sites and dig ponds. Bubba paid his own bills. He didn't want the government in his life.

"It gives my cheeks a warm glow, Bubba. It's delicious!" said Harry as he smacked his lips and gave a hillbilly chew.

"Thanks, Harry, it's my best yet. I used organic corn for the mash that I bought from a hippie in Knox County."

"Hell, organic moonshine, Bubba, it's genius!" said Harry, momentarily, thinking about going into business to make organic moonshine with Bubba. After another nip, he quickly decided it was too much work and passed the jug to Bubba. The jug looked small in Bubba's hands as he took a giant swig.

"Did you hear about the UFO Mac saw, Bubba?"

"Nope, but lots of folks have seen unexplained aerial phenomena for thousands of years, Harry. Although they've been reported in various sizes and shapes, typically, they're seen as an elongated moon shape. Daddy told us one chased him all over Bald Knob one night. Scared the dickens out of him so badly, he didn't leave the house at night for a year," laughed Bubba as he thought about his dad being afraid to leave the porch.

"Have you ever seen one, Bubba?"

"No, but I haven't been looking for them either. UFOs may be out there, but I don't really care, Harry. What difference would it make to my life? Could I wake up later in the morning? Could I stop working? Nope. I'd have to do the same thing I'm doing now. It wouldn't make a twit of a difference. As Sherlock Holmes said, it wouldn't matter a bit if the sun wasn't the center of our solar system," he said philosophically, waving the jug like a flyswatter daring the universe to prove him wrong. Everyone was always awed by how much Bubba read and knew.

"I haven't seen one either, but I'd like to see one," said Harry gazing off at the full moon.

"Wanting to see one and believing in UFOs are two different questions. I'd like to see many things, but there's little chance I will. I'd like to see a politician keep his mouth shut or keep his promises, but I don't believe I will." They both chuckled.

"Yeah, well, the government promises it's going to release files and videos showing UFOs. Lots of people are afraid,

Bubba. Lots of people claim they've even been abducted, enslaved, and even impregnated. There might be an alien here at your party," said Harry warily looking around.

"You really believe the government, Harry?" chortled Bubba, "That's strange for a Viet Nam vet to say. I don't think anybody can prove an actual close encounter with a UFO or an alien. Heck, even Elon Musk has said he hasn't seen any proof of aliens and he's flying space ships and launching satellites all of the time. I believe him more than the government."

Harry was perplexed and didn't know whether to believe in UFOs or not. Bubba gave some valid arguments. Oh, lots of movies and stories came out of Hollywood, but no one had a photograph of an actual alien. "You seem so sure, Bubba."

"It doesn't seem likely to me there are ancient alien civilizations smarter than humans who haven't left any proof. Aliens, Bigfoot and the Loch Ness Monster don't seem likely to me, but I love going to movies like *E.T.* and *Harry and the Hendersons*. Hollywood makes a fortune scaring people with movies like *Men in Black*, *Independence Day*, and *Aliens*. There's no proof, but everybody wants to believe. Some people even believe aliens are superior lifeforms able to smite earth on a whim. Heck, nobody'd go to the movies to see aliens the size of a germ, frozen in permafrost on some obscure planet."

"You might be right, Bubba, but I still like the thought of there being someone out there. I believe in them," said Harry.

"Are you and Dottie ready for Memorial Day weekend, Harry?" asked Bubba.

Memorial Day weekend, the official start of the Lake tourism season, was in two weeks. Simply the mention of the holiday brought maudlin memories to Harry. He solemnly celebrated it every year since his return from Viet Nam. He never wanted to forget all of the guys he knew, and those who died there. Several were standing right next to him when they were killed. He had mixed feelings. His tour in Nam left him feeling distrustful, but he loved America more than ever. Before Nam, Harry didn't think one way or the other about American politics or war, even though his dad served in Europe during World War II. Before getting his A1 draft notice, he enlisted in the Marines six months after graduating from high school. He spent the next four years trying to keep from being shipped home in a body bag. It was terrifying duty, and it took a lot of luck. Now, he was news-obsessed and watched and read everything he could about the current state of affairs with the greatest country in history, The United States of America.

"Oh, we're ready, but we need more tourism business this year." Harry and Dottie were self-employed small business owners. They had to pay for their own upcoming retirements. "We've been working and paying taxes our entire lives, and we've always paid our bills. Neither of us has ever collected an unemployment or disability check. We don't owe a dime to anybody, and we still can't afford to retire. We're not government employees who get cushy cost-of-living raises each year. We're not going to get any fat monthly government pension checks with the automatic cost of living increases. It's a crock, I tell you, Bubba."

Harry and Dottie worked and paid for everything they had. If the toilets were clogged and needed a plumber, Harry fixed them. If their roof leaked and they needed a carpenter, Harry fixed it. If they needed a painter, Dottie painted it. Harry hated painting more than plumbing and carpentry.

"We need to get more tourists into Sizzerbill's so we can retire with some dignity." They didn't want to work forever, even though they enjoyed having their friends stop by regularly for a cup of coffee and a wedge of homemade pie. The moonshine made Harry resolute as he whispered so he wouldn't be overheard, "Do you want to take a road trip with me, Bubba? I need to get to the city."

"Sure, I need a vacation," said Bubba as he rolled his eyes towards his wife, Hortense. She was tiny, but she was the boss. Their ten-year-old twin boys were taller than her, but she could talk the legs off an iron pot, and her tongue never got rusty from the lack of use. She was the ringmaster of their three-ring circus, and Bubba knew better than to call her bluff.

"It's time to call the dogs, piss on the fire, and holler; let's go, Bubba. They've all got someplace to get, and we've got chores in the morning, honey."

"Yes, Hortense. Drink up folk, thanks for coming. Hope you enjoyed yourselves, good night folks," said Bubba.

In the last few minutes, Bubba and Harry worked up an elaborate scheme to go on a foxhunt at a friend's farm. They toasted their plan with their last swigs of the night as the Practical Jokers finished their last song, *Your Cheatin' Heart.*

## CHAPTER 4

# On the Road Again

It wasn't easy getting permission from Dottie and Hortense for their trip to the city. Harry and Bubba needed a believable story to get out of their chores. They figured their best chance was taking the hounds to an imaginary fox hunt a couple of hundred miles away at Bubba's friend's farm. Bubba's friend, Red, lived so deep in the woods he didn't get the *Grand Old Opry* on his radio until Wednesday night. Their plan worked. Hortense was peacock proud of her hounds. They were bred from champion sires and dames for darn near a century from solid foxhound hill stock. Hortense was always keen on letting her hounds run and couldn't get Bubba out of the door fast enough. Dottie pretended she was disappointed, but she was happy to get some alone time. The guys were worried they'd get caught standing naked before the Lord, but they were free to go on their trip.

It took most of the day to unload the three cords of firewood in Bubba's stake truck and pack it with six rambunctious foxhounds, a couple of hundred pounds of dog food, a few jugs of moonshine, and the necessary camping supplies and equipment. Exhausted, Harry shook his head side-to-side as he hauled and lifted things off and on the truck. The six hounds were barking as much as his feet from all of the walking.

'Maybe, I should've just driven my own pickup truck instead of cooking up this cockamamie scheme. Why do I always get so elaborate? His dang hounds are giving me a migraine. How in the world am I going to survive this week? This is more work than staying at Sizzerbill's. I must be getting dementia from all of that agent orange to think this was a good idea,' sighed Harry.

"Are you okay, Harry? You look tired. Do you need a hand?" said Bubba.

"Why the heck do you need this? It's the size of a Japanese pickup truck."

"It's my rocking chair, Harry. I need to rock at night to relax my back," said Bubba as they heaved the gigantic rocker over the stakes onto the truck bed. The hounds started jumping on and off like it was a playground toy.

Harry sighed when they were finally driving and listening to KORN. Willie Nelson was singing *On the Road Again*.

"Where we going in Chicago, Harry?" asked Bubba as they cruised out of town.

"I've got the address on my phone. I'll give you directions."

"What do you have to get, Harry?"

"I need to pick up some security cameras for Sizzerbill's."

"Why didn't you just buy some on Amazon? That's what I did. Got a good price too."

"These are a special type of camera, Bubba. You'll see."

Harry had discovered a specialty electronics spy store in Chicago named *CYA* on the Internet. *CYA* specialized in stealth intelligence. It sold hardware and software technology for espionage and personal security to investigators, detectives, and security companies. The store supplied surveillance systems to equip the walled and fenced estates of actors, politicians, and other elites like professional athletes, and their ne'er-do-well families, from adoring fans and haters. Oddly, *CYA* didn't sell shotguns or dogs, the preferred security systems for hillbillies.

Harry didn't want anybody, especially Dottie, to know what he was buying or what he was planning to do. He trusted Bubba, but he didn't tell him either. He wanted to buy his supplies in Chicago because he didn't want locals to see what he was getting. Bubba was impossible to miss or mistake for someone else. Add Bubba's stake truck full of baying hounds, camping supplies, and his colossal rocking chair, and they stood out like a diamond in a goat's ass.

"I don't see the store's sign, Harry. Do you?"

"No, I don't, but we're supposed to be there. Oh, there it is." The storefront was painted a clandestine matte black. The windows and doors were blocked with dark screens, making it impossible to peer inside even when the lights were on, and the store was open for business.

"You can let me out here, Bubba. Park wherever you can find a spot. I'll find you when I'm done."

"How will you find me, Harry."

"I'm guessing I'll be able to hear you," said Harry smiling and happy to escape the barking dogs as he walked to the door of the store.

Bubba was lucky to find a parking spot on a quiet one-way street near the basement storefront. *CYA* employed a radio-wave stealth defense system that blocked spies from listening inside the store from outside locations. CYA was swept a couple of times each day for spy bugs and other covert listening devices. In the store, nobody used personal names or the real names of their businesses. It was a secure location. Cell phones were locked in a lead-lined safe at the front door.

Bubba stayed with the stake truck full of yowling hounds. Harry was dressed incognito as he strolled inside wearing dark sunglasses, a black t-shirt, jeans, and a bull rider's cowboy hat. He looked as out of place as a hog on a sofa.

The store's owner called himself Q. He looked like he was 16 and dressed like a skateboarder. He wore dark sunglasses and observed Harry warily. Neither trusted the other.

"Howdy, partner," smirked Q. "My name's Q. What can I do for you?" said Q, doing his best to imitate a cowboy twang while hooking his thumbs behind his belt buckle with a phony smile.

"You can lose your attitude and give me some respect, Q. I'm a vet. I need your help to find a hobby to manage my

PTSD," said a maniacally smiling Harry laughing to himself. "Call me, Bond, James Bond."

"Sure, James er, Bond. What kind of hobby are you thinking about? We don't carry any weapons here," Q hurriedly stammered.

"I'm not looking for any weapons. I've got plenty already," smiled Harry. "I'm looking for a badass drone, Q. What would you suggest?"

"How would you use it, Mr. Bond? What do you need it for?"

"It's none of your business, Q. If I told you, I'd have to kill you," snickered Harry. "Not really, Q. I'm not violent. It's got to be lightning-quick, easy to maneuver, quiet as a mouse with escape velocity acceleration, and easy to fly at night."

"Hmm, yes, we have a few models that would meet those specifications. Do you need a geospatial mapping application, Mr. Bond?" Harry could visibly see Q getting thrilled when discussing different drone features. How about exterior illumination to light up the target areas below? I'm assuming you want an infrared vision for nighttime flying, Mr. Bond."

"Of course, Q." Q selected and pulled a drone from *CYA's* inventory. Before Harry knew it, he had bought the XTX9 Ghost drone and a high-power surveillance spotlight. The Ghost was the fastest, most maneuverable, and highest-flying drone available on the market to non-military personnel. It was a stealth model, and it couldn't be heard by the human ear. It also had a 2,000-millimeter infrared night vision camera lens, giving the Ghost the nickname 'Cat's Eye.' Q preferred his payment in cryptocurrency, but Harry explained he hadn't brought any gold coins, laughed, and paid in cash.

Q helped Harry carry the matte-black, unlabeled boxes to Bubba's truck until Q saw two Chicago policemen waving their fingers and lecturing Bubba who was two heads taller than either officer. The hounds were acting as crazy as peach orchard boars. When he saw the police, Q put down his boxes, told Harry he was on his own, and scampered back to the dark recesses of *CYA* locking the door behind him.

With Bubba's family history of bootlegging, he wasn't afraid of cops. He was smart enough to be wary while he acted light-hearted. After all, he wasn't in the country talking to Mac. Bubba knew the cops wouldn't search the back of his truck with the hounds in it. So, his moonshine was safe. The hounds weren't afraid either. They were growling like they had a fox cornered. Fortunately, the cops couldn't stop laughing at the sight of Bubba, his six barking hounds, and the giant rocking chair in the back of his stake truck.

"Where are you from, Beverly Hills, Jethro?" asked the shortest cop while the other slapped his knee with tears running down his cheeks.

"No, sir, I'm not, and I didn't call Car 54 either. Did you, Harry?" asked Bubba as he stepped chest-to-face with the questioning officer, who felt uncomfortable staring into his massive chest. The cop took a step back to put some distance between them.

"Well, your dogs are too loud. We'll give you a ticket for disturbing the peace if you don't get them out of here, forthwith," said the officer trying to look confident while he stepped back even further.

"Thank you, officer, we'll be happy to get out of here as soon as possible. Bubba, help me put these boxes in the back of the truck, so we can get out of these officers' hair," said Harry.

•  •  •

"What's your friend, Red, like, Bubba?"

"We met years ago at a fox hunt in Washington County, Harry. We're both hillbillies who like hounds and making moonshine. He'll take any animal onto his farm. People constantly drop off their unwanted pets, and he's always finding animals roaming along the roads or out in the woods. He collects pets like some people collect coins or rare pocket watches. It doesn't matter what's wrong with the animals. Red takes them all."

Red called his farm Serenity. His neighbors called it The Ark. Serenity was a menagerie of mules, sheep, cattle, turkeys, goats, hogs, ducks, horses, geese, dogs, chickens, llamas, and peacocks. Red even had a growing herd of white-tailed deer because they knew they wouldn't get hunted on his farm. He didn't count his beehives or fish in the pond as his pets. His animals shared the same pastures and slept wherever they wanted. Red moved slower than sorghum in

January and talked even slower. He spent his time caring for his animals, moonshining, whitling, working around Serenity, and gardening. If he needed cash, he sold his moonshine or did odd jobs.

Harry and Bubba set up their camp near Red's spring-fed pond. It was nearly four acres, and its overflow created a nice fishing creek that ambled through his farm. Red and his pets loved having company, and everybody had a high old time. They stayed up late drinking moonshine and woke up whenever they felt like it. Red bred Blue Tick coon hounds, and he and Bubba let their hounds explore all over the countryside.

While Red and Bubba visited, Harry entertained himself by learning how to fly the Ghost by watching YouTube videos. Even as a former helicopter pilot, it was awkward flying by watching a screen. He had never played video games or had remote control cars or planes. Mercifully, the Ghost was a helicopter-style drone roughly the size of a small kitchen table. He piloted it from the ground. It made him nervous flying his new $10,000 spy toy. If Dottie knew what he had bought and how much he had paid, she would've had him committed to a mental hospital. Harry wanted to keep it a secret.

Once Harry perfected take-offs and landings, he practiced flying at night. Red, Bubba, and all of the animals thought Harry had lost his mind. They figured he didn't know 'come here' from 'sic 'em.' His biggest challenge was flying when he couldn't hear the Ghost. He had to watch the ground below from its Cat's Eye on his hand-held color monitor. Harry wasn't the nervous type. He had flown using only instruments with bullets whizzing through his helicopter. The Cat's Eye helped at night, especially after turning on the Hercules 100,000 lumens surveillance spotlight on its underneath carriage. The Hercules could light up almost an acre when it was turned on, and Harry could see all of the birds and animals in the meadow below. Harry was beginning to feel confident with his abilities and knowing the capabilities of the Ghost.

"It's quieter than a mouse pissing on cotton, Harry, and it's faster than greased lightning. What the heck do you need a bright spotlight for, though?" asked Red as he passed his jug of bourbon moonshine to Bubba. They'd been comparing moonshine mash bills while reliving the glory days of bootlegging and watching their hounds chase coyotes, foxes, and even a bear. Harry smiled. He'd been practicing his answer to Red's question knowing someone would ask it.

"Fishing. I got this rig for night fishing and frog gigging, Red. If I can see every bird in a tree, I can see every fish in the sea. Do you want to help me test it out?"

"Sure do," said a grinning Red. Bubba nodded agreement. They settled their jugs in the grass, and headed towards the pond. The plan was to fly the Ghost overhead, turn on the light, see a fish, and snag it out of the pond with a net. Once at the pond, Red and Bubba climbed in the boat and rowed out to the pond's center. It was so dark nobody could see the Ghost, and only the hounds heard it when Harry launched it. Harry was grinning from ear to ear, spying on his friends through the Cat's Eye. Bubba and Red were sitting in the boat, searching the night sky for the Ghost. It was two hundred feet above them. Unexpectedly, Harry flipped the Hercules spotlight switch on. SHAZAM! The spotlight was so bright, it blinded both men looking up into the night sky.

Juddered, Bubba bellowed, stood up, and precariously rocked the boat from side to side. He covered his eyes with his hands, but the bright light made his hands look transparent. He could actually see each vein.

"I'm blind! I'm blind! I can't see anything!" Blinded and off-balance, Bubba stumbled, tipped the boat, and heaved Red and him into the translucent pond. Seeing the men thrash in the water and lots of fish swimming in the pond on his screen, Harry chuckled, and turned off Hercules. He landed the Ghost away from the pandemonium while the hounds dashed into the water to rescue their beloved buddies. Bubba and Red instantly sobered up in the cold spring water. Fighting their wet clothes and a dozen dogs licking their faces made it nearly impossible to retrieve the boat and make it to the fire for long pulls on the jugs before bed.

After a whole morning of loading the truck and long goodbyes, Bubba and Harry left for home the next day. Everyone, especially the dogs, was exhausted.

## CHAPTER 5
# Take This Job and Shove It

**"S**orry, Agate, I can't make it. I've got to work all weekend," said Dan Blather. He was a joint half-smoked kind of pessimist. He never smiled and always seemed out of sorts. Blather didn't pay attention to life's blessings.

"What do you mean you selfish brat? You're too busy to attend your parents 40th wedding anniversary Saturday night at their country club? That's cold, Dan, even for you."

Agate, Dan's older sister, was a ball-busting lawyer. She was the assistant to the governor. Well, actually, she wasn't an assistant to the governor. She was the staff lobbyist for *Chief Tobacco Company*, which was better than being an assistant to the governor.

Agate wrote legislation to protect her company's interests which the state's assembly passed after generous campaign donations from her company. Her dream was to become a federal lobbyist. Then, she could escape all of the hick state politicians and their bumptious staffs who'd sell votes for a ham sandwich and a cup of coffee. She knew things wouldn't be any different in the District of Corruption but the paychecks were a lot bigger.

"I'll send Stella and Phillip my regrets. Don't worry. They'll be happy I'm not there."

Dan called his parents by their first names. They weren't emotionally attached. Dan's parents loved to brag about their rising star, Agate. They rarely mentioned Dan. He was an embarrassment. Fortunately, Dan rarely visited. If anyone asked, they'd say, "Oh, Dan is living a swinging bachelor's life at the Lake," even though he wasn't. He was miserable.

The one thing Dan, Stella, and Phillip had in common was, they all hated Dan's job. Phillip wanted Dan to be a structural engineer like he was, or at least an architect. Phillip dreamed about building a family business with Dan, but it was a pipe dream. Dan couldn't, or at least wouldn't, study math to become an engineer. Dan's job wasn't impressive like his sister's.

Dan had been stuck working at KORN an AM radio station for the last four years. KORN only played country, western and bluegrass music. The locals at the Lake loved KORN, but none of them would've recognized Dan in a police line-up. He never hung out with the locals. Locals only heard his hopeless baritone voice on the radio station. He was the station's news director and he read press releases about potluck church dinners and news stories from online websites a few minutes each hour. KORN didn't even let Dan choose which news websites he could use. Dan took the KORN job to work a year before becoming a national news correspondent for *Global News Network* or the *World Domination News Corporation*. He felt trapped at KORN with no prospects of getting out. It was depressing to think about staying at the Lake forever. At times, he felt homicidal.

"What are you going to do, send your regrets to Mom and Dad in a text, little brother? They're not going to believe you're busy. It's the least you owe them for all they've done for you."

Dan hated his sister's success. He had big dreams in college after he worked on his high school newspaper, TV station, and yearbook. He enjoyed writing stories and being a media celebrity. He dreamed about becoming an ace reporter for the *New York Times*, *Huffington Post*, or some other media outlet that would make his friends jealous.

Journalism school had been fun. When science and business students had to study for exams, Dan would say, "Pshaw," and party with his J-school friends. Dan used his time figuring out how to get around needing credible news sources for his campus newspaper's stories about police and campus corruption. He was busy and didn't have time to interview people and do actual investigative research. His teachers taught him to protect his source's identity by citing unnamed credible sources. It worked like a charm because his teachers rarely read his stories anyway. Dan knew first-hand how corrupt the police department was. The Honda Civic his dad bought him for his sixteenth birthday had a glove box full of parking tickets. Dan was furious the police didn't have anything better to do than harass poor students who already had a stack of worthless student loans.

The best thing about college was Dan's radical teachers. Their tests and assignments were easy. Every class they'd orate about the unfairness in the world. They didn't ask students questions because they didn't want to get poor course evaluations. Most teachers were bitter about their unrealized dreams too. They weren't sure who to blame, but they knew it wasn't their fault. They were the victims. They rarely found good-paying jobs like advertising, business or engineering students. After languishing four years at the Lake, Dan understood why they became teachers. He was thinking about going to graduate school to teach too. Working in the field wasn't nearly as much fun as going to school.

"I've got a lot to do this weekend, Agate. I've got a lot of deadline pressures that you wouldn't know about. You couldn't handle my job."

"I'm very sure I could, Taddler," said Agate sarcastically as she rolled her eyes. Dan visibly twitched with her personal insult. Dan and his friends obsessively played *Masters of the Galaxy*. His personal avatar was Taddler. Taddler's weapon of choice was a fountain pen that could be used as a magic saber to cut people or anything else in half. Taddler could also shoot different color laser bolts that killed, froze, or hypnotized his enemies. Taddler was a radical power in the galaxy, and Dan loved his life as a superhero.

"You're a bitch, and you don't have a life, Agate. You're as cold as your name. Why aren't you married? Don't you have any friends? Tell Stella and Phillip, happy anniversary." He clicked off his call quickly. He didn't want to give Agate a chance for a comeback. She had a silver tongue.

Dan's dream of becoming a national reporter in the elite progressive media didn't seem very likely. He'd tried everything to gain celebrity traction. He regularly made posts on social media, but still had fewer than a hundred followers. Most were his friends from school. The only Tweets, Tik Toks, and Instagrams that got him any traction were photos of hot chicks in bikinis at the Lake. Nothing ever happened at the Lake worth reporting.

Dan was Woke, appropriately progressive, angry, primed, and ready to save the world from corruption, inequity, and unfairness, but he was hopelessly stuck in a black hole called KORN.

• • •

Dan didn't like the locals or the tourists at the Lake. The Lake might've been okay to visit for a weekend, but he was more of an indoor cat. He didn't like hiking, boating, waterskiing, cycling, camping, hunting, or spelunking. All Dan wanted to do was hang out at his favorite heavy metal bar, *The Graveyard*, and play video games.

It was Saturday night at the Lake, and Dan couldn't wait to hang out with his two friends. He had his News Director position down cold. It didn't take much thinking or effort. Like college, it was simple.

After reading the 8:55 p.m. news report, he started the computer program to play a vintage *Grand Ole Opry* recording. It featured Johnny Paycheck and the only country-western song Dan liked, *Take This Job and Shove It*. After his news slot, Dan sped to *The Graveyard* to grab beers with his buds and listen to the *Rage Against the Machine* tribute band. He had to get back to the station before the *Grand Ole Opry* recording was over. He was dressed in his ripped and torn jeans and his favorite *Rage Against the Machine* homage t-shirt.

Dan's Lake buddies, Darryl and Stoney, worked at a marina renting boats to tourists. They did boat maintenance over the winter. Tourists journeyed to the Lake to party. Most boaters drank alcohol, and some drank heavily. If a slow-moving pontoon boat pulling towable floats with screaming kids wasn't off the Lake by mid-morning, it was swamped by the waves from 40-foot cigarette boats. Everybody raced to Party Cove by noon to reserve a special place to tie up for a kick-ass all weekend party. Families on luxurious rented houseboats stayed on the fringe of the party boats to watch through binoculars.

The *Rage Against the Machine* tribute band was bare-chested and sweating like professional wrestlers when they finished their second set with a mash-up of *Guerilla Radio* and *Bullet in the Head*. Mesmerized and blitzed, Dan slowly shook his head and mumbled, "I've got to get going, man," to no one in particular as he sucked down the last drops of his lukewarm *Natty Light*.

"Let's go outside and smoke a bowl first," suggested Darryl with a wink. The three amigos stumbled out the front door which was flanked by men as big as sumo wrestlers with beards as long as Santa's. They stumbled towards Stoney's Ford F-150 metallic red pickup. Once inside, Stoney lit a bowl of marijuana in a corn cob pipe and passed it around. Stoney and Darryl lived in an old rented farmhouse with a few acres south of the Lake on gravel road AA. They were hobbyist gardeners specializing in growing sensimilla pot which was very potent. Their pot was always in high demand, but they mainly grew it for personal use.

After coughing up a lung when he exhaled, Dan said, "Wow, this shit is blowing my mind, man. I'm tripping. What do you call it?"

"We're calling it, Ninja, man. It's killer!" said Darryl as Stoney silently slapped his knee while silently laughing. Neither of Dan's friends were local either. Darryl's family moved to the Lake when his dad took a job at the Home Depot store. He'd been laid off from a car dealership in the city. His dad told his family it was time for a new dream, and moved them to the Lake, where they vacationed one summer. The Lake was a booming countryopolis.

Its population swelled between Memorial Day and Labor Day weekends. Tens of thousands of city dwellers bought glamorous lakeshore condominiums with boat docks to have a place to party and spend their summer vacations. They didn't own huge boats. The long-nosed Donzis, Cigarettes, and three-bedroom yachts were owned by the wealthy elites who pressed class-action lawsuits, company presidents, and people who won the lottery. The Lake was a highly desirable tourist destination much to the chagrin of the locals. Locals yearned for the old days when the Lake was a fishing and camping outpost.

"Dude, I'm so stoned I can't even focus my eyes, dude," said Stoney. He had camped at the state park several years ago and stayed because he liked the Lake's laid-back vibe.

Darryl and Stoney were content with their lives. They liked working at the marina because it was a great place to meet chicks, especially those having bachelorette parties. They were able to use the marina's boats to go out on the Lake to check on the boaters and do maintenance when it was necessary. Late-night boating was especially useful when they met a receptive group of women who wanted to party. Darryl and Stoney had life by the ass.

"Oh shit, man, it's 10:45. The *Grand Old Opry* program is almost over, man. I've got to get my ass back to the station. Why don't you guys meet me there in half an hour or so?" said a hyperventilating Dan. "We can hang out then."

"Sure, dude, we'll meet you at the station," said Stoney as he exhaled a cumulus cloud of pungent smoke.

## CHAPTER 6
# Chug-A-Lug

"You go ahead home, Dottie. I'll be there as soon as I fix the ice-maker."

"It's too late, Harry. Do it tomorrow. You need your sleep."

"Naw, you're always telling me I procrastinate. You go ahead, dear. I'm getting this thing fixed tonight. Good night!"

Harry never let it slip to Dottie, and he told Bubba not to say a word either. He'd been wanting to fly the Ghost ever since his trip with Bubba. Tonight, was the night. He walked past the ice-maker to pull the drone and all the necessary equipment out of the basement. Then, he dragged all of it onto the field next to Sizzerbill's parking lot. Carefully, he laid everything out and silently launched the Ghost into the star-filled night sky. There wasn't much moonlight. First, Harry circled overhead in the field, testing his landings and take-offs. Patiently, he ventured over Sizzerbill's parking lot, making ever-larger loops, circling higher and higher. He had over two miles of range. The infrared Cat's Eye lens allowed him to see clearly on the full-color monitor of his controller. He watched himself wave at the Ghost. It brought a broad smile to his face, which he also saw. He was still amazed at how soundlessly the Ghost floated above him. He knew it was in the sky, yet he couldn't hear it or see it. It was creepy as he thought about the spying implications. What if somebody else, like a real space alien, was watching him? He shuddered at the thought of Mac's experience with the UFO.

Harry's mind started wondering about Viet Nam as it often did. What if they would've had drones when he was there? Who knows what would've happened with this technology? He sighed. Whenever he thought about Nam, it always made him mawkish, especially around Memorial Day.

The Ghost soared higher and higher, as Harry flew it over the neighboring woods. It was soon flying over the long, winding rock gravel road leading up the hill to the KORN radio station. KORN was built on a bald knob in the hills so everyone could receive its radio signal. Harry decided to challenge his flying skills by flying low and zipping along the twisting road simulating a chase. Suddenly, he came upon a Ford pick-up truck stopped in the middle of the gravel lane. Its taillights were on, but its headlights were turned off. Cautiously, Harry flew up to the truck's tailgate, paused, and hovered five feet above it.

• • •

It had been an enchanted evening staring into each other's eyes and holding hands across the red and white checkered table cloth. It was the most romantic evening either of them could remember. Mac was so captivated he had forgotten the time and couldn't remember the restaurant's name. He adored Faith and was scared as hell of her at the same time. He had a feeling his life would never be the same. Faith was bewitching and had cast a spell Mac couldn't break even if he wanted to break it.

It was unnerving being with such a beautiful woman. Everyone stared. Mac couldn't take his eyes off her. He was beguiled, and she knew it. She grilled him like a slab of ribs, slowly turning him over and over with a barrage of questions while he stammered to answer. The women at neighboring tables knowingly nodded with each of her questions and his answers. He didn't mind. He basked in her attention. Before he knew it, Faith, and all of the women at neighboring tables, knew more about Mac than anyone ever had. He didn't reveal any of his darker war stories, and she didn't ask. She felt his deep-down sadness. Faith knew about his family, students, favorite pets, Elvis and Honey, what he did for fun, and what scared him most—not being in control. She had already set up their next date by the time dessert arrived. All Mac could do was marvel at her. She handled him as easily as a kindergartener. He knew who was in charge.

Faith smiled, knowing Mac was hers, and she was his. She laughed at his jokes, even the bad ones, as she flirted with him and stroked his ego. She caressed his sinewy arm with her right hand and held his muscular hand in her left. She felt like a queen and was the happiest she'd ever been.

Abner knew it too. He had followed them from the Lake and watched them through the plate glass window as he sat in his truck in the parking lot. Mac had seen him early in the evening. Finally, Abner grumbled, accepted his fate, and quietly drove home.

"Your dad just left, so you're going to have to drive home with me now," said Mac as he smiled at Faith, both of them enjoying his joke.

"What makes you think I don't have the Uber app?" asked Faith. "I apologize for Dad. I know he's overprotective, but there's nobody else in his life except me. We don't have a big family like the other locals. It's him and me, and he still mourns, Mom. I feel guilty every time I go out and leave him alone. He mopes around worrying like a puppy waiting for me to get home. It's sad. He lost his Hope, and now he's afraid he'll lose his Faith."

"Well, if you were my daughter, I'd be fretting too. You're so trusting of everybody. You think everyone is good, but they're not. There are a lot of bad people out there, Faith. You need to be more cautious and less trusting of people."

"Can I trust you not to break my heart, Mac?" she asked. "I don't want to be suspicious of everybody I meet. It's not who I am. I'm sure as sheriff, you meet plenty of bad people, but I teach kindergarten. I've never met a bad kindergartner, just bungling parents who treat their kids the same way they grew up. It's frustrating, but I trust God will show them the way with my help."

"I promise I won't break your heart, Faith. What's the most important thing you teach your kids?"

"I teach them not to be afraid, Mac. Kids are taught to be afraid of everything. Spiders, school, especially math, bullies, scary movies, and kids they've never met. They're even afraid Santa won't give them a toy for Christmas if they're bad. You name the fear, and somebody uses it to control some kid. I want my kids to believe in themselves and not be afraid of everything."

"It's a tall order, Faith. I'm afraid of some things, and I think it's smart to be a little fearful. It's saved my life more than once."

"True, but you didn't let fear control you, Mac. You overcame it, and your courage saved your life. It seems to me fear is the mind-killer. Once we let fear dictate who we are, we've lost."

Mac realized Faith was more than a beautiful woman. She was the whole package. Faith was the woman of his dreams.

● ● ●

"What're you doing, man? Why'd you kill the engine? We've got to get to the radio station. Dan's waiting."

"Whoa, dude, I didn't kill the engine. It just died. I don't know what happened. I'm so stoned I can't remember how to start the truck," said Stoney as he exhaled another Ninja cloud while laughing hysterically.

"There's nothing to it, man. Turn the key and step on the gas," said Darryl as he waved Stoney forward.

"I can't find the key, dude," said Stoney. "Let's do another bowl."

"No way, man. Not until we get to KORN. Turn the key," said an agitated Darryl.

Feeling like a snoop, Harry decided to see how near he could fly to the truck without being detected. He wished he had bought the bionic ear listening device Q had recommended. It would've cost him another two- grand, so he didn't get it. Harry circled the Ford's cab to see what he could see. As the Ghost soundlessly crossed in front of the windshield, Harry clearly saw Darryl's and Stoney's disoriented faces. Harry dillydallied a moment too long when Stoney shouted and pointed, "Dude, what's that?"

Alarmed, Harry flipped the switch for the Hercules spotlight. It blinded the men in the truck as they covered their eyes with their hands. Harry clearly saw the panic in their faces before he elevated the drone up to 100 feet and bathed the Ford in 100,000 lumens of light. The background light made it easy for Stoney to see the truck's ignition key through his red-rimmed slit eyes. He turned the key, stomped the gas, and drove like a bat out of hell up the road towards the radio station.

"What the hell is it, dude?" asked Stoney.

"It's got to be a UFO, man. Our engine died, and I saw that happen to someone on X-Files. Get the hell out of here, man," said a frantic Darryl. "The aliens are trying to kidnap us. Hurry, man!"

Instinctively, Harry shadowed their truck from above, scaring the daylights out of Stoney and Darryl. The stark white light cast ominous grey shadows. Harry didn't even think about turning the Hercules light off. It made everything so much brighter. His Bell AH-1 HueyCobra pilot instincts took over as if he was in hot pursuit of a bogey. Rattled and confused at the prospect of being chased by a UFO, Stoney had a difficult time keeping his truck on the road as it skidded around the gravel curves. Darryl's screams were as loud as the truck's speakers blaring *UFO's Space Child*.

Dan was waiting in front of KORN, taking a selfie video, when he saw the eerie vision of a pick-up truck bathed in brilliant light racing towards him. Blinded by the light, Stoney's truck barely missed Dan as it swerved going past. Anticipating what would happen, Harry raced ahead and used his spotlight to light up the radio transmitter tower to warn Stoney. It didn't help. Stoney's truck crashed headlong into the tower. The Ford's airbags deployed, and the grill was smashed into a hideous smile. The tower bore the brunt of the truck's force as its transmitter was catapulted to the ground with an explosion of sparks setting the prairie grass on fire. KORN quit transmitting right in the middle of the song *Dixie Breakdown*. Shaken, Stoney and Darryl were trembling as they jumped out of the truck. Dan ran towards them, yelling to see if they were okay.

Harry turned off the Hercules. The Ghost rapidly ascended, and Harry watched the men walk away. The truck and the tower were wrecked, and KORN was off the airwaves. Harry hurriedly brought the Ghost back to the field and landed. He was shaken. Thankfully, it didn't look like anybody was seriously hurt. After hiding the Ghost in the basement, he drove home cursing himself. Dottie was already asleep. Grabbing a couple of beers, Harry sat up most of the night on his dock, remembering many bad memories.

"What happened, dude?" asked a shaken and confused Stoney.

"I'm not sure, man," said Darryl as he tried to shake the cobwebs out of his head.

"Did you see it? Did you see the UFO? It attacked your truck and threw you guys into the radio tower, man," shouted Dan as he darted around the chaotic scene. Stoney and Darryl were so scared they were quivering. Dan's nose-for-news was on auto-pilot. He started running around the KORN grounds taking photos and a video with his Samsung Galaxy phone of the truck, tower, burning grass, and sparking transmitter. Having a flair for the dramatic, Dan started posing the guys around the truck and tower as he took their photos. After the still photos and portraits, Dan video recorded short personal interviews.

"Did I see it? Hell, it chased us up the hill, man. We couldn't get away, man. We were driving for our lives. It was shooting lasers at us, man. Stoney was a stone-cold wheel-man. He's a hero, man," said a relieved but badly shaken Darryl.

"Did you see how fast it was flying, dude? It danced like a jitterbug. I couldn't see it because its light was blinding me, dude. It had to be going a thousand miles an hour. It picked my truck up with a tracker beam and threw us into the radio tower, dude. Whoa! There was nothing I could do but hold on to the steering wheel as tight as possible. I sure couldn't outrun it," said Stoney.

"Were you scared? Did you think it was trying to kill you?" asked Dan, the newsman.

"Scared? We were scared, but we were cool," said Darryl, grabbing himself to figure out if he wet his pants or spilled his beer. "The UFO tried to land on top of us, man. Stoney held tight and drove like Jeff Gordan, man." He mimicked having a steering wheel in his hand. "The UFO was a killer. We were lucky not to be killed by the aliens, man. We could tell they wanted to kill us. It was gnarly."

"How many aliens did you see?" asked Dan.

"Well, I'm not sure, dude. I might've seen a few, though," said Stoney.

"This is great, man," said a smiling Dan. "Call 9-1-1, man. We need to get the cops and the fire department up here."

"Are you crazy, dude? I'm buzzed to the max, dude. They'll bust me for driving under the influence," said a nervous Stoney as he ran to the truck to get his bag of Ninja and pipe.

"You don't have to worry about anything, man. It was the UFO's fault. It attacked you."

"Hey, do you think my truck's insurance covers UFOs, dude? I don't think so. Who the hell's going to believe a UFO attacked us, man? Nobody, that's who."

"Duh, look around. The transmitter is on fire, and so is the prairie grass," assured Dan.

"Dude, my truck ran into it. They're going to blame me and give me a DUI."

"No, they aren't, man. I've got a video of the UFO," said a proud Dan. He held up his phone and displayed the short video clip showing a pure white light with a slightly discernable silhouette of a pickup truck racing towards him. Then the video picture drops to Dan's feet and sandals as he yells, "What the hell, man! It's a UFO."

"Where's the UFO in the video, dude? I don't see one."

"You can't clearly see it because its light is so bright," said Dan as he dialed 9-1-1.

•   •   •

Before they wanted to believe it, their long-awaited date was ending. Faith and Mac both felt sad. It felt like they had been together forever. They were standing on Faith's front porch exchanging small talk when she suddenly grabbed him around the waist, tilted her head back, and reached up to kiss Mac goodnight. Startled, Mac clumsily swallowed his breath mint gum and awkwardly returned her kiss as best he could. He wished he wasn't so self-conscious, but it gave Faith an excuse to snatch another kiss. He was happy to oblige, and did much better on his second attempt. Faith knew Abner was spying from behind the living room curtains, wishing she had been a boy. Abner was as nervous as a hen on the roost when it came to Faith. He knew their lives were about to change, and he couldn't do a darn thing about it. He was going to lose his little girl and fishing buddy.

Blissfully on his way back to the squad car, Mac was replaying the evening when he heard the police radio squawk. He hustled to pick up the microphone and waved to Faith, still standing on the porch.

"Sheriff, we have a 911 call. Someone is claiming a UFO threw his pickup truck into the KORN radio tower. What should I do?" asked Thelma, the overnight operator.

"I'll take it, Thelma," said Mac as he waved goodnight, and shuddered at the thought of his encounter with the UFO.

In a matter of 15-minutes, the station's bald knob was lit up like Christmas. Sirens were screaming loud enough to wake up the dead. Without its tower and transmitter, KORN was off the air during the most important news story in its history. It was frustrating for Dan, who was always dreaming about covering a big story. There was no way he could report it over the air—live.

Everyone was suspicious of the men's stories about the UFO. Mac kept an open mind even though he'd busted these guys before for DUIs and pot. He didn't think they were bad guys. He felt they needed a tour in the military to give them some discipline.

Stoney and Darryl did their best to keep their acts together while Mac interrogated them. It seemed like he asked them to repeat their stories 30 times. To the best of their recollections, they re-told the same story they had concocted each time. Mac noticed their discrepancies and how stoned they were. It was apparent they were shaken and confused. They believed they had seen a UFO, and it had attacked them. As an eye-witness reporter, Dan stood behind them, taking notes and massaging their stories by giving his report based on what he witnessed.

Slim Carter heard about the station's fire when the music on his radio went silent, and his police scanner reported the fire in the fields. Slim was a self-styled star and the owner of KORN and the *Hillbilly Opry*. He was so skinny you could've painted lines on him and used him as a yardstick. Slim raced up to the ball of confusion and fire in his classic white 1964 Cadillac DeVille convertible. His 'Caddy' was modeled after a car he had seen when his daddy took him to see the *Grand Ole Opry*. The Caddy had red leather interior and a pair of Texas longhorns bolted onto its front hood. He also had silver dollars glued to the dashboard and every other flat surface in the Cadillac. Slim's clothing was based on styles created by Nudie's Rodeo Tailors. Nudie was the tailor for Elvis and other country-western stars. Slim dressed like he was on stage whenever he went out in public. He always wore his trademark white 10-gallon Stetson with silver medallions and a turquoise headband. Tonight, his white cowboy shirt was edged in dark green piping with sequin roses embroidered near its slit front pockets. A much larger embroidered red sequin rose with a single thorn and leaf was on the back of his shirt. A silver buckle, the size of a dinner plate shaped like a guitar, held up his slim-hipped pants with pant legs no bigger round than a shotgun barrel. His red-tipped, ostrich-leather pointed-toe boots added two inches to his height which was already formidable when wearing his Stetson.

On the *Hillbilly Opry* stage, Slim was as smooth as melted lard in a warm skillet and just as oily. Off-stage, he was meaner than a chicken-eating hog and hungry for an argument. Some folks wanted to buy him for what he was worth and sell him for what he thought he was worth. He was worth a lot. Besides KORN and the Opry, Slim owned a motel, bait shop, gas station, grocery store, and his family's original hillbilly farm.

"Can't you see those boys are drunker than Cooter Brown? Hell, Mac, they're graveyard dead. They're stoned," yelled Slim waving his arms like he was directing the Practical Jokers at the Opry.

"I know they are, and I want to throw them in the hoosegow, but the video raises doubts, Slim. What do you want me to do? They're claiming a UFO attacked them. Their witness is your employee and he has a video of the alleged UFO."

"They're slipperier than eels in a barrel full of snot, Mac. I know what they're trying to do. They're trying to confuse you with some outlandish story so they don't get arrested. You know I came up the hard way. I'm not buying it," glowered Slim.

"I understand, Slim, but disproving their stories is tougher than nailing jelly to the wall," said Mac as he walked away, disgusted. The glow from his dinner with Faith had already evaporated. Mac's recent experience with a possible UFO left him wondering if this might have been a real UFO.

Slim didn't buy their stories. He didn't believe in UFOs. He became a successful entrepreneur because his family was dirt poor, and everyone had to eat. His parents fed eight kids along with Granny and GranPappy. They all lived together in a 150-year-old dilapidated house. Slim started his first business at 12, when his older brother, Al, got his driver's license.

Slim's daddy rented a yellow school bus and Slim hand-painted a sign that read, 'Hillbilly Toors, See A Axsual Hillbilly Farm, $.25 per person.' The brothers parked at the dam and flagged tourists with red bandanas tied to bamboo poles. Soon pilgrims were lined up waiting to ride the bus to a genuine hillbilly farm. Once loaded, Al drove the pilgrims to their family's actual farm while Slim strummed his guitar and sang Hank Williams' songs. The 'Hillbilly Toor' was the number one tourist attraction when the Lake was a fishing mecca.

Pilgrims loved to pay to see impoverished people in an unpainted shack. It made them feel virtuous to give away their money, and it made them feel better about their personal situations. They went silly when a sassy spotted sow named Moonbeam strutted around like she owned the place. Moonbeam would saunter up and smile until the pilgrims threw the snacks Slim had just sold them out their windows. The snacks drew her piglets and more snacks were thrown out the windows. When enough snacks were lying on the ground, even the hound dogs would get up and walk over. At the next stop on the tour, mothers pointed out GranPappy sitting on the front porch rocking and swatting flies. Granny was washing and hanging their laundry using a boiling cauldron of water. Slim had placed an empty moonshine jug behind GranPappy's rocking chair even though GranPappy didn't drink.

Each week Slim had a new idea to make more money. He also started selling 'sooveneer' straw hats, cedarwood outhouses, corncob pipes, blue jean bib overalls, and anything else he could gather. In no time, his family built a new home on the backside of the farm and kept the old homestead just for the hillbilly tours. They hired family members and locals to be the actors. Yep, Slim knew how to make money and dress like a cowboy movie star, but he didn't know about UFOs or how to put out a grass fire.

When Dan, Darryl, and Stoney drove off in Dan's Honda Civic without being arrested by Mac, Slim shook his fist at them and yelled, "I'll get you boys for wrecking my damn radio station. You're fired, Blather!"

Smiling, Dan flipped Slim the bird as he drove away. He was determined to report the biggest story in his career.

## CHAPTER 7

# UFO

Dan had been practicing and planning for this moment ever since high school. He had the only ingredient he needed for success in the news business—a story that could be blown up in the national media. If he rolled it out to his best advantage, it would become his meal ticket to fame.

The UFO attack and supportive yet hazy video was the type of news story that fell into your lap once in a lifetime. If you were lucky. Dan was desperate to get away from the Lake area. He wanted more than a one-time 30-second feature on TMZ, cover on *National Enquirer*, or a story buried inside *People* magazine. If Dan played the story correctly, he could become a celebrity reporter like Wordrift and Bumsteer. One good news story could get him regular guest slots on all of the cable news networks forever. He'd be famous. He wanted this UFO story to be so big he'd be featured on the front page, top fold, of *The New York Times* and *The Washington Post*. This was his big chance. Dan figured he'd probably never get another story like this one and he didn't want to blow it.

Dan was on deadline, he had to beat the pack. He needed to release the story by sunrise before someone else caught wind of it and broke it. Darryl and Stoney were too shaken to take photos and too stoned to stay awake. If this story was caught by the national media, Dan would end up with a job as a national reporter. An impressive job, like his sister, Agate. He needed to show his dad and his phony sister, he was better than them. They wouldn't snigger when he was a reporter for a national network. They'd have to look at his face every Sunday morning.

"Payback is a bitch, Agate. Sorry, Phillip, my calendar is full. Maybe we can schedule something—like never!" he screamed at the top of his lungs scaring his fluffy cat, Ché, who darted under his futon and had to be coaxed out.

Dan wrote and re-wrote his headline until he was satisfied. In school, he was taught not to worry about headlines, but he knew wire service editors wouldn't read past the headline to decide if they wanted to buy his story. Sunday morning was always a slow news day until the morning TV news shows magically created stories out of thin air. Dan was hoping to get some live interviews on TV.

Dan dreamed, 'Am I crazy to think this story might get me a posting as a White House correspondent? Who knows more about UFOs than me?' He had always dreamed about a D.C. correspondent job before getting stuck in the KORN blackhole.

After writing the headline, Dan wrote and edited his story. It had to be letter-perfect, so there weren't any yellow or red flags raised. He wrote the story so he wouldn't have to be worried about fact-checking. Wire editors didn't want fact-checkers, or as some called them—fact-blockers, to kill stories because the checkers didn't agree with the stories politically. Wire services casually cared about grammar when it was appropriate. Editors didn't want to spend time editing much beyond a cursory Microsoft grammar check. Grammarly at most. Most of the time, editors didn't read past the first paragraph. The headline and the lede sentence had to grab the readers by the nose.

Writing an old-fashioned newspaper story was a challenge for Dan. He was rusty and constantly checking the AP Stylebook. He relied on social media to post photos, videos and blurbs to his news feed. He rarely read full-length newspaper articles. Like most people, he didn't subscribe to a paper. He preferred short video feeds.

Dan's gut instinct was to post his UFO video and photos on social media to generate mega-media buzz. He was forced to be patient as he took a massive hit from the gas mask hookah bong delivered by Amazon the day before. He knew this story needed to be established in mainstream media. Then, he'd release it on social media. Now that Slim had fired him, he was an unemployed news stringer. He wasn't a salaried reporter—yet. He didn't want to waste this once-in-a-lifetime opportunity as he exhaled a cosmic plume of Ninja.

After writing his news story, Dan sat back on his futon and proudly read it out loud as he scratched Ché's neck. The story was ready to peddle to his newswire contacts. It was an ass-grabber.

## UFO Attacks Radio Station
## Men Barely Survive

A UFO attempted a near-deadly attack on three men at the Lake last night. All men survived without life-threatening injuries. The UFO used an unknown magnetic weapon to hurl a full-sized pickup truck into the radio station's tower with the men in it. The KORN radio station tower and transmitter can no longer broadcast due to the UFO attack.

The UFO also used lasers in an unrelenting military-style attack aimed at the men, which set nearby fields on fire. The Lake Volunteer Fire Department fought the blazing wildfires most of the night to keep them from spreading to a nearby forest. Even with the deadly impact of climate change, the firefighters were able to keep the wildlife death toll to a minimum.

The three male victims were treated at the scene and able to return home after the life-threatening events. Two of the victims' names are being withheld for their safety.

Dan Blather, the on-the-scene reporter, captured video of the UFO while he was under attack. His video shows the aliens using white lasers to blind the men while using an anti-magnetic gravitational field to hurl the Ford pick-up truck into the radio tower.

It is suspected the aliens interpreted KORN's country and western music as hate speech before attacking the men and the station.

Contact Dan Blather at 573-555-1631'
or Blatherblab@cosmic.com.

Reporter's Note: Blather was an eyewitness at the scene when the attack occurred. He has a video and a library of photos to substantiate his eye-witness account of the events. Interviews are ongoing and were conducted with victims, law enforcement officials, firefighters, and locals.

●　●　●

"Hey, Dan, Mike Bitter with DPI wire service. We'd like to pick up your story. We need your video too. How much are you asking?"

Exhausted and sleepless, Dan said, "I need twenty-five thousand for the exclusive rights to the story and video. I need twenty-five hundred for each follow-up story with a guarantee of six more stories with bylines. I also need $500 for each photo used." He had gone through all of the negotiations in his head and jotted down his dream numbers beforehand. Dan planned to make more on this story than he had made all year at KORN.

"Are you crazy, Dan? We can't pay that much. We'll offer

two thousand for the story and video, and they have to be exclusive."

"Okay," said a weary Dan, "I'll call NP, and offer them the only video of a UFO attack, ever. Goodbye."

"Wait a minute, Dan," said a nervous Mike, who was always on a 24/7 deadline for more sensational news. "Don't get your bowels in an uproar. I had to ask. You know how tight news budgets are with the decline in subscriptions. I didn't realize you were such an experienced reporter. We'll give you what you're asking. Go ahead. Send your video and the first story," said a delighted Mike, who would've paid twice what Dan was asking.

"I'll send them when I see your payment hit my PayPal account, Mike, and it better be in five minutes, or I'm calling NP," said an agitated Dan.

"Of course," said Mike.

• • •

It was the Sunday. Everyone was gathering their breath for the upcoming summer tourist season. Nobody understood why they couldn't get KORN on their radios. KORN was always on the air, but it vanished like a puff of smoke. It was like KORN never existed.

By noon, everyone at Sizzerbill's was gathered around the life-size TV hanging on the wall. They repeatedly watched the video of the UFO attack. It was shown on every local and cable news network. Every station carried the same story, and the talking heads said the same things. Everyone sat whomper-jawed, especially Mac. The report on TV didn't come close to what he had witnessed and investigated.

'I should've arrested those guys last night,' he thought wincingly. Then I wouldn't be watching all of this hogwash. No one had ever experienced anything like the video was showing. Viewers wondered, "Are pickup trucks being catapulted into radio towers?' 'Are lasers being shot at men by a UFO and setting fields on fire?'

There hadn't been as much excitement at the Lake in a hundred lifetimes. In fact, there had never been a UFO attack in the history of the world much less at the Lake. Locals quietly wondered, 'Should we start locking our doors?'

The UFO story made Dan a media star and a social media diva. Mac watched him being interviewed by cable news celebrities on every channel. Bizarrely, nobody at Sizzerbill's recognized Dan. They'd never seen him around the Lake. He'd never been in Sizzerbill's. The UFO story was electrifying. Everyone in the USA started making plans to visit the Lake with the hopes of seeing a UFO attack or at least an alien or two.

No one at the Lake knew the story had already hit the front page of the online editions of *The New York Times* and *The Washington Post*. Harry felt guilty. He didn't know all of this would happen because of his test flight, but he didn't want to confess to Mac.

"What the heck is going on, Mac? Are we under attack?" asked a fidgety Fleagle. "Did you see the UFO last night? Is it the same UFO that chased you the other night? It didn't shoot lasers at you like those boys, did it?"

"Aww, slow down, Fleagle. I'm not sure it happened the way those boys are telling it. No, I didn't see any UFOs last night. This whole story is getting way out of hand. You can't trust the media to tell you a straight story. I'd better start my investigation before this story blows up and Blather gets a Putzer Prize."

"Did you see or hear anything last night when you were working on the ice machine, Harry?" asked Dottie.

"Were you working here late last night, Harry?" asked Mac.

"Yeah, but I didn't see or hear anything," said Harry as he acted disinterested. "No UFOs attacked Sizzerbill's."

"Well, you didn't get home until late last night. Didn't you see the firetrucks or hear the sirens, honey?"

Mac gave Harry a curious look, furrowed his right eyebrow, and listened as Harry tried to smooth talk his way out of the conversation.

"I said, no, Dottie. I didn't see or hear anything. I was tired and frustrated working on that ice maker. I didn't see any little green aliens running around, and I especially didn't see a UFO shooting lasers and starting fires." Harry sounded cranky and a little too exasperated. Dottie momentarily thought to herself, 'Does Harry have a girlfriend?' Then thought, 'No way, not Harry.'

In a gallant attempt to recoup his believability, Harry added. "I'm sorry, baby doll, I'm exhausted. I remembered some bad memories last night and couldn't get to sleep," he said, nodding his head to allude to his Viet Nam memories.

"I understand," said Dottie. She had lived with Harry's nightmares ever since they met. She understood how being a soldier in a war affected people. Mac knowingly nodded in solidarity with Harry.

"What in cornpone hell is that bean pole doing on TV?" asked an agitated Mac, pointing at the TV. Slim Carter stood there with a neck as long as a well rope in his Stetson, wearing a bright red cowboy shirt. He was being interviewed by Dan Blather. "Turn it up, please?" asked Mac shaking his head disapprovingly. Elvis stood up, walked in a circle and groaned sensing Mac's unrest, before laying back down.

Since that night driving home, Elvis knew Mac was unsettled. Elvis was more worried about Faith, the homewrecker. 'I like my life the way it is. Hero and I don't need some sweet-talking dolly trying to weasel her way into our happy home. The nerve of her,' thought Elvis as he dozed off to sleep.

Mac's personal cell phone was blowing up with texts from his parents and Faith as Slim's interview careened along with Dan leading the way.

"Why have you set up roadblocks with guards at the entrance of KORN's road, Slim?" asked a tense Blather. "The people have a right to know. Haven't you ever heard of the First Amendment and the free Press?"

"I'm keeping trespassers away from the station, Dan. It's private property and a dangerous site. I can't afford for anybody to get hurt in an unsupervised setting."

"Yeah, but you're charging people money to load up on your school bus and take them to see the radio station,

Slim," said Blather as the TV station videographer panned her camera over to the long line of people waiting their turn to see the site. They were sold soda and snacks while they waited for the next bus ride up the long hill. Slim performed songs as everyone waited for their turn.

"Yes, and it's only ten dollars a person, including a uniformed tour guide," said Slim winking into the camera.

"In the interest of science, public safety, and the free Press, do you think it's fair to be profiteering from this first-of-its-kind UFO encounter? Doesn't the public deserve to know what happened, sir?"

"Sweep in front of your own door, boy, and you'll get a shovel full. How much are you getting paid for your stories?" said Slim, using his fingers for quotation marks on the word 'stories.' "Besides, I'm giving people a fair trade for their admission fee. I've damages to pay for to get KORN back on the air. Do you have damages, Dan?" The camera panned back to Blather who looked confused.

"Well, don't you think you should let the Press tour the radio station so we can report the news to the public, sir?"

"I sure do," said Slim. "That's why I set up a special tour bus for the Press at five p.m. this evening. Admission comes with a complimentary barbecue dinner from *Smokin' Hot Barbecue*."

"It helps, sir, but you're not allowing the Press to take our cameras or phones up to the site to take photos or videos. It's not fair. We're the Press. The people have a right to know."

"I agree, Dan, you are the Press, and the Press plans to

sell photos, videos, and news stories about my property for a profit. I guess I'm the only person here who isn't supposed to make any money. Yet, I'm the only guy who lost any money and his radio station," said Slim.

At that moment, Harry and Mac recognized the whirly-bird sounds of THWOP-THWOP-THWOP and window vibrations from helicopters flying low over Sizzerbill's. The sounds were heading towards KORN.

"It sounds like an invasion," said Mac as Harry nodded in agreement.

"It must be those TV stations' helicopters doing a flyover to get photos of the area, Mac," offered Harry as Mac shook his head in agreement.

Then, dozens of shotgun blasts could be heard over the TV while Dan and Slim bantered.

"What're those sounds? They sound like gunshots," said Blather to Slim.

"I'm guessing it's my guards shooting at the news helicopters trying to illegally take photos and get video footage of KORN, Dan," said Slim as he folded his arms in defiance and smiled belligerently.

"You've got armed guards shooting at news helicopters? Are you crazy, Slim? It has to be a federal offense or something," screamed Dan.

"Not based on the castle-doctrine law, Dan. I've got a right to defend my property." They both watched the news helicopters turn-tail and swarm in retreat from KORN. Slim was smiling like a cat eating cockleburs.

"I've got to get over there, folks. See you later," said Mac as he hurriedly put on his sheriff's cap and hustled out the screen door. It almost slammed on Elvis' tail which seemed to have a mind of its own. Mac grimaced, knowing he had forgotten to text Faith back as he climbed into his truck, spun gravel, and headed to KORN.

At five in the afternoon, the bus lumbered up the hill. It was full of reporters from all over the country. The reporters were upset because the best Lake hotel rooms were already booked for Memorial Day weekend, and VRBO didn't have a home available. Everyone with a Lake home or condominium was planning a vacation as soon as possible. By six p.m., Sizzerbill's was sold out of Dottie's pies which were supposed to last until Tuesday. The UFO attack and all of the media coverage were good omens for Lake businesses.

• • •

"What do you mean you forgot about me, Mac? I thought we made a connection Saturday night. When I heard those shotgun blasts on the TV, I was worried about you. I thought you cared about me, about us," sniffed Faith into her phone. Feeling underappreciated and a little melancholy, she couldn't hold back her emotions.

"I do, Faith. Things have gotten crazy busy with all of this UFO stuff. I'm not sure what's going on, and that damn, I mean darn, Slim, is making my life even harder with those guys blasting their shotguns at the helicopters.

Now, I've got the State Police coming to inspect the station and see what they can do to help out. It's getting crazier all the time. I'm going to be busy until this thing gets unraveled and I can figure it out."

"So, are you saying we're not going to see each other for a while, Mac?" asked Faith, hoping Mac would say he'd be over tomorrow.

"Unfortunately, I'm sorry to say you're probably right, Faith. I'm not sure when we'll be able to see each other again," he gulped. "I'm sorry, but being sheriff is sure getting tougher with this UFO business."

"I understand, Mac. Go do what you've got to do. I'll finish up my classes, and we'll talk about doing something soon. Bye," said a sad Faith, hoping Mac would apologize and tell her he loved her.

Mac exhaled profoundly and said, "Good night, Faith."

## CHAPTER 8

# The Devil's Train

There were as many reporters as tourists at the Lake by Memorial Day weekend. Everyone was searching the night sky for UFOs and never-seen-before aliens. Reporters, especially those from New York and Washington D. C., were secretly hoping for an earth-shattering attack with phenomenal photo opportunities. Their editors and producers were already impatient.

"I didn't send you to the Lake for a damn summer vacation, Christopher! Make some news. Surely, the aliens are colluding with the sheriff's office about something. Write the story. You're on deadline," screamed his overbearing editor, Hillary, into the phone. "I sent you to capture a spectacular explosion where hopefully not too many people get killed, but I'll settle for an electrifying UFO and some thrilling action footage."

"I'm staying awake all night to see a UFO, Hillary. Nobody's seen anything."

"Then, make it up, Christopher. Show some enterprise. If you can't find a story, I'll send a go-getter down there to get it done." Hillary finished the last swig of her sweet white wine and clicked off her phone while she glumly stared at her ne'er-do-well husband who was using his phone to check out porn acting like he was reading news stories.

Out-of-town reporters didn't know where to look for UFOs. They spent most of their time on chartered boats lying on their backs or gossiping in a bar, careful not to reveal any sources or suspicions. Their expenses, especially bar tabs, were getting sky-high and it took all of their imaginations and energy to hide their expenses.

Reporters weren't interested in getting to know the locals, but they didn't know where all of the backroads would lead them. Logging roads weren't on their phone's Google maps. Reporters lived in cities with sidewalks, streets, and alleys. They could easily find all the buildings, sidewalks, and roads on Google's Street view at home.

Out-of-town reporters were afraid they'd get lost in the woods. Rumors were spread about mountain lions, bears, and even Bigfoot in the woods around the Lake. They felt lost and didn't trust anyone enough to ask where they should eat, drink, or stay. Reporters were terrified of the locals. Most locals were thought to be crazed gun owners and animal murderers. Out-of-town reporters were streaming Burt Reynold's movie "Deliverance" on *Nutflux*. Most reporters were house cats. They didn't want to be killed and buried where they'd never be found.

Locals and tourists smiled and talked with each other while they were in line at Wal-Mart and Piggly Wiggly. Reporters didn't smile or talk to anyone except themselves. Locals looked strange to reporters. They weren't dressed in Lululemon like reporters. Locals were dressed in camouflage and any other readily available clothing. They looked like people who watched Duck Dynasty and Jeff Foxworthy reruns.

For reporters, going to the Lake was like visiting a foreign country. They felt like foreign war correspondents without getting extra pay. Narrow country roads looked like reporters; neither had shoulders. Driving country roads made the reporters' stomachs queasy because they were twisting and winding. Lake roads didn't have regular street names. They had signs with letters or numbers or nothing. If the roads had a name, it was something dumb like 'No Name Road.' There wasn't one street named Broadway or Fifth Avenue.

The names of locations were dumber than the names of roads. Who wanted to live near Thief Hollow, Dead Indian Creek, Turkey Bend, Slave Row, or the worst name of all, Skunk Hollow? Reporters were more than a little afraid of locals who were thought to be ignorant rednecks with a touch of insanity.

When reporters drove on backwoods' lanes, they were liable to run over a pack of dogs lying on the shaded roads napping. Although driving the roads was scary, it wasn't as creepy as sleeping in a tiny rock motel cottage named the *Dew Drop Inn* or *The Love Shack*. Cringe. Redneck motels didn't have room service or WIFI, but they did have spiders. Reporters were upset that all of the rooms at Margaritaville were already reserved.

The Lake was the worst place they'd ever been assigned. At first, east coast reporters were excited to be assigned to the UFO attack story. Still, room accommodations, restaurants, and the bar scene sucked. The only pizza they could find was Dominoes. The only steaks were BBQ pork steaks smothered in hot BBQ sauce. They weren't able to find a good bottle of white Bordeaux or even a dry martini at the local restaurants. They were forced to buy their liquor at package liquor stores. The neon bar signs claimed the Lake was beer country, but they couldn't find any imported beer, only domestic lagers and bitter IPAs.

Roads encircling the Lake were buzzing with expensive Harleys, three-wheelers, and custom choppers driven by veterans with American flags flapping behind them as they rode. Biker mommas flaunted their cleavage, wore thick-soled boots, sleeveless black leather vests, and leather chaps. All bikers wore American flag headscarves and brightly colored sunglasses. Most hadn't shaved, and they called each other "road dawg." They looked rougher than a corn cob in the outhouse.

"Dan, if you want another fat paycheck, you better come up with some new UFO photos and stories," barked an angry Mike Bitter. He was used to screaming orders at his news stringers.

"Look, Mike, I'm doing the best I can. Sorry. I don't control the flight schedules for UFOs," said Dan as he muttered, "You..."

"What did you say, Blather?"

"I didn't say anything, Mike. The reception sucks here. I barely have one bar."

"What about that hick sheriff's story you promised me? You told me someone said the sheriff saw a UFO."

"I did, but the sheriff is pretty close-mouthed. He hasn't even held a Press conference. I'm working on him, though. I did send you the story from the local guy named Fleagle. He claimed he'd seen one before."

"Yeah, but he was squishy as an eyewitness. He didn't have any proof he saw it. Did he give you any ideas where to find another UFO?"

"He told me to go up on the bluffs to get the best view of the Lake. I've been there every night but I haven't seen anything."

"Well, keep an eye out, Blather. If you get beat on the story, you're out!" Yelled an exasperated and red-faced Bitter. He abruptly hung up while screaming at someone else on his end of the line. The UFO story was wildly profitable. Dan's video was a blockbuster and still running on all of the networks. It had 157 million views on the DPI website. DPI wanted to remain the UFO nerve-center of the world, and it needed to get the next big video or picture to keep its ranking.

Meekly, Dan hung up and muttered, "Kiss my go to hell," under his breath. It was the only phrase he'd picked up at the Lake. Dan was committed to finding the next UFO sighting to get a permanent job with a real media company. Right then and there, he decided to sell his next story to a different news outlet. DPI didn't give Dan much coverage anyway. 'Screw them,' thought Dan as he flipped Bitter off as if he was standing next to him.

Standing with his arm still fully extended in a full screw-you salute, Dan watched a white Hummer limousine envelop him and his dented Honda Civic in a cloud of Sizzerbill's parking lot gravel dust.

Coughing up the dust, Dan thought, 'Who's this, asshole?' A liveried chauffeur hopped out, put on his black cap, and hustled around the megalith to open the back door for its passengers. 'I'll bet there are some scorching hot chicks in there,' dreamed Dan while getting his phone ready for an *Instagram* post.

Dan's dream date quickly deflated. What he saw was a rotund sweating man rocking back and forth to launch himself out by clutching the limousine's roof. There weren't any hot chicks. The man had the whole limousine to himself. When the Humpty-Dumpty-looking man was finally able to pop out, which made a sucking sound, he was looking straight at Dan who still had his arm extended in a full screw-you salute aimed at him.

"Come here, son," said the red-faced and wheezing man staring at Blather. Dan dropped his salute. He couldn't will himself not to obey the commanding voice of the man. A forest green Outback Subaru skidded into a parking spot alongside the limousine. A couple of young, student-looking persons jumped out and ran to be near, but not too near, the extra-extra-large man. "Tell me where the KORN radio station is," said the man.

"It's over that way past the tree line," said Blather, pointing across the parking lot, a large grassy field and a wooded area. He couldn't help himself from asking in awe, "Are you Karl Bumsteer the famous reporter?"

Dan was pretty sure he was right. The man was heavier than he remembered from old photos, and he pinched himself to make sure he wasn't dreaming. Bumsteer was the, evidently, larger-half of the most outstanding reporting team in modern history. He and Nod Wordrift had won dozens of media awards from their colleagues, including a prestigious Putzer Prize. They broke a fake news story about collusion between the US president and The Duchy of Grand Fenwick. Their hoax got the president impeached fifty years earlier. They were still acclaimed in journalism schools for their investigative prowess. Wordrift had retired from journalism and was writing TV scripts for family sitcoms. Dan was surprised to see Bumsteer. He thought the legend was dead, but here he was in his corpulent flesh and blood.

"Yes, yes, I am Karl Bumsteer. Would you like my autograph?" hurriedly asked a much-gratified Bumsteer who was ecstatic to still be recognized.

"Sure," said Dan in a fawning voice, "Would you sign my Civic, right here?" He pointed to a spot he wiped clean as he handed Bumsteer the black Mark-A-Lot he carried, hoping someone would ask him for an autograph. "What are you doing at the Lake, Mr. Bumsteer?"

"I've come to report on the UFO story for the Global News Network," said Bumsteer as he signed the Civic in large, broad strokes. It was the first automobile he had ever autographed. Back in the seventies, girls in communication and journalism schools asked him to inscribe their naked bodies, he sighed remembering. 'Tempus fugit,' he thought.

"No way, man, I broke that story," said Dan as he gushed to be recognized by the celebrated reporter.

"Wait, you're Dan Blather?" asked Bumsteer quizzically looking at Dan who was wearing cut-off shorts and sandals. His unkempt hair, scruffy beard, and sunglasses made him look incognito. He had a tattoo of Taddler on his forearm.

Looking at Bumsteer, who was dressed in Brooks Brothers business casual, Dan thought, I need to clean up my act. "Yes, sir, I am," said Dan empowering himself by putting his hands on his hips while he tried to feel bold.

"We should collaborate on this story. I'm looking for a new partner." Bumsteer was experienced enough to know when to jump into the front of the parade when the opportunity presented itself. Let's go in here and have a piece of homemade pie to discuss it," said Bumsteer licking his lips. He headed inside, shadowed by Dan and the two persons dressed like twins.

"Who're these people?" asked Dan, indicating he'd been at the Lake too long. They reminded him of NPCs in a role-playing game.

"They're interns from the college helping me out." The three followed the waddling legend as he scurried for a couple slices of pie. Bumsteer had been dreaming about Chocolate Cream Pie ever since he saw the pie sign next to the hand-painted Bigfoot silhouette screwed to a giant white oak tree along the highway.

## CHAPTER 9

# Bonanza

"**G**rab us a couple of those UFOladas, honey. There's a good tip in it for you, if you hurry," shouted the smiling Parrothead over the noise from the crowd gathered around the Margaritaville pool. He and his girl-friend were dressed in lime green spandex bodysuits with hoods to look like aliens. They completed their ensembles with Maui Jim sunglasses, Hawaiian print shorts, parrot headdresses, and plastic-flower leis. The shapely younger woman wore a coconut shell bra. The older Parrothead had replaced his stuffed parrot with a miniature stuffed green alien strapped to his shoulder.

"You bet, darling," shouted the young scantily-dressed waitress over her shoulder. She was wiggling her way through the gregarious crowd dancing to 50-year-old Jimmy Buffett ballads. The Margaritaville staff were so exhausted they couldn't have yelled sooey if the hogs had them pinned down.

Tourists were scheduling their vacations earlier than usual. The Lake had been buzzing like a beehive ever since the UFO stories were broadcast. Everyone was traveling to the Lake to see an actual UFO. The Lake Airport had private jets and planes from as far away as Alaska and California breaking into the regularly scheduled flights. Looking up to see a UFO, which everyone did periodically, people would see dozens of planes circling overhead waiting to land. Planes running low on fuel were re-directed to the closest cities where passengers rented cars to drive to the Lake. Traffic looked like a big city's rush hour all day and night.

The holiday weekend was in full swing. Everyone hosted UFO parties anxiously anticipating another UFO attack. Every hotel and motel within 50 miles of the Lake had their No Vacancy signs lit. Vrbo, Airbnb, and FlipKey didn't have any homes available. Everyone wanted a chance to see an alien spaceship.

Perfectly groomed emerald green golf courses were packed with golfers using the new green alien headcovers for their drivers. Many wore garish fashions featuring space-ships and green aliens.

The Lake itself looked like a boat city. It was covered with every kind of boat and inflatable raft that allowed people to lay on their backs, sip their favorite beverage, and search the sky for UFOs. Families waded in floating mini pools which looked like UFOs, oases, and flamingoes. Their kids jockeyed swans, dragons, and unicorns around the Lake. There was barely a channel for boats to maneuver while they slowly towed swimming docks. No one doubted UFOs were flying during the daytime but seeing them was more challenging than spotting a gnat's wings. The Lake was more congested at nighttime because everyone caught up on their sleep during the day.

Mac and his deputies, Snuffy Smith and Barney Fife, were as busy as ants at a picnic taking calls from people claiming to have seen a UFO or alien. Many tourists were frantic and inconsolable. People from the coasts were the worst. They were afraid aliens wanted to abduct them and take them into outer space away from their families. When questioned about why aliens wanted to kidnap them, most quoted lines about Fox Mulder's sister's abduction. The Sheriff's office encouraged those most overwrought to leave, but no one did. They loved being scared and didn't intend to miss the most exciting event of their lives. It was like having a role in an actual movie like 'Close Encounters of the Third Kind.'

"I'm not sure what to tell these people, Sheriff. They're paranoid. They need a psychiatrist, not a sheriff. Why'd they come to the Lake if they're afraid of UFOs? Not one call we've investigated has panned out. There's not one scintilla of evidence about an alien or a UFO visiting the Lake except the crashed radio tower. What are we supposed to do?" said Snuffy.

"It's like somebody is beating the fear drum, Mac. People's brains aren't working," said Barney.

"I'm not sure what to say, boys. I've been reading everything I can find. I even ordered a book called *Flying Saucers* by Dr. Carl Jung to help me figure this thing out. Heck, Edgar Allan Poe was writing fake newspaper stories about a man flying to the moon in a balloon in the 1830s. And, Orson Welles broadcasted his fake *War of the Worlds* radio program in 1938. You'd think people would know what's fact and what's fiction. Keep investigating any credible lead though, and let's hope we find something to shed light on what's happening. I'm afraid we've got a psychological epidemic on our hands."

•  •  •

Real people are always creepier than a movie's characters which explained why David Ducktail flew to the Lake on his private plane. He was fretting about the environmental impact of the UFO sightings as he straightened his collar and checked his make-up before taking a selfie for social media. He had traveled to the Lake to keep himself relevant and sell autographed photos.

"Are you, Fox Mulder, the FBI agent? I've seen you on TV. If you're here, these UFO sightings must be real. I'm glad you're on the job, sir. Did you ever find your sister who was abducted by aliens?" asked a curious man dressed in a Tommy Valhalla ensemble which consisted of a baggy swim-suit, t-shirt, straw hat, sandals, and expensive sunglasses. The man's family was enjoying all of the UFO hubbub at the dam. The man really wanted to visit the black powder gun show on the other side of the Lake, but his wife wouldn't let him. He was looking for a muzzle-loading flintlock to hunt feral hogs.

"Hello, sir. I played Fox Mulder in the *X-Files* TV series. My real name is David Ducktail. *X-Files* is a fictional TV series. Fox Mulder isn't a real person," grimaced a frustrated Ducktail. Everyone called him Fox Mulder. *X-Files* had ruined his chance for a movie-acting career which never took off after *X-Files*. Nobody watched *Californication* except for drunk high school boys hoping to see naked women late at night.

Ducktail's autographed photos were accompanied by live readings of monologues from his favorite *X-Files* scripts. Tourists and locals thought Ducktail looked and sounded like Fox Mulder the real alien hunter.

"Would you like to buy one of my *X-Files'* photos, Mr. er?"

"Trueblood," said the sandaled man keeping his hands in his pockets.

"Mr. Trueblood, would you like to buy one of my autographed photos? I'm starting one of my monologues in a few minutes if you'd care to watch," said Ducktail with an insincere smile.

"Absolutely, yes, Mr. Ducktail," said Mrs. Trueblood recognizing the actor and hustling over to his booth to grovel for his attention. "We'd love one," she said, scowling at her husband, who kept his hands in his pockets.

"I guess we do, as long as you sign it 'Fox Mulder' and not David Ducktail," said a disgruntled Trueblood as he snapped a photo of his wife with Ducktail on her phone. Ducktail signed the photograph, Fox Mulder.

Slim was an actor at heart and a sucker for the dramatic flair. He was moved by listening to Ducktail's dramatic readings.

"Howdy pardner, I've been watching you. You've got moxy my friend and real talent. I like your readings, and I liked your TV program too. My name's Slim Carter. You probably saw me on TV."

"No, Mr. Carter, I don't believe I did see you on TV. I'm sure I would've remembered your hat," said Ducktail with an ever so slight sneer.

"Yeah, it's distinctive alright," said Slim affectionately caressing its brim with both hands. "Well, I'm not going to dink around, Mr. Ducktail. I'm going to hit the nail on the head. You deserve a lot better location than being a street vendor at the dam. Hell, you're at the top of your game with all of this UFO business. You should be selling your photos at the KORN radio tower. It's the scene of the crime, don'chya know."

"I appreciate your support, Mr. Carter, but I don't know anybody at KORN. I'm sure it'd be difficult to get a location there."

"You do now, Mr. Ducktail. You know me. I own KORN, and I'm inviting you to be a featured attraction at the KORN radio tower. I'm sure you'll be a big hit with the tourists. My bus tours are going gangbusters. There's usually at least a 30-minute wait."

"If tourists are actually waiting, I could sing songs to make the time go by faster," offered Ducktail.

"Wait, you sing too? How perfect. I'm the star performer at the *Hillbilly Opry*. I own the Opry too. We can sing a duet. How about *My Flying Saucer*? It was written by Woody Guthrie and Billy Bragg." Slim was smiling like the Cheshire cat.

After rapid-fire negotiations, Ducktail and Carter shook hands on a 25% agent fee, and they loaded Ducktail's booth into Slim's Caddy. As their partnership blossomed, Slim and Ducktail sang occasional duets. After singing their duets, tourists started asking for Slim's autograph too. So, they authorized a new 8x10 color photograph of the two of them dressed in cowboy clothes and hats, which quickly became a best seller. Ducktail even made several guest appearances at the Opry.

Smart-alecky kids dusted off the drones they got for Christmas and flew them around their neighborhoods. Many played Peeping Tom at bathroom windows and over the docks. There were so many lit drones buzzing at twilight, it was reminiscent of a summer sky full of bioluminescence from glowworms.

The constant media buzz after the UFO attack kept everyone in a distressed state wavering between ecstasy and depression. Since there weren't any new UFO attacks or bona fide alien sightings, reporters had to get creative. "We need some news to pay the bills," shouted editors and producers into their phones.

The easiest stories to report were interviews with B and C-list celebrities like Ducktail. Celebrities needed publicity to catch a role in a new Nutflux series. Any Press, even bad Press, was better than no Press unless stars were caught slapping someone at the Oscars. *Twitter* and *Instagram* were blowing up as over-the-hill starlet celebrities posted photos of themselves in bikinis, bubbly hot tubs, and everything they ate from morning until night at the Lake.

Celebrities treated interviews with desperate reporters like dramatic auditions for a role. They needed to pay their bills and get back into the media spotlight. Most stars had their publicity agents craft a story to explain why they traveled to the Lake. Personal tragedy stories brought tears to the eyes of their fawning fans.

The teary-eyed *New York Times* reporter asked Tiffany Blue, a much-loved child actor from the 90s, "Tiffany, when did you realize your parents allowed aliens to give you drugs and alcohol?"

"I'm not sure, Glenda. It's a blur to me. I was just a child worried about other kids liking me. I never wanted to disappoint my parents. I was about 12 when I realized my parents knew about the aliens. The aliens must've threatened my parents."

"It must've been crushing."

"It was, Glenda, but I felt responsible for everyone in my family."

After her interview, the Time's headline blared, "Tiffany forced to take drugs with aliens." Her story sold lots of newspapers, and her follow-up interview on GNN attracted lots of eyeballs. Tiffany's tragedy was so compelling it forced other Hollywood celebrities to stretch their acting skills. The news became dominated with stories about aliens harassing stars and forcing actresses to do housework and cook. GNN and other media claimed alien lifeforms came from male-dominated cultures. Hollywood's male actors were clearly at a disadvantage. It was hard for them to be a victim of the aliens. It was nearly impossible to break into the media cycle with the starlets getting all of the ink and screen time.

Wink Spacey had the cleverest publicity agent, Dave Draper. Draper came up with the idea of making aliens the actual victims not women. Wink Spacey, became the aliens' champion. It was masterful.

"Today, Wink is here at the dam to announce his *Go Fund Me* campaign to support space-alien rights," said Draper as he presented Spacey to the thrilled crowds.

"Good afternoon, folks. When I heard about the aliens' history of unfettered capitalism, crushing poverty, and declining galactical climate conditions, I had to do something to make a difference. These unstable conditions force aliens to leave their planets," said Wink as he dropped his head in abject grief.

Onlookers became visibly emotional and jumped on their phones to make contributions. They wanted to be part of Wink's solution. Other male actors, some of whom were forced to act in ketchup and adult diaper commercials, supported Wink's allegations of intolerance. Spacey's din of declarations ultimately forced women celebrities to ask their alien attackers for forgiveness. They were afraid of being called alien-phobic and speciesists.

"We're making history—today," screamed Spacey into his new 50-watt megaphone. The crowd rose up and waved their fists hysterically. His megaphone was so large, someone had to hold it while he spoke. Daily protests led by Spacey and his army of actors and actresses attracted gawkers taking selfies to document they were part of the alien-rights protests. It was a watershed moment. Most protestors wore colorful and angry t-shirts with pictures of aliens and grappled with other protestors to buy an illegible autograph for $20 from the unrecognizable aging stars.

Spacey was standing on the makeshift stage with Ducktail who was jumping and pumping his fist in the air to the beat of the people's chants. Sensing a change in the wind, Ducktail abandoned Slim. Ducktail and Spacey publicly declared country-western music was hate speech. Crowd control was becoming a pain-in-the-neck issue for Mac and his deputies as politicians rolled into the Lake for their share of publicity.

CHAPTER 10

# Against the Wind

Under extreme duress from the army of reporters and TV cameras camped out in his front yard and at his office door, Mayor Delbert Klaxon called an executive session of council members, prominent business people, and Mac.

"What in Sam Hill are you going to do, Sheriff? This fiasco is out of control. I can't find any privacy. Yesterday, a damn fool reporter followed me into the toilet asking me questions with his phone in my face. I WAS IN THE DAMN TOILET, MAC! Excuse me. I apologize for screaming. What are we going to do about these UFOs, Mac?"

Before Mac could say anything, Slim Carter arrogantly interrupted. "I don't know what you've got in mind, Delbert, but I disagree. My businesses are going gangbusters. Every day is like the Fourth of July. You politicians better not do anything stupid to screw it up. I'm making more money busing people up to the crashed radio tower than I ever did broadcasting country and western music on KORN! Think of all the sales taxes we're generating from your so-called fiasco. Delbert, don't screw it up, or we'll impeach you and push you out of office. I guarantee it!" said Slim as he pointed a threatening finger at the mayor. Slim was acting like the big dog on the porch threatening everybody from climbing the steps.

The other business owners vigorously nodded their bobbleheads in unison agreement with Slim. Business at the Lake was booming, and their wallets were bulging. Everybody, including Sizzerbill's, was making money hand over fist. Mac didn't have half of the deputies he needed to manage the safety and well-being of the people at the Lake. Hotels and motels, state parks and private camping grounds had packed tourists like sardines in a can. Restaurants and grocery stores were busy from morning until midnight. Traffic was always backed up, and parking lots were loaded with campers. The Lake was filled with boats and bodies. Everyone wanted a chance to see the shimmer of a UFO and a glimpse of an alien. The growing horde was so crowded for Memorial Day weekend, there were food shortages. To fill the scarcity, locals brought in food from their gardens, and the Sam's and Costco's in nearby cities to sell from the beds of their pickup trucks.

All of the heads in the room spun towards Mac. No one had any idea what to do to get control of the situation. Most people in the room secretly hoped to see a UFO, and their families were part of the crowds collecting at the dam. It was exciting!

Resolute, Mac stood up and walked to the front of the room. He made other people feel confident by sharing space with him. When he got up front, he gave everyone his confident smile and looked everyone in the eyes as he scanned the room. His eyes came to rest looking Slim Carter squarely in the eyes. Mac's stare made Slim visibly twitch as he sat down, and folded his hands in his lap covering his crotch. Mac didn't flinch.

Nodding his head, Mac said, "Thanks for asking for my thoughts, mayor. I'm not the kind of guy who runs around like a chicken with his head cut off." Everyone, including Slim, nodded their heads in agreement. They trusted Mac to get them through this chaos. "We've got a situation that can easily get out of control if the media keep stoking the fire. Folks like Spacey and Ducktail have 12-gauge mouths and .22 caliber brains. My deputies and I are outmanned. We need to be able to rely on all of your help to get control."

"What do you need us to do, Mac?" asked the mayor.

"I need everyone to stay calm, mayor. Don't say much to the Press. You can't trust them to accurately report what you say. I'm holding a Press conference later today. You're welcome to attend. Please don't say anything until you hear what I have to say. We all need to be on the same page. We don't want to create more disorder."

Everyone nodded agreement except Slim.

• • •

Mac hated the idea of holding a Press conference. It brought back memories of when he and his team caught Osama Bin Laden. He didn't see himself as a hero like the Press made him out to be. Mac wasn't proud of killing even someone as hated as Bin Laden. Still, the Press insisted on painting him as a hero. Mac saw it as a job he was trained to do. He took an oath to protect his country from terrorists, both foreign or domestic.

He'd been hoping this UFO mess would blow over like a storm on the Lake, but the tempest kept growing, especially with the Hollywood characters arriving and tweeting every day. Avoiding a Press conference was harder than pushing a wheelbarrow with rope handles.

Mac wasn't prepared for the horde of celebrity and citizen reporters waiting for him. Initially, he had scheduled the conference to be held at City Hall, but it was too small. There were more than 500 reporters, photographers, and videographers. Mac moved the conference to the high school gym because of its oversized parking lot. Reporters ran and jostled for position as soon as the gym doors were opened. *The New York Times*, Karl Bumsteer, and Dan Blather felt they deserved the front row positions being occupied by a group of local high school journalists who published a website and produced a podcast. After bickering with the students, who arrived first, as to who was more deserving and essential, the Times, Bumsteer, and Blather resigned themselves to the second row.

There was a mountain of microphones set up on Mac's

podium. He took a deep breath and stepped in front of the swarm of reporters. Mac's first words were drowned out from the sound of clicking cameras, and he was temporarily blinded by the flashes and spotlights.

"Hello, I'm Sheriff Rob MacGregor of Lincoln County. Most people call me, Mac. Thank you for attending this Press conference. I have just a few comments to make today. There is no credible evidence a UFO attacked the KORN radio tower and the men there at the time. We have thoroughly investigated the site and combed the grounds for any evidence we might have overlooked. At this time, we haven't found anything linking a UFO to the site. The damage was caused by a pickup truck when it ran into the KORN radio tower. We are continuing our investigation.

Also, we haven't identified any other credible UFO sightings at this time. Additionally, no one has come forward with a credible claim or evidence proving they saw or interacted with an alien life form.

Thank you for attending this Press conference. I will post a daily update on the Sheriff's website with any new evidence we may discover in our investigations." He wanted to bite his tongue when he said, "Are there any questions?"

Mac grimaced at the unintelligible questions being shouted at him. He couldn't understand anyone. Everyone was shouting over everyone else.

Mac smiled at the students sitting in the front row and pointed to them as the crowd quieted down. "Do you have a question, Stacey?"

"Hello, Sheriff, should we be afraid?" asked a confident young woman who had taken Mac's automobile mechanic's class. She held her phone to video record Mac's response.

"No, Stacey, there's no reason in the world to be afraid at this time. Live your life like you normally do. Everything will be fine," said Mac as he pointed to an out-of-town reporter as Stacey said thank you.

Yelling to be heard, a disheveled and hungover woman reporter from a Fresno newspaper screamed, "How do you explain the video we've all seen of a UFO attacking the radio station tower, Sheriff? Aren't you being too cavalier when you tell us not to worry?"

"No, I don't think so, ma'am. No one can clearly see a UFO in the video. People see a bright light that puts a haze over the rest of the picture. There isn't any concrete evidence proving that what we're looking at is a UFO. We can't tell what is causing the light in the video."

"Well, Sheriff, what is it, if it's not a UFO?"

"I'm not sure. It could be a helicopter, a drone, or even a kite. Anything that flies is a possibility. We haven't found any evidence that proves it's a UFO."

"But you can't prove it's not a UFO. Right, Sheriff?" battered the reporter as the rest of the corps nodded in agreement. She was agitated because she was stuck at the *Love Muffin Hotel* and hadn't had a good story in a week.

Without any acknowledgment from Mac, Karl Bumsteer stood up from his extra-large folding chair, which his interns had set-up and saved for him. The corps waited with bated breath for the gotcha question from the country's sage reporter. Videographers trained their lenses on Bumsteer as he straightened the knot in his tie while his interns tugged on the tail of his wrinkled sport coat.

"Karl Bumsteer, Sheriff," his voice was full with gravitas. "Excuse me, sir, but aren't you forgetting three important facts about this case?"

"I'm not sure I am, Mr. Bumsteer. What facts are you referring to?"

"Harumph, the three eyewitnesses at the scene of the UFO attack." He used his hand to dramatically gesture toward Dan Blather, who was standing on his left side with a rat-eating-cheese smile.

The smug corps stayed silent. They were all thinking, 'Checkmate, cop.' Bumsteer had done it. He had cornered the lying cop in a trap with a straightforward question. He was the preeminent investigative reporter. No question. Self-satisfied with his riposte, Bumsteer's mind wandered as he thought about a slice of coconut cream pie and contacting Wordrift to do a documentary. UFOs and documentaries were spicy right now. He and Wordrift could throw a documentary together in a month for Nutflux.

"You bring up an excellent point, Mr. Bumsteer. Three eyewitnesses claim to have been attacked by a UFO. They also claim it destroyed their truck and the KORN radio station tower. The witnesses' testimony and the video are still under investigation by my department," said Mac as he nodded to Blather.

Dan's mind spun like a roulette wheel assessing proba-bilities, which wasn't easy for a guy who didn't understand math. 'What did the Sheriff mean by still under investiga-tion?' Dan wondered. He needed to get with Darryl and Stoney later today so they could coordinate their stories again. The three made extra money at the tower autograph-ing photos of Stoney's crashed pickup truck, the leaning KORN tower, and the prairie grass fire in the background. Slim had bought the crashed Ford pickup truck from the insurance company to keep the display intact for the tourist attraction. Slim dubbed the highly sought-after attraction *The Leaning Tower of KORN*, since he thought Italy's leaning Tower of Pizza was catchy.

Feeling under attack, Blather blurted out, "Have you ever seen a UFO, Sheriff?" The corps went silent. Dan relied on his interview with Fleagle who had told him Mac saw a UFO one night driving home. Dan hadn't shared this bit of infor-mation with anyone else. Bumsteer stared quizzically at Dan wondering. Why hadn't Dan shared this information over the slice of delicious lemon chiffon pie they had together? He licked his lips, remembering. His stomach growled. He decided to stop by Sizzerbill's after the Press conference.

Mac looked at Dan piercingly and wondered how the little weasel had heard about his UFO experience. Then, Mac remembered Fleagle being at Sizzerbill's. Fleagle had lips that could sink ships. "Yes, I did have an experience one night when I thought I might've seen a UFO," said Mac.

"Well then, why don't you believe it could've happened to me, Sheriff?" asked Blather with a smug smile. Most of the people in the corps knew Dan. His credibility was growing by the moment. They'd seen his face on the TV hundreds of times being interviewed, and he was a local celebrity at *The Graveyard*. Everybody wanted to buy him a drink and hear a first-person account of the UFO story. Most reporters did their first stories at the Lake, interviewing Dan, Stoney, or Darryl after buying one of their $20 autographed photos.

"I didn't say I didn't believe you, Mr. Blather. I said your case is under investigation."

"Is your sighting of a UFO still under investigation too, Sheriff? Don't you believe your own eyes? What else could it have been if it wasn't a UFO chasing you through the backroads?"

Mac wanted to confront Fleagle and ask him what the hell he was thinking when he talked to the reporter. "You're asking great questions, Mr. Blather. What could it have been if it wasn't a UFO? My investigation isn't personal. I believe, you believe, you saw a UFO. I was taught not to believe anything I hear and only half what I see. I'd like to thank everyone for coming today, and I want to remind you to check our website for any updates. Thank you."

It was the end of the Sheriff's Press conference but just the beginning of Blather's. All of the reporters raced to shout questions at Dan about the Sheriff's UFO sighting. Blather's celebrity status was growing. Bumsteer was crushed and ignored by the swarm of reporters.

## CHAPTER 11
# Achy Breaky Heart

"You sure looked striking and in command on TV, Mac," said Faith over her cell phone. "How about I take you out for dinner tonight to celebrate your Press conference?"

"I'd love to go out, Faith, but we'll never find any place to eat out tonight. The Lake is crazy busy. How about you come over to my place. We'll barbecue, and there's an Intel aerial show we can go watch later tonight," said an exhausted Mac.

He was still stinging about the UFO question from Dan, and he was ignoring the calls and texts from Slim and the business people. They were angry he expressed doubt about the UFO sighting. Mac walked into a crowded Sizzerbill's and looked around, hoping to see Fleagle. He didn't recognize a soul and was lucky to find a table in the back.

"You did a great job with the Press conference, Mac," said Dottie as she set down a cup of black coffee that could've floated a horseshoe. Mac's eyes were so bloodshot they looked like a roadmap. He waved off the piece of pie Dottie offered. "Well, you must be in love, Mac. You're watching your weight," she laughed.

"She's sure special, Dottie," said Mac nodding his agreement.

"Well, you better get romancing. You aren't getting any younger, and Faith's as pretty as a rose in the sunshine. Somebody's going to pluck her, and it may as well be you."

"I know, Dottie, I'm doing all I can. Things are out of my control right now. She's coming over for dinner tonight. Did you see Fleagle today?"

"He jumped up and left as soon as he saw Blather ask you about seeing a UFO on the TV."

"I knew Fleagle must've told Blather. I knew it," said Mac nodding his head up and down.

"His wheels don't spin too fast upstairs, Mac. You can't be angry."

"Hello, Hero," said Harry as he walked inside through the backdoor. He was struggling to carry boxes full of sugar and flour, which he bought at a Sam's store 50 miles away. Local suppliers were out of food. After he set the boxes down, Harry poured himself a cup of coffee, headed over to Mac, and sat down.

"Harry, did you ever see a UFO when you were flying helicopters?'

"No, can't say I ever did. Why?" asked Harry as he squirmed, wishing he hadn't sat down.

"I don't know. I'm just wondering about the UFO I thought I saw. What else could it have been? The only things I can think of are a helicopter or a drone. Can you think of anything else?"

"Well, maybe it was a top-secret aircraft the military is testing. You might've gotten caught in a test maneuver. We're only 100 miles or so from the Airforce base."

"Yeah, I thought about that too. I don't think it's likely though. I'm baffled," shrugged Mac as Harry nodded. They both sipped their coffee at the same time.

"How're you investigating and tracking the UFO sightings? What can you do to get ahead of the next sighting? They don't seem very predictable."

Mac looked at Harry. "It's as tough as sacking wildcats. Who knows where they're going to show up next? Unless I'm lucky or iron-assed, I imagine the best I'll be able to do is answer a phone call from a person claiming to have seen one."

"Well, I'll keep an eye out, but I'm not expecting to see anything."

They were both gazing towards the front door when Bumsteer rolled into the dining room, followed by his interns. Bumsteer shuffled over to Mac.

"Hello, Sheriff, may I buy you a slice of their delicious pie?" asked Bumsteer as he smacked his lips.

"No, thank you, Mr. Bumsteer. I've got someplace to be and was just leaving."

"I understand, Sheriff. You're a busy man. May I ask one question, please?" pressed Bumsteer without stopping, "What color of lights did the UFO you saw have? Did it attack you?"

"That's two questions, Mr. Bumsteer. It had a bright white light, and, no, it didn't attack me."

"Thanks for the coffee, Harry." Mac stood and headed for the door. He felt uneasy looking at the TV and seeing a recording of himself saying, "Yes, I did have an experience one night when I thought I might've seen a UFO." He knew his statement would haunt him while he investigated what was happening.

Mac ran around like a madman the rest of the day. He and Faith barbecued at Ironwood and then they watched a lighted drone display sponsored by Intel over the dam. They watched it from a deserted stone hotel on the bluffs, sitting on a blanket and drinking a beer. Intel used hundreds of color-changing drones the size of basketballs to put on the whimsical spectacle. It featured 3-D oscillating drone formations 600 feet in the sky which created all types of UFO and alien images. Mac was the most relaxed he had been since their first dinner date.

"I've had a wonderful time tonight, Mac. I wish we could see each other more than once a week though. You seem so distracted, even when we're talking on the phone, which is only once a day if I'm lucky. I was hoping we'd see more of each other and get involved with each other's lives."

"I know I'm distracted, Faith, and I'm sorry. The UFO reports, alien abductions, and crazies pouring into the Lake are running us ragged. Everybody's seeing UFOs these days."

"Abductions? Are people being taken by aliens? That makes me scared. How many people have been taken? I need to be more careful?"

"No, you don't need to worry, Faith. Nobody can prove they've been abducted. The reports are from tourists who claim they've been abducted. One woman said she was impregnated by aliens. Her husband doesn't believe her, of course. It was a big fight, and it took most of an evening to settle. He was trying to kick her out of their camper. But, unfortunately, we've got to answer all of the calls and complaints received in the Sheriff's department. It's exhausting."

"Maybe you need to set regular office hours and let your deputies handle the cases when you're off, Mac."

"Easier said than done, Faith. They depend on me to be there, and I feel more comfortable knowing the facts. It'll get better. Don't worry."

"I hope you're right because we're not sharing much of our lives. I told you how much I've always cared about you and how I'm ready to settle down and raise a family. I was honest with you, and you told me you felt the same way. I love you!"

"I love you too, Faith, and I know things will get better. Things are going to settle down. It's just going to take a little time," he reassured her.

# CHAPTER 12

# My Flying Saucer

Afterbeing crushed by the Memorial Day crowds, Harry got nervous about getting caught and being sued. He wasn't sure if he'd committed a crime, but he was too old to go to prison and couldn't afford to hire a lawyer. If Dottie found out, she'd kick him out of the house. The first UFO incident happened accidentally, but it turned into a bonanza for Sizzerbill's and the rest of the Lake businesses. He wanted to keep it going while the interest in UFOs and aliens was high, but Harry didn't want anyone to get hurt or get caught. Mac told him those guys were stoned out of their minds the last time. He needed to be careful if he purposely did it a second time.

Harry needed a plan built like a good fence—hog tight and bull strong. He needed to choose the best location for enough people to video record it, but he didn't want too many people. People increased the chances of things going wrong, which would get him caught. He didn't dare ask any of his friends, like Bubba, for help. Friends might get careless and tell somebody. He had to do it alone, and it wasn't going to be easy. The KORN episode was too close to Sizzerbill's.

Harry didn't want to use his truck to haul the Ghost on any public roads in case something happened. He decided to take the Ghost out on the platform boat they kept at Sizzerbill's. He decided to launch it at night a half-mile away from Lazy Bear Cove. From Lazy Bear, Harry planned to fly over the trees on the 'Possum Cove isthmus.

His planned route would make it seem like the UFO appeared a few miles away from Sizzerbill's. After the launch and sighting, he'd have a quick boat ride home while everybody looked for the UFO on the other side of the Lake. 'Possum Cove had a KOA campground, but it was smaller than the state park or the resorts. Things were too crazy to launch from Party Cove, people partied hard all night.

"I'm staying late tonight to fix the ice machine again and clean the fryer, Dottie."

"It's time to go home, old man. We've had a long day. Let them go until tomorrow. They're not going anywhere. I need to be back here at 5:30 to bake pies and get breakfast going."

"It'll make tomorrow much busier for me, Dottie. I'm going to get them done tonight."

Dottie was too tired to argue, so she agreed and headed home to get to bed. After she left, Harry loaded the Ghost into the boat, covered it with a camouflage tarp, and cruised across Turkey Bend to Lazy Bear. He didn't want to be seen by anyone.

The boat's canvas top was lowered so the drone could take off and land on the boat. The Lake's dark water looked foreboding. It had Spoonbill paddlefish which often weighed over 100 pounds. Water on the main channel was calmer at night even with the tourists' ongoing UFO watch. There weren't any boat islands tied together in the middle of the main channel to watch for UFOs at night. They were set up in the coves.

Harry had planned his drone sortie carefully. He went through a detailed military checkoff list like when he was flying his 'Snake' in Nam. Considering details was part of the reason Harry got home alive. Well, studying details and luck is what got Harry home alive. A lot of his friends weren't so lucky. He blocked his memories. His plan was to fly over 'Possum Cove and get seen and video recorded. He planned to retreat in such a way as to misdirect everyone investigating the UFO sighting. The Ghost had to fly higher and faster than ever before. It was dangerous, and he felt the adrenalin rush he always felt before a mission. He needed some luck.

Harry dropped the boat's anchor about 30 yards off the bluff shoreline and listened to its splash. He uncovered the Ghost and launched it into the night sky at a reckless ascent speed. He hid under the camouflage tarp so no one could see the colorful reflection from the monitor on his controller. Since he was flying blind, it didn't matter where he was when he flying the drone. It was a little warm under the tarp, but he couldn't be seen. He had done a reconnaissance tour and mapped the shoreline of 'Possum Cove a couple of days earlier. He knew where the campsites, houses, and the parking lot were. He saw where the people were hanging out.

The Ghost cleared the tree line at the top of the bluff and started its flight pattern to survey 'Possum Cove below. The infrared lens gave Harry a clear view of the people. There was a group of laughing high schoolers and college students on air-filled rafts floating in the middle of the cove. Harry could even see the reflections from their cell phones. Another group of isolated couples was hanging out in the cove in canoes and kayaks.

A luxury houseboat was moored closer to the main channel. People were on the top deck. Everybody Harry saw was searching the sky, but nobody saw or heard the Ghost spying on them from 400 feet above.

"Okay, Ghost, let's do your thing," said Harry to no one. He started his strafe strategy by turning on the Hercules while flying above the campground in the woods. After clearing the woods, Harry dropped the Ghost to about 100 feet above the Lake and was flying with the throttle wide open. He figured everyone would be blinded by Hercules before they knew what was happening. He hoped they'd recover their sight too late to get a high-quality close-up video of the Ghost as it flew towards the main channel away from Sizzerbill's.

Harry laughed aloud as he watched people flip off their rafts and out of their canoes, blinded by the light. His flight plan worked like magic as the Ghost jetted toward the titanic houseboat. He couldn't stop himself from quietly screaming, "Okay, sailors, all hands-on deck."

The Cat's Eye focused on a naked couple standing on the deck pointing toward the Ghost's light. They looked familiar, and seemed to be in disbelief. Their mouths were agape as they covered their eyes, which exposed their privates to the blinding light. Hovering a moment directly overhead, Harry recognized the people with their arms outstretched towards heaven.

"Holy sassafras, that's Bumsteer with his college intern." They were bathing in Hercules' light while doing an awkward dance.

After a momentary pause, Harry altered his flight path by rapidly ascending and doused the light. He continued to climb as high as he dared until he made a beeline back toward the boat. That's when Harry's luck ran out.

Harry became alarmed when he heard the guttural sounds of a boat's motor and saw a searchlight from under his tarp. Quick as a hiccup, Harry flipped the switch on the controller to put the Ghost into the 'Follow Me' mode and let it hover at 250 feet. In 'Follow-Me,' the drone would hover and follow wherever the controller went. Then, Harry jumped up as the boat cruised towards his. The Ghost's battery strength was under 20% and dropping fast. Harry stood up, walked to the rail, and winced when he recognized Mac in the Sheriff's cruiser.

"Ahoy, Harry, I thought I saw your boat. What're you doing out so late?" said Mac with a quizzical look.

"The same as you and everybody else, Hero. I'm looking for a UFO and little green aliens," fake-laughed Harry, "Please don't tell, Dottie. She already thinks I'm as crazy as a soup sandwich." Harry wasn't feeling any cheer and was starting to sweat. He wanted to look up to see if the Ghost was where it was supposed to be, but he didn't. "It seems like everybody's seen a UFO but me."

"Yeah, I get it," said Mac. "People are acting crazier than a bunch of outhouse flies."

Then an excited but matter-of-fact woman's voice came over the Sheriff's intercom and interrupted them. "Come in, Mac! We've got a situation. Do you hear me, Mac? Come-in."

"Go ahead, Mabel. I hear you," said Mac in his calm in-command voice.

"We're getting tons of calls about a UFO spotted over 'Possum Cove. Everyone's scared but no one's hurt. Are you nearby, or should I send Snuffy?"

"Roger, Mabel. I'll take the call. Tell Snuffy to stay where he is and keep his eyes out for the UFO."

"Roger, Mac, affirmative," said Mabel.

"Hot damn, I missed another one," said Harry acting disappointed.

"Do you want to come with me to see what happened, Harry? We can leave your boat here and take mine."

"No, no thanks, Mac. I'm not interested in hearing what everyone else thinks they saw. I'm not interested in it if I can't see it," said Harry. "Besides, it's getting late, and I'm old and need to get to bed."

"I get it. Good night, Harry," said Mac as he throttled up his throaty engine, careful not to sink Harry in his wake.

Harry exhaled his relief as Mac motored around Turkey Bend, Harry landed the Ghost with less than 5% battery left. Quickly, Harry covered the Ghost with the tarp and headed for Sizzerbill's. Harry knew Dottie would hear about Mac seeing him on the Lake. He needed to be proactive and tell Dottie beforehand. His mind ran like a rat in a spinner wheel developing the necessary details to make his story believable.

As he thought of his story for Dottie, he laughed out loud, thinking about the naked reporter and intern on the top deck of the houseboat.

"You must've been having a religious experience, Bumsteer, you old dog. I hope everybody got a video or photos of you, you lech," chuckled Harry as he played the event repeatedly in his mind. Harry felt self-satisfied his 'unidentified aerial phenomena' or UAP as the media called them, had gone as well as he could've hoped. Nobody got hurt, no boats ran into anything, and he didn't get caught. He hated creating such a big mess for his friend, Mac, but all things considered, it was good for business. Besides, it was just a hoax.

## CHAPTER 13
# Devil Went Down to Georgia

The 24-hour news-cycle airwaves were alive by midnight with talking heads who had 50-cent brains and two-hundred-dollar hairdos yakking away. They echoed the news reports about the new UFO sighting at the Lake. The news shows' producers were giddy about the frenzy of news 'enhancement' opportunities. They discovered sleep-deprived UFOologists and Extraterrestrial experts who were willing to discuss the ramifications of the aliens' arrival. 'Experts' were interviewed about the ET's political preferences, gender designations, and diet. The most provocative alien experts were concerned about whether aliens were herbivores or carnivores.

Roland P. Clegg, a semantics professor at Ivy Towers University, raged to Penelope Bombast, his former student and late-night newsreader. "Not to sound ghastly, Pen, but Earth will be much better off if these aliens are carnivores with a preference for human flesh. This would solve our existential threats of overpopulation, environmental degradation, and the unethical treatment of animals, especially cats. Aliens would be the Earth's savior from human encroachment." Bombast nodded and smiled in agreement while at least half of her viewers shook their heads in wonderment.

Clegg continued his wrath as the other experts on the panel approved. "It will definitely be best if the aliens conquer all humans, especially Americans because of their speciesist policies, which impact animals and the environment."

Not to be outdone, Adam Jamoke, president of the Alpha Tribe, interrupted Clegg via his video feed from the Lake. "Alphas agree with Professor Keg. I mean Clegg." Jamoke's followers were standing in the background dressed in handmade hemp clothing. They held signs with messages like 'Take Me' and 'Go First Class' to announce their breeding availability to the aliens.

Jamoke explained, "We, Alphas, believe ETs are coming to Earth to mate with us and produce a new species. We've come to the Lake to offer ourselves as human breeding stock to create a super species like Superman and Wonder Woman. To stay pure for the aliens, we only eat organic wild plants and organic bugs to avoid any type of human chemical contamination. ETs are pure energy, Penelope, and they are the highest form of life in the universe."

"Wait, are you saying ETs are a higher form of life than God?" asked Bombast, whose mind was clearly blown.

"Alphas believe ETs are god, Penelope. Further, ETs inspired Ron Howard to make the movie 'Cocoon' to give us a preview of who they are."

"I'd like to apologize to Mr. Jamoke and my panel for this upcoming interruption in our programming. We are able to bring our viewers actual video footage of tonight's UFO sighting. We will interview the person who recorded the actual UFO video. Hello, Bard Nightingale, can you hear me?" asked Bombast to the grainy video image on the screen.

"Hello, Penelope, yes, I can hear you," said a round red face covered in mottled-gray facial hair. Bard was wearing Ray-Ban sunglasses and a Hawaiian shirt even though it was nighttime.

"Can you tell us about the supernatural event you witnessed tonight, Bard? Take us through how you got this amazing footage. We're very excited to hear your story!"

"Well, I'm still trying to absorb what I saw tonight, Penelope. My friends and I were hanging out on the Lake, hoping to see a UFO. We were laying in our huge 'Woman on the Moon' raft, doing 'Jell-O Moon Shots,' and taking selfies. This bright light flew over us out of nowhere and almost blinded us. I did everything I could to keep my telephone screen on it, but it was flying faster than shit. Excuse me. I'm sorry, Penelope, but I was scared. I apologize."

Quietly laughing, Penelope said, "We understand how scary and exciting it must've been, Bard. Why don't we run the video, and you explain what we're seeing, okay?"

"Sure, Penelope. Here you can see my beautiful girl-friend, Yvette, who is available for modeling jobs. The UFO's light shone over her head, but it was actually flying like a bat out of hell. Uh, sorry. Can I say hell? The UFO's light flew out of the woods, straight towards us, and then directly over us. I rolled on my side to keep it in my viewfinder as it headed towards that houseboat. Then, the UFO paused over the houseboat before it disappeared into heaven."

"Wait a minute, will the producer please freeze the video when the UFO is paused directly above the houseboat?"

"What do you see there, Bard?"

"It looks like two naked people dancing to me, Penelope?"

"It does to me too, Bard. Can you augment the video back there, please, so we get a better view? Oh, my gawd, is that Karl Bumsteer on the boat?" said a clearly flustered and embarrassed Penelope.

"I'm not sure who it is, Penelope, but the guy is at least three times bigger than the woman. She's pretty hot, that's for sure," laughed an uninhibited Bard. "Penelope, please remind your viewers, Yvette is available for modeling gigs."

"We need to pause for a station break," deadpanned a rattled Penelope.

● ● ●

Everyone who was on the houseboat was watching Penelope's show as they surfed through various networks for UFO news in their hotel rooms. Bumsteer needed a 'brain control' story to manage the damage from the bizarre incident. His Facebook page claimed he was a feminist. Karl was always an excellent storyteller, which began as a young boy, when he couldn't overcome his compulsion for sweets.

He was a chocoholic, and had eaten his mom's entire chocolate birthday cake one sunny summer day before her party. He still felt pangs of guilt. He blamed his dog, Bacon, who was beaten with his mom's hairbrush as punishment. His storytelling improved with age. Throughout his education, he made up excuses about missing assignments, cheating on tests, and multiple accountings about his grandfather and grandmother dying horrible deaths at crucial moments to explain his absences and failing grades.

Needing to muster a defense to preserve his career and reputation, Bumsteer called a Press conference at the dam. It was time for the free Press to go to work for him. None of the locals attended except the Sheriff and his deputies. A growing number of representatives from every kooky club and organization, like the Alphas, had found their way to the Lake for the second alien encounter. The Press conference looked more like a religious revival and baptism down at the river than a serious news event.

Bumsteer looked as ugly as homemade soap, standing behind the podium. He was swaddled in a white king-size bedsheet. He had taken the sheet off his bed at the *Love Shack Motel*. It was tied around his vast waist with a golden drapery cord taken from his room. He used a section of the drapery cord to secure a matching headband around his newly-shaved head, which framed his fat-rimmed eyes. He looked like he was going to a college toga party except for his trenta iced caramel macchiato. The podium was jammed with dozens upon dozens of microphones. Bumsteer was joined by a beaming Dan Blather and his modestly dressed interns. The inexperienced, scared, and star-struck female intern trusted everything Bumsteer, her mentor and spirit guide, told her.

The media swarm was so quiet, or dumbstruck, you could've heard a hummingbird fart. Bumsteer had decided to follow the maxim from his favorite college PR teacher many years ago. She instructed him to deny the most damning facts during a crisis upfront with swagger. When he was conjuring his story last night, Bumsteer created his own title—Alien Oracle, and set out to make it true. He knew how the media worked, and he knew how to deploy it by stating right up front, "I'm not an oracle, merely a messenger for the great ones." The Oracle continued his narration by sharing the divine knowledge he acquired from his transcendental conference with the aliens the night before.

"I was teleported from our boat's deck to the interior of the UFO." The crowd gulped. He continued with quiet patience, "The UFO hovered above me to test my resolve. We were fully dressed, looking up into its beckoning light, when it suddenly sucked off our Earthly garb. Rather than feeling fearful, I felt peaceful and accepting. I felt their awe-inspiring power."

The spellbound crowd gasped in unison when they realized they were standing in the presence of the first person to ever visit inside a UFO.

Only Bumsteer knew he was making everything up to save his gasping career. Even his interns weren't sure if he was telling the truth. They wanted to believe him. Blather, a cynic by nature, was awestruck at Bumsteer's brilliance in creating blockbuster news. He recognized Bumsteer wasn't creating a fake story as he would've done. Bumsteer was creating a lifetime of fake stories making him the hero and chief source of his own story, forever. Blather was disappointed he hadn't thought of this ploy after the KORN tower incident. He recognized he was learning from the best.

Whenever Bumsteer got confused recounting his story, he would prattle a few unintelligible utterances. After his second garbled outburst, he apologized and explained that he was actually speaking in the ET language. He learned the ET language during his summit with them. With forbearance, he explained there weren't equivalent words in the English language for various ET concepts. The people were thrilled as Bumsteer spoke in the ET mother tongue. Onlookers raised their arms and shook their hands halleluiah style. Spacey and Ducktail were in the back of the crowd, grumbling about Bumsteer's good fortune.

"Can you believe that guy's good luck?" groused Ducktail.

"No, I can't," said Spacey in an all-knowing smile. "But, hey, it will be lucrative for all of us."

If people knew the truth, they would've thought Bumsteer was delusional. Truth be told, he didn't think of himself as a scandalmonger. He saw himself as a seeker-of-truth who interpolated interpretive facts about what ETs would've told him if he had, in fact, been teleported inside a UFO for a meeting. The stories he was telling could've been actually true. Bumsteer was helping people find truth in a way they would accept without prejudice or bias. He had gotten closer to a UFO, hence an ET, than any known human in history. It was astounding. The UFO had selected him. He was definitely qualified to speak on behalf of all ETs throughout the universe. He was one with them and he was chosen to be their oracle.

During his 30-minute soliloquy, which looked and sounded like the sermon on the Mount, Bumsteer recounted the Ancients' declarations about Earthlings' desecrations against the universe, and other lifeforms in other galaxies.

In his fiery finale, Bumsteer screamed, "Ancient Aliens will terminate Earth in 10-years unless Earthlings transform themselves and become simpatico with the universe." The boisterous cheering crowd gave off a Woodstock vibe, and Bumsteer became emotional at everyone's exultation. "I promise to appear whenever the Ancients reach out to me with new celestial epistles."

After his sermon, each of his three acolytes took turns giving their eye-witness accounts of what happened during the UFO encounter. Each confirmed Bumsteer's version of supernatural events. Bumsteer had already sold stories to various media outlets and promised one-on-one interviews with various talking heads. Blather was appointed his chief-of-staff. The outhouse-poor interns were left out of the payday bonanza until they got more experience. The female intern, who was as soft as a raisin in the hot sun, enjoyed the limelight and attention from the gaggle of reporters. After seeing the attention Bumsteer's toga got, she decided to dress in a sheet too, but decided on a pastel color instead of white. After all, her clothes had been sucked off also. After their statements, Bumsteer took questions from the gaggle.

"Hello, Karl!"

"Hi, Tom."

"Karl, uh, I mean, Oracle, you said the aliens, er' Ancients, talked to you directly. I'm sure everyone is wondering what happened. Since you're the only person to ever have a conversation with an Ancient, can you tell us how you had such a deep dialog with them so quickly, please?"

"Sure, Tom, thanks for your question. I'm as perplexed as everyone else as to why the Ancients chose me. I'm not sure I'm worthy of their belief in me. I'll be happy to explain what happened. First, our extraterrestrial guests aren't confined by our normal time continuum. They don't wear glow-in-the-dark Mickey Mouse Apple watches or set alarms on their smartphones, Tom," everyone giggled. "Ancients don't even have a word or term for time in their language. To our outer space neighbors, time is irrelevant. Time doesn't have any dimensions, limits, or measurements. Time is our meaningless earthly social construct, not theirs. My visit with the Ancients lasted a fraction of a moment in the way we measure time. Still, in a fraction of our moment, they could accomplish what would've taken over a week in our normal time construct. I don't believe my colleagues even saw me leave the boat deck when I was tele-transported to the UFO. Am I right?" asked Bumsteer opening his arms to his acolytes. They all shook their heads in unison and agreement like NPCs in a video game.

"In a moment, or a year, depending on your time construct, they imparted to me all of the knowledge I have been able to tell you here today. I can tell you this, Tom, it blew my mind. I'm still processing everything they imparted instantly to me. It was like a skip in the time warp."

Next, the Oracle pointed to a friend who had appeared with him when he was her guest on countless news panels over the years. Earlier this morning, he had locked up a profitable contract with her network, GNN, to host his own upcoming show, *Ancient Oracles*, for the next five years.

"Katie Balderdash, I'm a fake-fact-checker from GNN, Oracle." Katie was always very matter-of-fact and looked the part of a bimbo trying to look intelligent. She had all of the Hollywood-news requisites. She was blonde, busty, and didn't have time for a trifling chat.

"How were you able to speak with them? Earlier, I heard you utter certain sounds. I couldn't understand what you were saying. Did you learn their language during your visit, or did they speak to you in English?" asked the bewildered yet beguiled reporter.

"Thanks for your question, Katie," said the indulgent star seer with a knowing nod of his now sunburned and sweating head. "Our outer-world friends didn't use language to interact with me. Language has no use because it slows down the communication process. It was an omni-directional dialog of thought-exchange. They don't speak as we do. Every being exchanges thoughts at the same time. They're capable of transmitting what they know to others in less than a nano-second and receive feedback simultaneously without any discernable conversation or body language. In the fraction of a moment that I was in the UFO, our guests educated me about everything I could possibly absorb so I could tell you," grinned Bumsteer.

"The Ancients assured me they will tell me what you need to know through divine mediation. I will joyfully relate their lessons as soon as possible with the constraints we must bear here on Earth," said Bumsteer as he spread his arms high towards the universe with his palms up looking to the stars.

"What did the aliens look like, Mr. Bumsteer? Were they short and green?" shouted an impatient high school reporter from the high school.

Dan smirked at the snot-nosed reporter he'd seen around the Lake with an air of indignation. However, he thought she looked hot. They had covered the same local news stories before he'd become a recognized correspondent across the globe. The Oracle sensed Dan's inner conflict and touched his shoulder to soothe him.

"Let me handle the little one, Dan. She doesn't know any better," said Bumsteer, thinking she looked hot too.

Chuckling until his belly shook like a bowl full of Jell-O, and with the patience of an egg-stealing fox, Bumsteer said, "No, no, our guests aren't short and green or tall and translucent. They don't have physical manifestations like you and me. They're not Spielberg's E.T. We can't see, hear, smell, or even touch them. We merely sense them and feel their presence. They give us a peaceful feeling. It's a soulful and emotional experience. An interface with them is like looking over a vast ocean of water and listening to the calming waves. They're an energy lifeform, and that's all there is. I didn't see any aliens. I knew they were there because they were. My meeting with them put my soul at peace. It was like taking a deep cleansing breath."

"Are you saying they're spirits? Like God or ghosts? Does this have anything to do with the occult?" asked the persistent teen journalist.

"Now, now, please don't put words in my mouth, young one. I didn't say I believed in God or ghosts. This wasn't a paranormal phenomenon. It is real. Our outer-worldly guests invited me to share their thoughts. I'm not a speciesist. I accepted their invitation without prejudice or pretense. They have evolved to the point where physical form is unnecessary. They don't want or need to be judged by whether they're tall, short, heavy, strong, weak, or green. They are beings without physical manifestation or dimension. Think of René Descartes. I assume you know him," he said with a smile of beneficence, knowing he only knew one quote from the man. Descartes could've been a stonemason for all Bumsteer knew.

"They think, therefore they are," said Bumsteer as the entire Press corps broke into raucous applause and wild approbation. The gobsmacked cub reporter and her colleagues shook their heads to see if his confused answer made any more sense. It didn't.

Another impatient high school reporter who covered the science beat blurted out, "Do you follow the science, sir? To quote *The Hitchhikers Guide to the Galaxy*, 'Space is big. Really big. You won't believe how vastly, hugely, mind-bogglingly big it is.' Can you please tell us what the aliens used for energy to get here? If they're so smart, and don't have bodies, why didn't they simply set up a Zoom meeting instead of traveling here?"

Frazzled by the student's rational questions and not having any prepared answers, Bumsteer decided to end his Press conference by acting like he was fainting from his psychic exertions.

Drenched in sweat, Bumsteer's saturated sheet looked like he'd been standing in the rain. He was thankful he had decided to wear a headband. Under the strain of his re-found celebrity, Bumsteer was voraciously hungry. Divining truth and prophesy were exhausting. His acolytes surrounded him, and he concluded with his promise of more revelations as long as the Ancients continued to grace him as their messenger. Everyone cleared a path for the Oracle and his acolytes as they made their way in a slow procession to his white limousine. They were going directly to Sizzerbill's for a couple of wedges of chocolate cream pie with whipped cream on top.

Sizzerbill's was about to become the hottest restaurant on the Lake, and Dottie wasn't prepared for the onslaught of celebrities. She and Harry were going to have to hire a platoon of local pie bakers to create new-fangled varieties of pies to fill the demand of their new customers.

The dam area was starting to look like a California homeless encampment. Businesses near the dam were constantly calling the Sheriff's office to complain about vagrants. Dam area parking lots were filling up fast with expensive self-contained RVs, 5th-wheels, and pull-behind campers. Factions of people representing spirit rocks, hellbender salamanders, and voluntary human extinction set up makeshift tents, tarps, and all styles of cardboard box tiny houses. The various alien tourist groups were anti-everything, including deodorant. They gave the gathering the musky scent of a Lollapalooza festival. There was constant hand drumming on all physical objects, including plastic buckets, glass bottles, backpacks, open cheeks, and bare chests painted with various slogans.

All of the campers and RVs weren't the worst part of the mob building up at the dam. Many black SUVs with dark tinted windows were gathering also. Men and women in dark suits and black sunglasses whispering into each other's ears were sneaking around and standing in the shadows.

They listened to the crowds with every technological listening and monitoring device invented.

Looking around disgustedly, Mac thought, 'Dang, even the FBI, Homeland Security, and the CIA are moving into the Lake. This is getting out of hand. It is like everybody has had their brains highjacked. It doesn't make any sense.'

"Okay, I want Snuffy and Barney to hang out at the dam the rest of the day. Look for anything out of the ordinary, boys. Stay in touch with me in case things get out of control. Don't let the ne'er-do-wells block the doorways to the businesses with their boxes and tents. I've ordered a bunch of Johnny-On-the-Spots to set up along the parking lots' back walls. They'll be here around noon. They should take the pressure off the stores' bathrooms. I don't want any situations. Keep the peace and call for help if you have any problems. I'll be out tonight, but you know how to reach me if anything escalates. Keep your eyes on the black SUVs. I want to know who's in them."

"You've got it, Sheriff," said Snuffy with a smart two-finger salute from the bill of his Sheriff's department cap.

# CHAPTER 14

# Crazy

Mac spent his time investigating UFO sightings, landings, and abductions, but was only able to solve one alien abduction. Elvis sniffed out an abducted big screen TV, which was hidden in a livestock stall under a haystack. The farmer's wife, Seraphina, hauled it away and hid it because her husband, Fabian, wouldn't stop watching episodes of X-Files. He had bought a signed set of DVDs from Ducktail.

"How'd your TV and DVDs get out to the barn under the hay, Seraphina?" asked a smiling Mac.

"I've got no idea. Aliens must've taken them, but they're innocent because that no-account TV program is driving them, and me, insane. The aliens told me the X-Files were assault and battery on their sense of good taste," laughed Seraphina placing her hands on her child-rearing hips.

"Your voice sounds like a buzz-saw cutting on a cast iron skillet, woman," whined Fabian, who was normally as tight as a bull's butt during fly season. "She's narrow-minded,

Mac, she can see through a keyhole with both eyes. What do you know about good taste, woman?"

"Well, he's got me there, Sheriff. I freely admit I don't have good taste. He's living proof. The aliens must be worried about his health. They're probably afraid his blood turned to lead and settled in his butt. They wanted him to get off the sofa and do some chores," smirked Seraphina.

"I don't have time for domestic disputes, Seraphina and Fabian. If you've got irreconcilable differences move to opposite sides of your house." They scratched their heads knowing their house was so small they had to go outside to change their minds.

"Legally, not having good taste isn't against the law. Unfortunately, I don't have time to arrest both of you for wasting my time. I'm taking these DVDs to the Sheriff's office. Fabian, you can check them out for two weeks once each year," said Mac as he picked up the box of DVDs and drove to Faith's house.

• • •

It was a beautiful June evening. The setting sun painted a pink and azure sky with a lacy veil of white clouds. It looked like a watercolor painting. The new moon was starting to rise. Faith and Mac could see the planet Venus on the side of the moon. The spectacular view from Lover's Leap overlooked the Lake. It was full of cruising boaters. UFO madness had put a damper on their smoldering relationship.

Faith wondered why such a brave man was so afraid of a woman and his own feelings. Faith's feelings for Mac, and his for her, were growing, but he was always too busy to make plans. To her, Mac seemed disinterested. She, and she thought he, wanted to spend long summer evenings together. It wasn't happening with all of the alien hullabaloo. Her school was out for the summer, and Faith was bored. Mac was busy. She was tired of fishing with her dad and wanted her relationship with Mac to blossom.

Without Mac knowing, Faith had driven to Ironwood to help him. She wanted to demonstrate how much he needed a best friend, a wife. She straightened and cleaned his home and did chores like collecting eggs from the clutch and brushing Honey.

"You didn't need to do all that work at the farm, Faith, but it really helped me out, thank you. Everything looks great and I don't feel as pressured. I would've done it as soon as I had a chance. It's just I'm busier than an ant hauling an ear of corn. You wouldn't believe how crazy things are. Bumsteer, the one they call, Oracle, lies so much other people have to call his dog. People who follow him take his word to be the Bible. I'm not sure what to do with all of the crazies. They're coming to the Lake by every open road. We don't have any room, but they just keep coming. You'd think the good Lord himself was visiting."

"Don't worry about me, Mac. I've got too much time on my hands. I can't leave a neighbor in a tight." She smiled. "Do you believe in UFOs now?

"I don't know, Faith. I haven't found any real proof except for the videos which don't show any details just a white light. The challenge is reporters use those videos to scare their audience and get rich. Reporters are so crooked sharks wouldn't eat them out of professional courtesy."

"I know you're right. I wish it would all go away. You need help, Mac, and I want to help you the rest of my life. Don't you want my help?"

Her innocence and honesty left Mac feeling unworthy. Faith was the best person to ever come along in his life, and he didn't want to ruin her life or his chances of marrying her. He wanted to settle down and have a family, but his sense of duty made him feel obligated to get these UFOs figured out first. He was torn between his sense of responsibility and his own needs.

"I do."

"There you said it, again, Hero. Don't say it unless you mean it. Don't tease me."

"I do mean it, Faith. I'm not as happy when we're apart. I feel the happiest in moments like this, when we're together. I want to be with you forever, but I've got to get these UFOs figured out and get all of these crazies out of town first. Then, I can concentrate on you, on us."

Sad, Faith asked, "So, you can't marry me until you figure out these darn UFOs? Then, you better get them figured out by Labor Day, Mac. If you don't, I'm planning our wedding Sadie Hawkins style, and maybe Daddy's shotgun."

They smiled, they hugged, and they kissed. Faith was torn and wondering if Mac had been a bachelor too long. Maybe he'd never marry her even if he did love her. Her dad had told her about his friends who came back from Viet Nam. Some were never quite able to readjust to civilian life. Maybe Mac was like those men. Perhaps she needed to find someone else, but even the thought of not having Mac in her life brought tears.

# CHAPTER 15

# Summertime

O sage Indians considered it paradise, before high-powered masters of the universe built colossal homes with marina-style boat docks filled with adult toys like cigarette boats and personal watercraft. Their massive Lake estates celebrated their prominence in the universe. Still, no one, even insurance executives, had insurance covering a UFO attack. Panicked, most execs slept on their massive multi-story sundecks with loaded guns hoping to repel an attacking alien spaceship.

The Oracle's daily UFO epistles was one of the top tourism attractions along with Moonbeam's featured appearances at KORN and the Opry. Bumsteer and his acolytes were treated like Hollywood movie stars. None of them had bought a slice of pie, meal, drink, or souvenir in weeks. Their adoring fans were happy to shell out $30 for lunch to get a signed photograph or a selfie with an acolyte. The public's curiosity about the Oracle was limitless. Talking heads and news readers filled their 24/7 time slots with endless puff pieces about his visions.

Even Cooper Vanderbilt did a *60 Minutes* segment on the Oracle. Celebrity privilege helped him feel deserving and superior, and he worked hard to conceal his conceit. He wanted to appear grounded during their sanctimonious interviews.

The Oracle was now residing at *Margaritaville*. He'd been evicted from the *Love Shack Motel* for stealing sheets and drapery cords. *Margaritaville* had to hire guards to control the crowds. Vacationers wanted an up-close view of the Oracle and his trailing acolytes. Those that could afford them snatched up his $50 autographed photos. Those less eager, or fortunate, satisfied their curiosity by stealing a gaze into his contented yet sweating red face. After a huddle one morning, the acolytes decided to wear complementary pastel-colored sheets to increase the donations to their *GoFundMe* page. The page promoted outer-space diplomacy. The colorful sheets worked, and the college interns were finally given small shares of the fund to encourage intergalactic diplomacy at their college.

Crazy rich people bored by the natural beauty of the Lake rented all of the luxury yachts, massive houseboats, and sleek cabin cruisers. They didn't care whether they supported local businesses. Their personal chefs and staffs imported premium wines, liquors, and food so they could be properly entertained while they cruised the Lake. Many invited the Oracle, accompanied by a princely fee of course, as their guest of honor to teach them about the existential threat of the galactical crisis.

The UFO phenomena was a psychic epidemic. Most tourists were giddy about an alien showdown. No one wanted to miss the electrifying event. UFOologists descended on the Lake like locusts to conduct interviews with the Oracle and his acolytes. They were especially interested in Blather because he had witnessed two verified UFO sightings. Astrophysicists considered UFOology a pseudoscience based on rumors from people claiming to be enslaved, programmed, bred, and in contact with aliens throughout the universe.

Compounding the mass confusion, the *UFO World Enclave* moved the celebration of *World UFO Day* to the Lake for July 4th. They planned to reveal the truth about extraordinary alien lifeforms from around the galaxy.

The most useless alien tourists were gas-filled politicians. They were the best money could buy, and bumped into each other like bowling pins whenever they saw a TV camera. Politicians either echoed everything the Oracle said or called him a philistine depending on who was with them. They walked around shaking hands and flashing big smiles. They made big promises they couldn't afford or keep. Most politicians were as useless as whitewashing horse manure and setting it up on end. Politicians had one practical skill. They could speak out of both sides of their mouth at the same time while drinking free coffee and eating a free lunch.

"Good morning, Sheriff! How are you on this fine day? You're doing a wonderful job managing this UFO mess. I'm sorry. I don't mean that it's your fault that it's a mess. Like you, I'm excited to meet our new galactical constituents. We need to give them the right to vote as soon as possible. It's their country too. I'm also working with Homeland Security to find the funds to help them get started in business. The Oracle says they're natural entrepreneurs. Is there anything I can do to help you, Sheriff?" asked Senator Amos T. Moldy. He waved his hand towards Mac with a grand gesture over his expansive government-filled belly. His belly was covered by a red, white and blue plaid vest with a gold watch chain.

Moldy was walking alongside Governor Portentia Smugg. Taken together, they had all of the qualities and habits of a dog except loyalty. Portentia stuck her nose so high in the air she would've drowned if she got caught in the rain. Their entourages of fund-raising assistants could take an electronic transfer on their phone faster than greased lightning. They were like graveyards; they'd take anything.

Mac jumped on their offers like a chicken on a June bug. "Yes, sir, thank you for your offer to help. My Sheriff's budget isn't half big enough to handle this crowd. We need officers, vehicles and gas. My department is running on fumes. Lincoln County can't afford to pay overtime either. We're working 80 plus hours a week. Is there any way you, or the Governor, can help us find extra budget or get folks from Homeland Security or the National Guard to help us? This "mess" is wearing us down to the nub," said Mac as he looked them square in the eyes.

"You can count on it, Sheriff. I'll have my staff manager reach out to you as soon as she's able. It's shameful no one's offered any help. Portentia, can you help the Sheriff?"

"National Guard? Goodness, no. We don't want the Ancients to think we're going to attack them, Sheriff. We need diplomacy not militancy. I'll see what I can do and have my chief-of-staff get back to you when I return to my governor's mansion. Thanks for efforts, you're a true patriot."

"Well, there you go, Sheriff. You can count on the District of Corruption and your state of Despair to give you a hand in your time of need. You can count on us!" said Senator Moldy waving his forefinger high in the air.

'Well, butter my butt and call me a biscuit,' thought Mac. He walked away, knowing the Sheriff's office had as much chance as a head without a chicken of getting help. Mac knew he had to figure this out and take care of it alone. The government wasn't worth dried spit.

CHAPTER 16

# Good Hearted Woman

"I'm not sure why we needed to meet with Slim Jim Carter today, baby doll. Our entire day is rush hour. We've got a never-ending line of mouths to feed from open to close. We can't keep up. We're too darn busy for people our age," said Harry.

"Don't I know it? We're selling more pies every day than we used to sell in two weeks. Praise the Lord, we were able to hire the woman's church auxiliary to make pies every morning."

Much to Dottie's vexation, Harry had created flamboyant names for her pies, such as 'Dottie's Moon Pie,' which was the Oracle's favorite. Sizzerbill's sold 10 Dottie's Moon Pies every day as takeout items. She didn't like the special attention from her fans, but sales were better than ever. She and Harry were dreaming about retirement.

"Good morning, Miss Dottie, Mister Harry," said a smooth-talking Sawyer tipping his 'Sizzerbill's Out of this World' ball cap. Sawyer and Josie were stylish local college kids hired to run Sizzerbill's booming dock business for the summer. Sizzerbill's was more popular than any Lakefront bar, with the Oracle stopping for fresh pie, often, twice a day.

Sizzerbill's had a well-worn, vintage dock that had a 'dive' vibe which was popular with the Lake crowd. Sawyer and Josie, and the friends they hired, slathered themselves in sun lotion and wore stylish Hawaiian print swimsuits, Ray-Bans, and ballcaps. They pumped gas, served food and drinks, and flirted for tips while they listened to their favorite music on loudspeakers. Everyone stopped on their way to Party Cove to ogle the pretty kids and see if the Oracle was there.

"Hey, Sawyer, how're the tie-dyed UFO t-shirts selling?" asked Harry.

Sawyer and Josie were entrepreneurs. They had a new idea every day to make more money from the burgeoning tourist traffic. Josie curated their *Tik Tok*, *Instagram*, and *Snap Chat* accounts. They were called #OutofthisWorld. The posts featured short videos of the hottest-looking men and women, and cute little kids, doing their favorite dance step on Sizzerbill's dock. They had two million followers.

"They're selling great, Mister Harry. We've sold 50 already. Josie's working on some new designs for our next order. We don't want to get stale," grinned Sawyer. "By the way, heads up, Cowboy just pulled his boat into the dock."

"Thanks, Sawyer. Keep up the great work!" 'Cowboy' was the code name for Slim Carter. Slim had his new, low-slung cruiser fitted with long bull horns on the bow, so he was easy to recognize.

Business was booming at all of Slim's enterprises including the bus trips to his hillbilly homestead which featured Moonbeam. She and her piglets had become more popular, with some people, than the Oracle. Fact was, Moonbeam had more personality than Bumsteer. She had an Internet fan club, her own hashtag, #Moonbeam, and her own YouTube station with millions of followers. Her dancing video climbed to ten million likes on YouTube in a week. It was mind-boggling. Harry even named Sizzerbill's banana cream pie after her.

Once the media did feature stories about Moonbeam, her photos and videos popped up everywhere. She was a media phenom, and beloved by everyone. Slim had a special trailer built to tow her behind his Cadillac. She'd go with him to KORN and Hillbilly Opry for special guest appearances. Tickets to the Opry were a scarce as a hen's teeth. People paid a 20% premium for Opry tickets on Stub Hub even though some visitors didn't enjoy bluegrass or country and western music.

Bored social elites hired Slim, Obie Blevens and the Practical Jokers for private performances. They did it secretly because they didn't want to be accused of spreading hate speech. They'd never met a hillbilly, and taking Moonbeam with him made it exclusive. When Slim sang *Good Hearted Woman* to a smiling Moonbeam, swaying to the beat, the audience went gaga. Elites thought of Moonbeam with a crooning hillbilly as 'native.' Slim didn't care what people thought. After the show, he charged folks a premium to kiss his pig and have their photo taken with Moonbeam.

Slim tipped his Stetson and cooed, " Hello, Dottie, Harry, thanks for meeting with me. I appreciate your time. You've always been great neighbors." Then, he aimed his trademark cheesy smile and winked at Dottie.

Harry took umbrage with the snake oil salesman's overture and brusquely asked, "How're your helicopter tours going Slim? They're mighty loud. Sounds like a war zone over here."

"I apologize. I'm sorry to hear they're so loud. I'll see what I can do, folks. Crazy rich people spend money like water when they're bored. They love my nighttime helicopter tours of the radio tower. My Opry lighting and sound production crews have made it a Universal theme-park ride. I'll send over some complimentary tickets," smiled Slim.

"The helicopter acts like the UFO. My sound techs installed Dolby speakers into the helicopter's cabin to play the Jokers' recording of *Dixie Breakdown* during the flight. The lighting techs put dramatic theatre lighting around the station and tower. The helicopter chases an identical pick-up truck to the tower. The grand finale is an explosion of laser lights and fireworks hidden in and around the tower. After the explosion of lights, the helicopter lands for a private tour of the station and an appearance of me singing a serenade to Moonbeam," said a sunny Slim. "It's a smasher. Totally life-like."

"I can't wait to see it. It sounds exciting, Slim, really, it does," said Dottie in an unconvincing manner.

"Come on, Slim. We've been neighbors over 30 years, and we've got a two-hour line of folks whose stomachs think their throats have been cut. If you've got something on your mind, spit it out. We're busy."

Chuckling, Slim forged ahead. He knew he had Harry's nanny goat. "That's what I like about you, Harry. You're as direct as a schoolmarm. No one ever wonders what you're thinking because you tell them. Well, I'm going to be direct with you too. I'm not going to beat around the bush. I want to buy Sizzerbill's. Right now. Today. It's time you and your beautiful bride retired and enjoyed yourselves. You've worked hard. You don't want to work until the day you die. Do you? Don't you want to spend the money you've been saving? Don't you want to sleep as late as you want and stay up as late as you want? You two lovebirds don't want to stay chained to Sizzerbill's. I'm here to give you two things. I will give you freedom, and I will give you money to spend any way you want. And hell, I'm going to throw the biggest damn retirement party for you two anyone has ever dreamed about. I'll provide the entertainment free of charge. Your proverbial treasure ship has come into port. Don't be foolish. Take my offer."

"Heck, Slim, you like to talk, but you're not saying anything. How much money will you pay us for selling you the hottest restaurant and dock on the Lake? What kind of retirement are you going to give us? Do you want us to eat chicken necks or beef tenderloin? We're working hard, but we're making bank too. Aren't we, Dottie?"

Then Harry looked at Dottie to see what she was thinking. They'd spent so much time together between home and

Sizzerbill's; they knew each other's thoughts by the way the other person said, Good morning.

"Yes, we are, Harry, but I'd like to hear Slim's offer." You could've knocked Harry over with a turkey feather. He didn't think Dottie would ever leave Sizzerbill's and all of their friends. Harry thought he'd have to work at Sizzerbill's until the day he died if he left it to Dottie to decide when to retire. No matter, he was prepared to do whatever she wanted. She was the real boss and the only person he wanted to be with the rest of his life. He knew he'd plain out-married himself. They both got anxious, waiting to hear Slim's offer.

Slim took pride in his ability to sell anything to anybody. He figured he could sell chastity belts in a red-light district if he needed to make a living. Harry didn't trust Slim any further than he could throw him. The trading was about to begin, and Harry and Slim were dancing like two wood rattlers standing on their tails.

"Wonderful," said a grinning Slim, clapping his hands together, thinking the bobcat was in the bag. "I will help you two finance a comfortable retirement, and I'll have another great business to manage. There are lots of ways to skin this polecat. We can do it anyway your accountant wants. We don't want the government to get too much of your money. Old Moldy and his revenuers will skin you alive with taxes if it's left to them. I want to offer you a million dollars in the main." Harry interrupted Slim with more energy than a year-old colt.

"A million dollars?" laughed Harry as he slapped his thighs and stood up. "You're crazier than a screen door on a submarine! How about I sell you the Brooklyn Bridge instead?"

Slim cut Harry off quicker than small-town gossip, "Each." Then, Slim clapped his hands and sat quietly like a mouse stealing cheese. He looked at both of them with a smile as big as a Jack-O-Lantern.

Dottie and Harry sat mute while they collected their thoughts. They didn't know what to say. They figured Slim would offer too little, they wouldn't come to terms, and they'd walk away. Dottie and Harry were born dirt poor. Harry grew up in a house so small everybody had to turn around at the same time. Dottie's family used an outhouse until she was ten years old. They never dreamed of being a millionaire, much less a two-millionaire.

"The smell of those greenbacks takes your breath away, doesn't it?" smiled Slim. Harry had to admit Slim's offer left him breathless. Slim wanted Sizzerbill's. It was an ideal location since it abutted his KORN property, and it had the best shoreline on the Lake. There was plenty of room for a large parking lot, and Sizzerbill's business grew leaps and bounds over the summer. Slim was sure he'd make back his investment in no time. He had big plans for Sizzerbill's.

"Well, if you'd pay two million, how about two and a half million, Slim?" countered Harry.

"I knew you were a horse trader, Harry, but I didn't know

you were this much of a hardcase. Are you trying to put me in the poor house? I'll have to do some figuring, hmm."

"Maybe you should be looking for a smaller restaurant without a spectacular location, Slim," said Harry as he leaned on the back legs of his chair and folded his arms across his chest.

Inside, Slim was smiling. "Well, there's nothing I can say, but two and half million it is." Slim smiled big as he stuck his hand out to shake Harry's.

"Well, you might be able to buy Harry's half, Slim, but it's going to take four million to buy both of our halves," said a sharp-eyed Dottie. Slim and Harry did a double-take of Dottie. They had forgotten she was even at the table. Slim thought, 'Damn her. Why couldn't she keep her mouth shut? I had him.' Neither of them had even wondered what Dottie was thinking. Both figured the negotiation was over.

"Well, I don't know, Dottie," said Slim as he tipped his Stetson back upon his head and slowly rubbed his chin, thinking. Then, he pulled his silver toothpick out of his front shirt pocket and stuck it into the corner of his mouth. Observing, Dottie knew she'd hit Slim's maximum, and smiled to herself. "I guess I can do four million, but I need concessions, folks. Both of you need to stay and help me hire and train people to replace you. If you do, I'll pay you four million."

"Done," said Dottie sticking her hand out to shake. She was grinning from ear to ear. Harry shook his head in disbelief at his marvelous wife.

"We're going to be a four-millionaire," laughed Harry. It was the perfect trade. Each thought they'd gotten the best end of the bargain. Everyone was giddy. Their handshakes sealed the deal.

Harry was relieved. He'd been worrying for years how he and Dottie would ever be able to retire to their Lake bungalow. He wanted them to finish out their years traveling to all of America's national parks. In the back of his mind, he started thinking about what kind of RV they'd buy. When he wasn't traveling, he planned to fish and watch the sunset from their dock. He wasn't worried about having something to do in retirement.

Dottie didn't have a care in the world as she watched Slim write a down-payment check for $200,000 and fill in the blank contract with a four-million-dollar price tag. She'd never seen so many zeroes following a number. She was stunned. Dottie loved working at Sizzerbill's and seeing her friends, but she was ready to retire. She knew she'd have plenty to do being retired, and she was ready to travel America with her man.

After the contract was signed, and the check secreted away, Slim pulled away from the dock with a big grin on his face. Dottie and Harry did the two-step and the do-si-do out to the dock and back. Their ship had come in, and they were ready to climb aboard.

## CHAPTER 17
# Small Town Throwdown

All of the homes, stores, and buildings were decorated with American flag red, white, and blue bunting for the Fourth of July. The Fourth was the biggest tourism weekend at the Lake. Tourists took advantage of the extra day off to plan a long holiday weekend. Shopkeepers usually held big sales to 'move the merchandise' to the large crowds. This year was different. Shopkeepers were so busy they didn't want the crowds to get any bigger.

The scene at the dam was becoming more and more bizarre. It looked like a bijou movie theatre showing the *Rocky Horror Star Trek Show*. Hundreds of enthusiastic Trekkies were hanging out at the dam dressed in their favorite *Star Trek* character's costume. They were constantly scanning the skies for UFOs hoping to meet an undercover alien. Some costumes were homemade. Most were expensive replicas bought from a booth looking curiously like a half-moon outhouse. It had been built by Spacey and Ducktail.

Trekkies spent their days re-enacting their favorite scenes from *Star Trek*.

Tourists co-starred with Spacey, Ducktail, and a couple of the original *Star Trek* cast members in video-recorded segments for a 'modest' professional fee. Original cast members were brought onto the make-shift stage on walkers and wheelchairs to raucous applause. The glow of cellphones, lighters, and the silent *Star Trek* hand sign for 'Live long and prosper' created a Comic-Con happening.

Everything was copasetic until a company of 40 *Star Wars* Stormtroopers laid siege to the stage area. The Storm-troopers indiscriminately shot the peaceful Trekkies with gas-propelled rapid-fire high-pressure paintball guns. The guns were filled with frozen paintballs that stung like a hornet, and they left swollen angry welts with green, red, blue, purple, and yellow paint splotches. The community theatre scene turned into pandemonium. Trekkies scuttled and screamed like small children stranding those in wheel-chairs and walkers as sacrificial lambs. It was alleged, but later denied, Stormtroopers were screaming, "Die, muthas, die!" as they shot their victims. Replica Trekkie phasers, which only made high-pitched sounds, were no match for the attackers.

Acting as dumb as a box of rocks, some onlookers wanting to share the pain and feel the fun, pleaded the psycho-crazed gatecrashers to "Shoot me! Shoot me, please!" Stormtroopers were only too happy to oblige. Colorful bruises and paint blotches left the twittlepated crowd looking like tie-dyed hippies at an oldies concert. It was as much fun as a boatload full of rattlers.

Snuffy and Barney were outnumbered. Womper-jawed, they called Mac. He was on the other side of the Lake answering Faith's call from the *Clearview Christian Church*.

"What's going on, Mac? Are you and Faith alright?"

"Yeah, I'm evicting some grumpy RVs, and tent and pop-up campers from her church's parking lot. The congregation couldn't park in their own church lot. It's a mess. What about you, guys? How are things at the dam?"

"It's nuts down here at the dam, Mac. A gang of Storm-troopers attacked the Trekkies with paintball guns. It's bedlam."

"Don't shoot anyone. Keep your guns holstered. Use your tasers if you need force. Arrest anyone who shoots someone without permission. Keep the peace, and arrest all lawbreakers who don't do what you tell them. I'll send deputies over as soon as we hang up."

The crowd was quickly put under control with the extra deputies and some arrests. Things got as quiet as church when the Oracle's white limousine snaked through the crowd and pulled up to the cattywampus stage. Fans craned their sunburned necks for a better view. Bumsteer and his acolytes strode in unison onto the paint-splotched stage. They looked like a 70s Motown review, except they were white, and Bumsteer didn't look like a lead singer.

Many in the audience had one burning question. 'Were the Oracle and his acolytes wearing underwear?' No one was sure, so side bets were placed.

As Bumsteer struggled up the stage steps to deliver his epistle, Stormtroopers were ordered to line up shoulder-to-shoulder at the front of the stage daring the audience to get rowdy. None of the Trekkies budged. The 'Dark Force' was dominating. Stormtroopers came to parade rest cradling their paint guns in their arms.

Today's 'UFO Epistle,' as Bumsteer's homilies were commonly known on cable news shows, centered on the environmental imbalance humans placed on the galaxy. Bumsteer's inspiration came while snacking on a Moon Pie and watching a *Wife Swap* re-run. He loved the show. He felt it was a subliminal alien intervention for one of his favorite shows to be broadcast while he was eating his favorite pie.

Bumsteer stood in prideful self-satisfaction with his stubby hands on his saddlebag hips as his acolytes' pastel-colored sheets swayed to the EDM music. A fog machine created a mysterious colorful mist.

"Citizens of the universe, I don't feel noways tired. We've come too far. We've come too far from where we started. Nobody told me the road would be easy. I don't believe the aliens have brought me this far to leave me. The Galaxians have said, let us not grow weary in doing good for the universe. We shall not lose heart. Humans have imbalanced the Milky Way Galaxy which will imbalance our universe. Our galaxy will implode in ten years unless humans change how they live. The Ancients have told me you need to disband your families. Your families create primitive and selfish social tribalism. After we break up your families, you need to join other families to re-balance the Milky Way Galaxy and the Universe."

The docile mob stood in stunned silence until the enthusiastic Alphas clapped jubilantly. Alphas wanted to curry favor with the Ancients to become a ruling species. The majority of the mob stood scratching their collective heads and other body parts with painful paintball bruises pondering the possibilities. Some thought of it as a chance to dump their insufferable spouses and spawn without paying child support. Others weren't so sure. They mostly loved their families except for various insufferable kids, obnoxious siblings, and extended family members.

By the time Mac arrived to check on Snuffy and Barney, Stormtroopers were popping off their helmets to scratch their sweating heads while they shuffled away. The media slipped into overdrive as a frenzy of reporters dragged their videographers for an interview with Bumsteer. The time had finally come to rebalance the universe by breaking up the patriarchal human family structure so hated by the media.

# CHAPTER 18
# Dixie Breakdown

Slim wasn't about to be outdone by the bruising mayhem at the dam. He had a show to produce, and it was going to be the best darn show anyone ever watched. After his afternoon Opry show, he had a private nighttime tour of the KORN tower scheduled for a special group who was paying a royal sum. Under his breath, Slim called his guests Bossie, Mossy and Boggy.

Priscilla Cameo, or as her friends called her, Prissy, or as Slim called her, Bossie, made the reservations and handled all of the arrangements. Bossie had such a cold personality ice wouldn't melt in her mouth, and she was so thin it looked like she needed worming. Bossie was the producer and director of *Alien Astronauts* the late-night cable show. Under her breath, Bossie called Slim, hillbilly, redneck, or yokel, depending on which came to her tongue first.

Because of the size of Bossie's group, Slim had to rent two helicopters to fly everyone over the KORN tower. In addition to the videographers in the helicopters, Bossie set up three videographers on the ground to videorecord the event. Her show's guests included two prestigious UFOologists.

The stodgy pompous professor was Professor Roland T. Mossback. Slim called the professor, Mossy. Bossie's other guest published *Ancient Astronauts* magazine. He was Percival Boggs or as Slim called him, Boggy. Boggy was a mess of white and grey stringy hair. Both men were unkempt according to Slim's standards. Slim was dressed in his best cowboy attire. It was his rhinestone American flag cowboy shirt. It took Slim's breath away thinking about being featured on a national cable news program.

"We're taking off now and heading to the tower," said Bossie alerting her techs on the ground. "I don't want anyone asleep at the wheel. Let's get this done on the first take. We're way over budget. Wake up, here comes, Momma!"

Bossie couldn't contain her exhilaration. It was going to be the most significant episode she ever produced. She was going to make sure it launched her movie directing career where the real money and fame was. She secretly planned to edit out the smarmy redneck before the episode aired. Knowing the dumb hillbilly didn't even know what the word 'smarmy' meant made her chuckle.

"Make sure your cameras keep rolling after the tower gets all lit up from the pyrotechnics, ma'am. You don't want to miss anything," said Slim yelling to be heard over the din of the whirling helicopter blades.

This was the most significant media opportunity he'd had since this whole UFO gold mine was discovered. Slim planned on KORN becoming a bigger tourist attraction than the *Bass Pro Shop* after this *Alien Astronaut* episode aired. He needed everything to be perfect.

"Get ready, boys. We're coming in hot, and I'm buying the beer if it goes according to the plan," said Slim into the microphone to his flight and ground crews. He rubbed his hands together thinking about the profits.

"Don't fly too fast, Jack." Jack was the captain in charge of both helicopters. "We need to fly nice and slow, so everybody gets a chance to film everything happening down there. Take your time. Remember, you're getting paid by the hour. There's no rush. I don't want them missing anything."

"Roger, Slim. We're taking it nice and easy. We won't land until you give us the word," said Jack, thinking Slim must be sick because he wasn't worrying about money.

"Keep your cameras rolling," said Bossie commanding her team into action. "We're knocking at the door!"

The edge of the spotlight from the first helicopter barely touched the pickup truck's tailgate when it started speeding away, but not too fast, towards the radio station. *Dixie Breakdown* was playing over the speakers at a feverish pace, which matched the excitement of the re-creation of the first UFO attack ever videorecorded. The video cameras were recording from every direction. As the pickup truck drove past the KORN station, it turned off its lights, and ducked to the side undetected by the cameras.

The KORN tower exploded into colorful flames at that precise moment. Flames reached a hundred feet in the air.

Green, red, and gold lightning sparks shot all around the metal tower which engulfed the crashed pickup truck. It was magical.

While the helicopters hovered above the exploding tower, one camera on the ground recorded a colossal but slightly hunched shadow that materialized from behind the tower. The shadow seemed startled and began trotting across the field at a rolling pace towards the woods.

Bossie saw it too. "What the hell is that, Rosie? Put your camera on the shadow moving across the field. Do you see it?" asked Bossie screeching into the microphone to her ground crew. "Tommy, keep rolling on the tower. Shoot from a lot of different angles and be sure and get a shot looking up at the tower."

You got it, boss," returned Tommy.

"Rosie, what's running across the field? It looks huge from up here. What is it?"

"You're not going to believe this, boss. It looks like a Sasquatch to me. I mean, I'm no expert, but it's huge. I don't have great light, only the reflections from the tower, but that's what it looks like to me. It's the silhouette of a Sasquatch, and it just looked back at me," stammered Rosie. Everyone's head snapped to the left side of their helicopter so they could see too.

"What? Repeat what you said, Rosie. You're breaking up a bit. I think you said a Sasquatch. If you said a Sasquatch, you better have it in your camera lens, Rosie. You better be filming it right now."

"Yes, boss, I think it is a Sasquatch. I've got it, boss. It's heading for the woods though."

"Chase it, Rosie. Stay on its ass. Stay on its ass, and that's an order."

"It's huge. I'm not following that monster into the woods, boss. What if they eat people?"

Bossie was so excited she would've had to walk sideways to keep from flying. "Damn it. You better set this frigging helicopter down right now, Jack. Set it down, now," demanded Bossie. "We've got to get video before it disappears. Chase it, dammit, Rosie. You better stay on it."

Nobody was paying attention to the dazzling flames of the tower any longer. All eyes were glued on the dark silhouette escaping across the field.

"First of all, Miss Prissy, I'm the captain of these helicopters. I'll give the order to set down when it's safe to land. Right now, I'm concerned about everyone's safety. I don't know if it's Old Sheff or not. I'd prefer no one get eaten on my mission," said Jack proving he was a hillbilly by calling it Old Sheff.

"Hey Jack, it's a Bigfoot, not Old Sheff," said a chuckling Slim. "I think it'd be safe to land over there by the station, but it's not safe to chase a Bigfoot or the one-eyed, one-horned flying purple people eater into the woods at night, ma'am."

"I say, old man," said Mossy, the plump folk studies professor from the mediocre private east coast college, clapping his fingertips together. "It's a magnificent specimen of a cryptid whether you call it Bigfoot, Yeti, Wood

Ape, Skunk Ape or Old Sheff. They're quite mysterious, but they're herbivores not carnivores. They won't eat anyone," he assured chuckling at their needless worry. "This is indeed a rare moment in modern history. We're witnessing a Bigfoot at the site of the first UFO attack."

"I quite agree, professor," said Boggy. "It's smashing. All of this outer-world activity must be related to the ancient global energy grids. Perhaps, this is an ancient burial site for ET astronauts. Stunning discovery. The government needs to step in and take over this site to be preserved and studied."

"It proves what I've been claiming for years," said Moss-back, the noted cryptozoologist. "Bigfoot, as you call it, is an interdimensional being. It is one with the ancient alien astronauts."

"What are you talking about?" asked Slim, who was feeling as ornery as cat manure at the thought of having his private property being taken over by the government. "How do you know it doesn't eat people? Have you ever fed one? Why should I let the government have my property?"

"Let me put it in terms you may understand, my good man. For the good of everyone, this site is one of the galactical wonders of the universe. I am sure it is an Ancient Alien monument of some sort. It was part of the Ancients' global energy grid, which they networked around Earth to supply all of the necessary energy. This is probably an ET burial ground like the pyramids in Egypt. ETs, or as many call them, aliens, needed a body to inhabit Earth, hence, Bigfoot. Bigfoot is an interdimensional being. He, she, or they, as the case may be, is the earth lifeform of the ancient ETs who have been directing man's evolution since before the pyramids. It's fascinating. Simply fascinating!"

"I didn't get your name, sir?" asked an incredulous Jack.

"Percival Boggs, cryptozoologist and publisher of the *Ancient Astronauts* magazine, at your service. I've written several books on various cryptids, including those I've already mentioned and MoMo, the Abominable Snowman, The Ohio Grassman, Yowie, and the always ill-tempered Wendigo. It's my distinct pleasure to be here, sir. Thanks for the invitation, Prissy. I can't wait to investigate this site further."

"No problem, Percy, now it's time to earn your keep. We've got a lot of work to do. Get this damn thing on the ground. Where's the Sasquatch, Rosie?" asked Bossie.

"It ran into the woods, boss. I only chased it a little way because it is so dark. I can't see anything through the lens. We should've brought our infrared lens."

The rest of the night was a whirr of activity. Slim called the Sheriff's office, which alerted the media on the police scanner and created a full-blown media event. Every reporter in the Lake area rushed to cover the story. Slim asked Mac to secure the site since it was under investigation for the Bigfoot sighting.

The combination of a UFO and Bigfoot sighting at the exact location created a media frenzy never seen before. A mob of journalists collected at the entrance demanding access to the property for investigations, interviews, and photographs.

It took all of Snuffy and Barney's ingenuity to keep the raucous reporters off the site. They even had to close down Sizzerbill's and its parking lot next door to keep reporters from sneaking their way onto KORN property.

Even Bumsteer and his acolytes, who were getting a late-night snack at Sizzerbill's, appeared at KORN's gate demanding immediate entry.

"I demand to see Sheriff MacGregor immediately. I need to personally examine these premises right now. The Ancients are telecommunicating with me. They want me to have access to receive a deeper understanding of this Bigfoot appearance. Begone, Earthlings!" said Bumsteer with a dismissive wave of his hand.

"I'm sorry, chief, but you're not going anywhere until the Sheriff tells us you're welcome. Now, please vacate these premises before us Earthlings put our boot in your butt and throw you in the hoosegow," said Snuffy smiling at Barney. They were fed up with the reporters, including these sheet-wearing blowhards.

While interviews were conducted with Mossy, Boggy, and Slim, various crew members made excursions into the woods to get sound recordings of Bigfoot.

"Tell our crew members to imitate wolf howls, Rosie. Percy thinks the howls might attract Bigfoot," said Prissy.

"They're afraid, boss. I am too."

"This is the discovery of a lifetime, Rosie. I don't care who's scared. Fire them. I'm calling the editing crew back at the hotel. I'm ordering them to find as many menstruating women as possible so they can bring them up here. Percy thinks their musk might attract Bigfoot."

"I'm sorry, ma'am. Nobody is allowed to come up here for any reason. These premises are under an active investigation. I am allowing you and your crew to video record the premises because we need as much evidence as possible. Please recall your crew from the woods immediately. It's not safe for them to be there at this time," said Mac.

Bigfoot had vanished, and it wasn't seen or heard from the rest of the night.

## CHAPTER 19
# My Heroes Have Always Been Cowboys

It was bedlam at the Lake after the Bigfoot sighting. Lodging was tighter than last year's underwear. The most recent arrivals were Bigfoot fans. The excitement of the UFO sightings and now a bona fide Bigfoot sighting created a honeypot for the honeybees. Lake life was at a fever pitch.

"We're running out of rooms in the asylum," said Mac.

"If you've seen a UFO, why don't you believe in Bigfoot, Mac? I do," said Faith.

"I don't know, Faith. Bigfoot doesn't seem real to me. It's like being told about the boogeyman when we were kids. It was fun to be scared, but we didn't believe in them. That's all. Fact is, I'm not sure I ever saw a UFO. I know I saw a bright light following me before it flew off. How can I be sure it was a UFO? Maybe it was a drone or some other kind of radio-controlled plane or helicopter. With the technology I've seen this summer, nothing surprises me. I figured I'd seen it all when I was in the service. Today, civilians have more technology than I did in the military. Why do you believe in Bigfoot?"

"I've been told about Old Sheff my whole life, Mac. Daddy says Grandaddy even saw one crossing Cow Creek in Dogwood Valley. I know I've never seen one, but they seem believable. I get anxious walking in the woods alone when it's getting dark. I always wonder who's watching me. Speaking of alone, let's talk about us. I'm not making it any secret, I want to marry you, and I have wanted to for a long time. I don't want you taking up with a younger woman because I'm getting too old. I want to get married, and I want a family. Am I being too forward?" Faith giggled, feeling uncertain.

"Old? You? Faith, you're the woman for me. I wish I would've been brave enough to ask you out before I went into the service. I never thought you even knew who I was. All of the guys at school and everywhere else were always hanging around you. Gosh, you're so beautiful. Who would've thought you'd like a lunkhead like me? You could've dated anybody. Why would you want to be with me?"

"Well, I do, Mac, and I always did. See, now, I've said it too. Let's get married. Please."

"I want to in the worst way, Faith, but I don't want all of this madness over our heads. I want the Lake to be peaceful again, like when we grew up. Don't you want to be able to relax and concentrate on our family? I don't want to go out at all hours of the night tracking down imagined Bigfoot and UFO sightings. It's crazy. All I need now is the Loch

Ness Monster showing up in the Lake. Then, we'll have a three-ring circus," said Mac rolling his eyes, clapping his hands, and laughing. "I'll figure out how to make the Lake peaceful again, Faith. Don't worry, and once I do, we'll get married right away. I promise."

"I know you will, Mac, but nothing stays the same. Everything changes even the Lake. I don't care if things are the way they used to be. I don't care if you're going and coming at all hours of the night. It's what marriage is all about. We'll figure it out."

Mac's police radio sprang to life as Faith wondered if Mac was so set in his ways as a bachelor that he'd never get married. He'd never give up being Sheriff. Maybe she needed to move on with her life.

● ● ●

Walking through the crowd to find his deputies made Mac's stomach do a double-belly-flip-flop. He was so aggravated at what he saw he wanted to spit. The dam looked like a Halloween scene. Everybody was wearing a costume. Half of the mob looked like a zoo full of animals. The most popular was a one-piece Chewbacca costume being sold at Wal-Mart. The Chewbacca costume worked as a UFO and a Bigfoot costume.

Mac had missed Bumsteer's latest UFO Epistle, when Bumsteer proclaimed a celestial bond between Bigfoot and the aliens. According to Bumsteer, Bigfoot's sighting was guided by the Ancients, who wanted humans to stop harvesting all animals. He claimed Bigfoot was put on Earth by the Ancients to be the ambassador for all domestic and wild-borne lifeforms.

Mac buttonholed Snuffy and Barney. "Howdy, boys, what's going on with all these barmy out-of-towners?"

"I'm exhausted, Mac. I feel like I've been run over by a steamboat in shallow water. This crazy never stops. Those drummers in loincloths over there make my head feel like an anvil. They never stop pounding. What can we do to get these people out of town? They just keep coming," whined Snuffy.

"I don't know how to get them out of here if you won't let us taser a few to set an example. We're as busy as bees in a bucket of tar keeping the peace," said Barney, who seemed as confused as the hen who hatched a duck egg.

"Bumsteer is the source of my consternation," said Mac. "If hot air was music, he'd be a marching brass band."

In unison, the three of them put their hands on their hips, shook their heads, and stared at the menagerie collected around them. Bruised and battered Trekkies had armed themselves with pepper gel spray on one side of the street. Stormtroopers held their ground on the other side without their paintball guns. Mac's deputies had disarmed them. They re-armed themselves with super-soaker water guns. There was an uneasy peace between the two gangs.

Mac's head flinched when a hairy hand put a piece of jerky in his face. "Howdy, Sheriff, how about a free sample of Jack Link's Teriyaki Beef Jerky?"

Mac smiled and said, "Thanks, but I prefer Original." The costumed Bigfoot laughed and gave Mac a whole package of Original jerky sticks to share with his hungry deputies.

"Can we take your picture with Bigfoot, Sheriff?" begged a swarm of people dressed like various Trekkies and Chewbaccas. Mac laughed, acquiesced, and mugged for photos. He acted like he was arresting Bigfoot and taking his jerky. Everyone, including Link's advertising agency, pulled out their phones and cameras. The photos and videos were immediately launched into the digital world. Snuffy and Barney felt like movie stars.

It was all fun and games until a group of animal rights activists got offended.

"Why are you dressed up like Bigfoot?" shrilly shrieked a young college coed named Polar. She pointed her expensive, long contoured brightly-painted fingernail in an accusing manner. It had a polar bear painted on it. "You're appropriating the fur and culture of Bigfoot. Don't you have a soul or anything better to do with your time? You're a sellout, you freak!!"

In the breath of an instant, her animal rights group, who was dressed in nude-color bodysuits splashed in red paint, started chanting in unison, "Freak, freak, the sellout is a freak!!"

Roger, the advertising agency account executive in charge of the Link's account, protectively stepped between the angry animal rights mob and the Bigfoot actor. Roger offered free Teriyaki-flavored samples to settle everyone down.

"Are you a college flunk out, you dunce? It's beef!!" bellowed Polar. Everything Polar said was at a volume louder than a jet engine. "Why would we eat your death sticks?" said Polar pointing at the Bigfoot actor. "He's an abomination!! You have appropriated Bigfoot's very soul and culture!! There's blood on your hands!!" Her group created a new chant.

"He's not the Abominable Snow Man," countered Roger.

"He's an actor acting like Bigfoot. Bigfoot's not real. The Abominable Snow Man isn't real either. They're a fantasy like a unicorn. We put Bigfoot in our commercials because they don't offend anyone. They're cute. Our ads are funny. Our ads are made to make people laugh. People love them," explained Roger proffering another box of Link's samples to the group. This time it was Original flavor.

"Dunce has blood on his hands!!" chanted Polar, pointing at Roger as her group joined her new chant in unison.

Sighing, Mac walked over to the animal rights group and told them they'd be arrested for peace disturbance if they didn't lower their voices. They insisted on ear-piercing chants, so Mac had Snuffy and Barney load them into their Suburbans and take them to the Sheriff's office for booking and processing.

The animal rights group couldn't have been happier. They took photos and videos of each other being arrested to post on *Instagram* and *Tik Tok*. Nearby reporters saw what was happening and shot videos of the entire event. They were on deadline and needed a story for the evening news.

Producers loved police brutality stories.

Climbing into his SUV while chewing his jerky, Mac shook his weary head and surveyed the foolishness. He couldn't get Faith or her beautiful face out of his mind as he recalled the sincerity in her voice. Mac knew. There wasn't one thing he wanted to do more than marry Faith. He was willing to quit being Sheriff. He didn't want to investigate people playing a prank with a drone or a Chewbacca costume. Mac vowed to get to the bottom of the UFO and Bigfoot sightings. He needed to get rid of all the crazies who had invaded the Lake.

## CHAPTER 20
# Hound Dog

Mac was sitting in his favorite rocking chair on his folk's wrap-around porch sipping coffee after dinner. He was chatting with his dad. His mom was taking dinner to a sick friend.

"You've been hunting these ridges since you were a little boy, Pop. Have you ever seen anything like a UFO or a Bigfoot? I'm getting desperate. I want to marry, Faith, but I want to get rid of this mess at the Lake before we get married."

"I don't believe I've ever seen either one, Mac. What do UFOs and Bigfoot have to do with getting married to Faith?"

"I don't want this chaos to interfere with us getting married. I get calls at all hours of the day and night about UFOs and Bigfoot sightings. She doesn't deserve that kind of life. She deserves a man who will help raise a family and be there when she needs him."

"Then, it seems like you're in the wrong line of work, Mac. Perhaps you should find another job. What would make you happier?"

"I don't think so, Pop. I like being a sheriff, but these UFOs and Bigfoot sightings are making life miserable. Being sheriff used to be fun. I used to be able to visit and help people when they needed it. Now, I'm running from one silly incident to the next. I've never seen so many crazy people in my life."

"Not even when you and your team were chasing Osama bin Laden? Do you think crazy will ever be out of your life, Mac? It's always been in my life, and it will be in yours. Faith can help you manage the crazy in your life. Your mother helps me with mine. You've got to accept you'll never be able to control crazy. It'll always be in your life, and Faith will always help you when it is. Now, with the matters of UFOs and Bigfoot, what facts do you know?"

"I know a strange bright light chased me one night, and I know the boys who ran their truck into the KORN tower were stoned and drunk. I also know many locals claim they've seen UFOs before. Heck, everyone who has come to the Lake this summer claims they've seen a UFO or a Bigfoot."

"If those boys were stoned and drunk, why'd you let them off of the hook, Mac? Why didn't you arrest them?"

"That's a great question, and I've asked it myself a thousand times. It would've made my life a lot easier if I had arrested them. Sure, they were stoned and drunk, but they weren't on crystal meth or hillbilly heroin which are my biggest problems. Nobody was hurt, and it was on private property. They said they got drunk immediately after the attack. I gave them the benefit of the doubt about the UFO because I wasn't sure if I'd seen one or not. Now, I'm not so sure I did. It could've been a drone or secret military spy craft. Who knows what I saw? I don't believe a lot of things I see anymore."

"What facts do you know about Bigfoot?"

"I know even less about Bigfoot. We've hunted almost every acre around the Lake, and we've never seen anything like a Bigfoot. Sure, I've heard sounds in the woods, but they could've been bears, deer, or panthers. I've never seen a clump of fur on a branch, or a Bigfoot footprint, except for the one in front of Sizzerbill's. Now, I've got dozens of eyewitnesses and actual video footage of a Bigfoot running across a field at night."

"Yeah, I've seen the Bigfoot video clip on TV. It looks pretty convincing, but you know what I've always said. Don't believe anything you hear and only half of what you see. You've got to let the facts determine where you go with your investigations. Don't let yourself get rattled. If it's a three-ring circus, make sure you're the Ring Master. What's Elvis think?"

"Elvis? Well, Pop, I haven't asked Elvis what he thinks, and it's time I did," said Mac breaking into a broad smile as he rubbed Elvis's ears and petted his head.

'It's about time you brought a professional detective into this case,' thought Elvis as he moaned with his ears getting scratched. 'What'd you think you'd find with those two untrained deputies on the case anyway? You should've quit leaving me at home and brought me onto this case weeks ago. I hope it's not too late,' thought Elvis as he moved into Mac's scratch, moaned and stretched.

●　●　●

The early morning songbirds were singing, when Mac pulled into KORN's lower parking lot. Tourists were already in line dressed like their favorite space movie or Bigfoot character. They were waiting for one of Slim's school buses to visit the tower. Moonbeam was making a special appearance later, so there was a larger crowd than usual.

Elvis was sitting on his haunches in the passenger seat with a big smile looking out the window at the crowd. He was as happy as a dog with two tails.

"Sorry, Sheriff, Slim told us not to allow anyone who wasn't a paying customer go up to the tower. It'll cost you $15 each for you and your dog."

"Well, I'm here on official sheriff business, Milo. I'm not paying for ol' Elvis or me to go up there. This place is the scene of an active police investigation, and I'm shutting it down as of right now while we investigate."

"Wait a minute, Sheriff, this is private property. You and your dog can't walk in and out like you own the place. You'd be trespassing."

'Let me handle this whippersnapper, Mac. He's mine.' Elvis crept toward Milo, "Grrrroowwl." Milo jumped back.

"I'll tell you what, Milo. If you haven't opened the gate by the time, I count three, I'll get a warrant from Judge Tuttle. Then, I'll shut this site down for weeks while we investigate. What do you want to do? One, two..."

"Hold your horses, Sheriff, and get your hound under control. I'm opening the gate, and I'm calling Slim. You better believe he will be madder than a wet hen."

"Thanks, Milo. Tell Slim I'm at the tower if he wants to meet. Don't let anyone come up to the tower as long as I'm here. Understand? Tell everyone I'm doing a safety inspection."

"Yes, Sheriff," said Milo as he shuffled in the dust to open the gate.

Mac drove up the hilly road surveying the landscape for missed details during his many trips up to the tower. Nothing stood out. The grounds were heavily trafficked by people and vehicles looking for souvenirs from Bigfoot or the UFO. Mac didn't know where he and Elvis should even search for clues. At the top of the bald knob, he parked Buster by the station, and he and Elvis jumped out of the front seat.

"Look around, Elvis. Find some clues about Bigfoot or the UFO. Anything would be helpful. Go find something, buddy"

Elvis grated, thinking, 'It's about time you brought in the professional detective. You've kept me locked up at the farm for weeks while the trail was getting cold. Thank goodness my allergies aren't acting up. My sniffer is in great shape.'

Then, Elvis set his remarkable nose to the ground and started smelling everything in his path. His floppy ears roused the scents hiding on the ground.

The lonely tower and radio station looked like the dreary dystopian *Star Wars* attraction at Disney. It was a time capsule except for the dramatic lighting and attraction signage explaining the UFO attack and Bigfoot sighting. KORN's tower was reinforced by welding the pickup truck into the structure. They also added extra support legs. The KORN radio station equipment had been moved to another site and was broadcasting while still under construction. Slim used KORN advertising to promote all of his enterprises which were going gangbuster.

As Elvis worked to pick up a scented trail, Mac examined the truck welded into the tower. Both of their heads turned when they heard Slim pumping the horn on his Caddy which kicked up a cloud of dust as he charged up the hill like a Pamplona bull. Both smiled.

"What in the name of all good things are you doing, Sheriff? Why'd you shut us down? I've got a business to run. I've got people on the payroll who want to get paid. Now, either you let me open up, or I'm sending everyone home without logging any hours today. What's it going to be?"

Elvis thought Slim was all hat and no cattle. "Hold your horses, Slim. Insulting and threatening your sheriff is as dumb as a bucket of worms. I've got an ongoing investigation here."

"Investigation? To have an investigation, you've got to have a crime. What crime's been committed? Is it a crime when a UFO attacks your radio station? I don't think so. Is it a crime when a Bigfoot runs across your property? I don't think so. You should be looking to arrest the aliens in the goldarn UFO for willful destruction of private property. You should be looking to arrest Bigfoot for trespassing on my private property. I am the aggrieved party here, Sheriff. You're treating me like a criminal. I'm asking you again. What crime do you think I committed? Why are you harassing me?"

As bold as an eagle on the attack, Mac smiled and said, "Insurance fraud and filing false police reports for starters. If I find evidence of a crime, you will be in trouble, Slim."

Quick as a rattler's bite, Slim countered, "Are you accusing me of a crime, Sheriff, or are you blowing smoke? You know I didn't have anything to do with the UFO attack. I wanted you to arrest those boys. They were so stoned they couldn't stand, but you didn't. If you don't have any proof, you just slandered me. I've got attorneys too, and they'll have a hay day with your interpretation of the facts." Slim put his hands on his schoolmarm hips with a 'dare me' look in his eyes.

"Now, Slim, you better stop threatening me, or you're going to make my mad come," cautioned Mac. "The Lake is going nuts because of events that happened on your property. I need to investigate them. Elvis and I will nose around here for another hour or so. You go down the hill and give everyone a free song and dance, so they stay in line. I'll come down the hill when we're done up here."

Faster than a knife fight in a phonebooth, the argument was over. Slim bit his lip, walked over to the Cadillac and drove down the hill leaving an angry cloud of dust in his wake.

Mac and Elvis walked all over the hillside, searching for unseen and overlooked evidence. Frustrated, Mac and Elvis looked for any nook or cranny where Bigfoot could've been before or after he was seen crossing the field.

Speaking out loud, Mac said, "Where in the heck was Bigfoot before everyone saw him, Elvis? Why can't we find a footprint or something he left behind? Come on, find something, ol' buddy. We need a break in these cases."

'I was doing detective work while you were jawing with the music man.' Sniffing and tracking for all of his worth in ever-widening circles, Elvis discovered a gang of wild turkeys which rushed from the brush. The tom gobbled, hissed, and spread his tail feathers threateningly. Elvis didn't pay the tom any mind. Continuing to track, Elvis came upon an interesting scent. It was in a shallow grassy depression under an ancient Burr Oak away from the open field. It smelled like sweat and fear. Elvis howled to Mac, who rushed to find him.

'It took you long enough to get here. Were you taking a nap?' thought Elvis.

"What'd you find, ol' buddy?" said Mac walking up to pet Elvis's head. Mac was a vigilant tracker too. He scanned the area until he noticed a considerable area of tall matted-down grass. It looked like a large animal had been lying down. When Mac hunted, he'd find places where deer or other large animals slept. This animal had to be very large.

Mac's eyebrows arched up when he paced the area and realized it was almost nine feet by nine feet. "Either a small herd of deer or a Bigfoot napped here. Good boy, Elvis," smiled Mac as he scratched Elvis's ears and took photos of the area with his phone.

Perturbed with Mac's pathetic nose, Elvis again put his nose on the ground. He woofed to indicate something shiny laying under the matted grass.

"Hello, what've we got here, Elvis? You might've found an important clue," said Mac. "Bigfoot must carry a well-worn Old Timer two-bladed pocket knife with a chip out of the handle."

Carefully, Mac picked the knife up with an evidence baggie to preserve any fingerprints. Elvis moaned, 'And Bigfoot uses his knife to clean his fingernails and whittle wood, Mac. Case solved,' thought Elvis as he high stepped it back to their Bronco.

Once loaded into Buster, Mac and Elvis drove down the road past the costumed tourists listening to Slim sing. They drove to Sizzerbill's. Mac wanted to investigate the fields between Sizzerbill's and KORN to see if Elvis could pick up Bigfoot's scent again. Mac was feeling better than he had all summer until Bumsteer's white limousine pulled up next to his Bronco.

"Ahh, good morning, Sheriff MacGregor! Don't shoot. We come in peace," smirked Bumsteer with his hands up.

"We're just the messengers. Would you like to join me for a piece of Moon Pie? My treat. I'm sorry you missed the epistle from the Ancients this morning. Their message is one of acceptance, peace, and love. They see you as a friend not an enemy, Sheriff. Open your heart to their warmth and benevolence. Today, the Ancients expounded on their age-old relationship with Bigfoot around the globe, including China's Yeren. You need to accept we are one speck of this vast universe. We must bow to their awe-inspiring power. They know best. Please, join me for a delightful slice of Moon Pie. You won't be sorry." Bumsteer beckoned Mac with an air of superiority.

"No thanks, Bumsteer. I've already eaten breakfast. Besides, I've got work to do to keep this tiny speck of ours safe." Mac thought Bumsteer was as worthless as bumps on a side of bacon.

"Indubitably. I appreciate your sense of duty, Sheriff. The Ancients' power is vast and cosmic. It's impossible to resist. We must obey. We exist because they created us, our technology, and our society to do their bidding. We can't survive without the Ancients. They've controlled humans since the beginning of time."

"Look, Bumsteer, let's be frank and earnest. I don't believe you're an oracle for anyone, including some alien lifeform from somewhere in the universe. I ain't buying your flying saucer conspiracy theories. I don't even believe what some people claim happened in '47 at Roswell. No one has any proof aliens exist other than talking heads spouting the news stories that say aliens exist." Mac was on a roll.

"Further, I don't believe any UFOs or aliens have visited the Lake. You wouldn't know an alien if it came up and took your last piece of pie. You're as big of a cryptid phony as Bigfoot and, in my mind, a lot more useless. He at least gives away beef jerky. Now, I hope the rest of your day is as delicious as a slice of Moon Pie. Good day!" With a tip of his cap, Mac smiled and followed Elvis into the woods.

Elvis thought, 'It's about time you told that fake fortune-teller off, son. He smells like yesterday's trash and needs a shower.' Elvis was on the scent of the Old Timer in Mac's shirt pocket.

With a virtuous nod towards his acolytes, Bumsteer gave a wry smile. "Let's hope the Ancients are compassionate and don't treat the Sheriff and all non-believers harshly for their blasphemous behavior."

The acolytes' heads all bobbed in agreement as they shadowed Bumsteer into Sizzerbill's. Their newfound cult celebrity and wealth were apparent. Each wore expensive matching leather sandals with straps laced up their calves—Roman style. The leather was dyed to match the color of their robes.

Despite the fact Mac was big enough to hunt bears with a switch, he was always vigilant. Even though he didn't believe in Bigfoot or MoMo, he didn't want to walk into a bear or cougar unarmed and unprepared. He always carried his 9 mm Glock sidearm.

Mac and Elvis hiked through the woods to the bald knob to search for Bigfoot's scent. They had to guess where Bigfoot entered the woods after the helicopters spotted him trudging across the field. Tourists were at the tower looking around and taking photos. Since it was a daytime tour, none of the lights or explosions were working.

There were orange ropes with 'Danger: Bigfoot Zone' signs set around the field's perimeter to stop tourists from exploring the woods. Several extra-large-size wooden Bigfoot cutouts were placed around the area so tourists could take photos of themselves with Bigfoot. The costumed tourists could hardly contain their delight.

They snapped videos and photos to post on their social media. Slim had commissioned an extra-large fiberglass statue of Bigfoot with real coyote fur. It was scheduled for delivery next week. A professional photographer had also been hired to take photos with the 'real life' Bigfoot statue.

At the top of the hill, Mac opened the bag with the Old Timer pocket knife and put it to Elvis' nose so he could get a good deep sniff.

'Not so close, youngster. I can smell it in your pocket,' sneezed Elvis.

"Find the trail, ol' buddy!"

Wrinkled and relaxed, Elvis wasn't the excitable type. He could pick out a grain of salt when mixed with 1,000 grains of sugar. 'Stand back, son. Let a professional work,' thought a smug Elvis. He loved showing off for Mac. They were, after all, best friends.

After a quarter-hour on the knob, Elvis found the scent from the knife along an overgrown wildlife path leading down the hill to the far corner of Sizzerbill's parking lot. Mac rewarded Elvis by scratching his ears and head with both hands.

The knife didn't prove anything. It was circumstantial evidence and inadmissible in court. All Mac knew for sure was somebody had lost their knife. It could've been lost, stolen, given, or forgotten anytime in the past, although it wasn't rusty. There was one thing Mac knew for sure; Bigfoot didn't carry an Old Timer two-bladed pocket knife with a chipped handle.

CHAPTER 21

# Wanted

**"W**hy in Sam Hill did you close down Slim's business, Mac?" said a red-faced and distressed Mayor. "He's an upstanding and respected businessman at the Lake," said Klaxon, nodding toward Slim, his most prominent campaign contributor. Slim was hornet mad.

"I'm doing what you told me, Mayor. I'm keeping reporters from following you into the bathroom," said Mac. "We've got to get to the bottom of all of this madness."

"Madness? What are you talking about? Businesses at the Lake have never made more money than they're making right now. Locals are making real money, and they can pay all of their bills. The hotels and motels are full. The supermarkets can't keep groceries on their shelves, and mom-and-pop shops can't keep fish bait in their coolers. It's Christmas in July, and you're fretting like a hen on the nest. What's the matter? You need to enjoy life more," shouted Mayor Klaxon.

"Now, look here, mayor. I'm willing to listen to what you have to say, but don't start questioning the need to preserve and protect the peace at the Lake. This madness has attracted unsavory characters who don't give a hoot or a holler about the people who live at the Lake," said Mac with a stare that would've melted a piece of iron. "It's time to put an end to it."

"Are you accusing me of not caring about the Lake, Sheriff?" asked Slim. "I've got almost 200 people on my payroll. I put my money where my mouth is. How many people do you hire?"

"Look, Slim. I'm not getting into a shouting match with you. You're a good businessman who knows how to make money. I'm a good sheriff, and I know how to keep the peace and keep people safe. Elvis smells a rat, and I plan to catch it. I don't think we've had any aliens or UFOs visit the Lake, and I don't think there was any Bigfoot."

"A rat? What's the rat done, Sheriff? Has it done anything illegal? I hope you're not calling me a rat or a liar. I have video proof there was a UFO and a Bigfoot on my KORN radio station property. Do you have any proof there wasn't a UFO or a Bigfoot on my property? Because, if you don't, you better take back what you just said."

"I didn't say you were a rat, Slim, and I don't have any proof you are—yet. You're right. It's not against the law to dress up as Bigfoot, but it doesn't make it right if you're trying to fool people to make money. I plan to figure out what's going on and fix it."

"Do you and Slim have anything else to ask me, mayor? Remember, I'm not appointed. I'm elected. If you can beat me in an election, take your best shot. Have a wonderful day, gentlemen. I've got more investigating to do."

• • •

"Morning, boys. Would you please come in here?" asked Mac as he walked into his office. He was disappointed but not surprised to get back to the Sheriff's Office, and find out the FBI fingerprint repository didn't have a match for the fingerprints on the pocketknife.

"What's up, Sheriff? What do you need?" asked Snuffy as Barney nodded hello.

"Have you heard anything suspicious about the Bigfoot sighting over at KORN?"

"No siree, sir. We haven't heard a thing. There does seem to be a Bigfoot sighting every day though. Yesterday morning one was spotted crossing Leatherwood Creek near the old grist mill. Another one was spotted in Defiance last night, which is just a stop sign with a mayor. I didn't know there were so many Bigfoot living around the Lake. Did you, Sheriff?" asked Snuffy as Barney nodded in wonderment.

"There isn't any such thing as a Bigfoot, boys. Who told you there was?"

"True, folks might be confusing Bigfoot with a MoMo or Sasquatch, Sheriff. They're hard to tell apart. Look around. Every car and truck have a 'Believe' sticker with a picture of Bigfoot on it. You might be mistaken, Mac. There're lots of eyewitnesses. All of the TV stations and newspapers have stories about Bigfoot and UFOs," said Snuffy as he folded his arms across his chest, challenging Mac. "They've even got photos. Dang. I feel cheated. I've lived here my whole life, and I've never seen one. Now, everybody sees them every day except me. I'm guessing Bigfoot are migrating south from up north."

"Oh, my Lord. Do you boys believe this hogwash? You don't believe the TV or the newspapers, do you, Snuffy? Barney?" asked Mac as he shook his head in disbelief.

Elvis carped and rolled over on the floor at the deputies' innocence. 'If they had any sense, they'd get down on all fours and take a giant sniff. Then, they'd know the difference between a blueberry cobbler and heifer dust,' thought Elvis.

"Sure, I believe the media, Sheriff. Why wouldn't I? It's their job to report the truth. Ain't it? Why would they lie to us? If they lied, nobody would believe them. Would they?" asked Barney.

"Do you believe Bumsteer is telepathically communicating with aliens?" asked Mac.

"I'm not 100% sure of that, Sheriff. He says he does, and we've listened to him talk at the dam a lot. I guess we should give him the benefit of the doubt. Why would he lie?" asked Barney as Snuffy shook his head slaunchwise in a confused state of mind. "Bumsteer's even got his own acolytes following him like baby ducks. I think a lot of people believe him, Sheriff."

"Don't you believe Bumsteer, Sheriff?" asked Snuffy.

"I don't believe Bumsteer any farther than I can throw him, and he's gained a lot of weight eating Dottie's Moon Pies," said Mac as he laughed and sat back in his straight-back wooden office chair. "I've got my work cut out if my own deputies believe in Bigfoot and UFOs. I'm not sure I'll ever change anybody's mind about whether they exist. What the heck am I going to do? Anyway, I need a couple of sharp detectives to volunteer for an important investigation. Are you men available to work with a detective I'm bringing on for a special assignment?"

"Are we ever, Sheriff!" said Snuffy in a rush of excitement. "We love detective work more than anything. What do you need us to investigate? I haven't heard about any murders or bank robberies. Did you, Barney?"

Barney shook his head 'no' when Mac whistled for Elvis, who ambled over to his chair.

"Here's what you need to do. Take this pocketknife and Elvis down to the dam. Then, give Elvis a good smell of it so he can walk through the crowds to find the owner of this pocketknife. Make sure to put his Sheriff's Office vest on Elvis, so nobody gets scared.

"Pocketknife? You want us to help Elvis find the owner of a pocketknife, Sheriff? That's all? We're supposed to follow him around the dam while he sniffs everyone until he finds the owner of this pocketknife?"

"That's right. I'm sure you and Elvis can handle it?"

"Sure, of course we can, Sheriff, but don't you need us for more important Sheriff work than following a dog around to return a beat-up pocketknife?"

Elvis grumbled as he looked first at Mac and then at the two deputies, 'Why are you assigning me to work with these two pecker heads, Mac? What'd I do to you? Without me, you'd still be walking around on the Bald Knob looking for Bigfoot's tracks. These two don't have a whole brain between them. Give me a break.'

"Nope, men, finding the owner of this knife is important detective work. Don't say a word to anybody about your assignment. Keep it secret and stay there all day if you must. I want Elvis smelling everybody in the crowd if that's what he has to do to find the owner," said Mac. "Here's money to buy yourself lunch at Big Ray's Silverfross. Get Elvis a double-cheese burger with everything, except onions, and a root beer in a frosted mug.

Elvis's voluminous ears picked up. He hurried out of the office towards the deputies' truck licking his chops. He was on point.

Mac had other matters to tend. He was supposed to have coffee with Faith's dad at the Kittyhawk Coffee Shop in Defiance. He didn't want to be overheard by Dottie or anyone else. He knew small-town gossip at the Lake traveled faster than a UFO.

• • •

"Howdy, Abner, how's your day going?" asked Mac as he smiled and sat down in the cushy red vinyl upholstered booth opposite Abner. They looked each other in the eyes.

You could tell Abner had been muscular as a young man even with his paunch. He was dressed in his denim work overalls with a couple of days of grey-beard stubble. He'd been working in his well-loved garden, thinking about their meeting this morning. Abner knew it would be a shootout, but he didn't have any bullets. Heck, he didn't even have his gun. He figured there wasn't much he could do to change Faith's mind or Mac's intentions. He mostly thought he'd already lost the fight. He was banking on a strong bluff to bully Mac away. He didn't figure his plan had much chance, but he wasn't the quitting type.

"It was going fine until you called, Sheriff. What's on your mind? Do you want to arrest me?" asked Abner sarcastically.

"Yeah, I do, Abner," mocked Mac, as Abner did a double-take ending in more grimace than smile as Mac intended. "I'm kidding, Abner," said Mac. "As you know, Faith and I are seeing each other, and we're very fond of each other. We...," Abner interrupted Mac.

"Look, let's get straight to the point, Sheriff. The Lake wouldn't be a doggone mess if you spent more time searching for those UFOs and Bigfoot instead of sparking my daughter. We're loaded with weirdos dressed like they're on a movie set. The dam looks like a Star Wars freak show. Lake folks can't even take a drive to watch the sunset anymore because the darn roads are so busy. We can't get out to a restaurant or get out on the Lake to fish because all of the boats are filled with partiers. You need to do your job and leave Faith alone. She's doing fine. We don't need you messing up our lives. Shoo-fly! Don't bother us," said Abner with a dismissive wave of his hand.

Rubbing his chin, Mac tried to understand what Abner was actually thinking, "Hmm, Abner, you're making this harder than I hoped. Let's get a cup of coffee so we can get to know each other better."

"What would you like this morning, Sheriff," said the fresh-faced young woman who hurried to stand at the end of the booth. She was one of Mac's former shop students. "Two cups of black coffee, please, Skye," said Mac looking Abner square in the eyes, hoping to break the ice with the kind of smile you'd give your parents.

"I know you plenty good already, Sheriff. I've known you since you were a boy younger than her," said Abner, pointing his thumb to Skye as she hustled away. "You're a politician, and you work day and night. You don't have any room for anyone in your life, much less my daughter, whom I cherish."

"I love your daughter too, Abner, and I want to marry her. Further, she loves me, and she wants to marry me. I'm coming to you for your blessing. We want you in our lives too."

"Blessing? Why should I give my blessing? You don't have my daughter's best interests at heart. You can't take care of her better than me."

"I'm not saying I can, Abner. I'll try as hard as I can. You can't love her any more than I do."

"You don't know, Mac. You've never had a child. You've never held a child so small and so innocent their life depends on you. Don't tell me you can love her any more than I do. You can't. It's impossible."

"You're right, Abner, I can't love Faith any more than you do, but I love her as much as possible. I'm going to do right by her. I'm going to ask her to marry me as soon as she'll have me. I want your blessing when I ask her. It'll mean the world to Faith if you and I can be friends. I want to be one of your best friends. We want you to be a huge part of our lives—our family." Abner was dripping teardrops on the table when Mac quit talking.

"Here's your coffee. Can I get anything else?"

"No thanks, just give us some time, please, Skye," said Mac reaching across the table to touch Abner's hand in friendship and comfort. "It's all going to work out, Abner. We'll be one big happy family."

He felt so emotional Abner couldn't look up at Mac. The moment he had always feared had arrived. He had lost his Hope, and he never wanted to lose his Faith. Abner knew Mac was a good, loyal, trustworthy man who would care for his daughter, whom he loved more than life itself. Abner gave his blessing but never touched his coffee. He had to leave.

Mac sat alone, sipping his coffee. He felt a different kind of scared than he ever felt before in his life. He was going to ask Faith to marry him. He would take responsibility for having a wife and a family who counted on him. His emotions hit him like a charging bull. It was a sobering moment filled with many memories and people from his life. He was excited and terrified at the same time to get started on his next adventure. Now, what was he going to do about these UFOs and Bigfoot?

# CHAPTER 22

# Mountain Dew

Elvis moaned as he stretched out on Mac's cool office floor, looking up at Mac through his droopy eyes. He was exhausted from smelling thousands of butts, legs, and crotches walking around at the dam with Snuffy and Barney. He used his prodigious proboscis to goose people he didn't care for, like Bumsteer, to make them jump. He licked his chops, thinking about how Bumsteer smelled like Dottie's pies and coffee. Most people, especially the kids, exhausted him to distraction. Their stinky deodorant, hairspray, and perfume made him sneeze. Elvis didn't care for other dogs, especially rhinestone-collared, spa-groomed, yapping lap rats.

Elvis was a hound dog, a sleuth on the scent. He wasn't a golden retriever anxious for acceptance from every hand in the crowd. Nose-frisking people wasn't any fun. It was work. Everyone wanted to pet him, especially kids with sticky hands and faces. Couldn't they see he was a detective working the scene? Mac had given him an assignment, and he wanted to get it done, but he failed. He knew he'd earned his root beer, but he never found the owner of the pocketknife.

"Whew, our trip was as worthless as teats on a bull," joked Barney as Snuffy chuckled. Mac pushed back onto the back legs of his chair, biting his lip while mulling it over in his mind.

"I don't understand. Are you sure you kept giving Elvis a fresh scent of the knife and kept the knife in the evidence bag? Did you let the knife touch anything? I would've sworn we had a good chance of catching, er, finding the knife's owner at the dam. You can try again tomorrow. Everybody goes to the dam to watch the UFO-Bigfoot freak show every day."

Hearing Mac, Elvis sighed as he stretched out on the floor. He knew he had to find the owner soon, or his life would go from unbearable to impossible.

"Don't get too comfortable, Elvis. We've got to run by Sizzerbill's before my date with Faith tonight. Let's go, buddy! Good night, boys. Get a good night's sleep. Let's get started early in the morning at the dam. We'll meet you there."

"Okay, Mac, but why is that knife so darn important? Was it used to kill someone?" asked Snuffy.

"Not yet, Snuffy, but it breaks my heart to know a hunter can't whittle a turkey call without it," smiled Mac.

Elvis creaked as he clambered up to follow Mac.

•  •  •

"I can't believe you sold out to Slim, Harry. What about you, Dottie? You'll go loopy sitting at home with this joker all day," said Mac backhanding Harry on the shoulder.

"Slim's paying us enough money to afford the good life, Mac. Of course, I'll miss this place, but I can always find things to do. I hope this old coot can keep up with me after we're retired. I might have to chase down a young buck," laughed Dottie while Harry smiled.

Harry had a tough time keeping up with Dottie as it was. Resigned, he sighed, knowing he'd do his best, and spend the rest of his time fishing off of a new dock, or the new bass boat he planned to buy. Harry chuckled to himself, thinking about the good life. He didn't like waking up every morning at 4:30 to open Sizzerbill's.

"When are you closing the sale?"

"We're closing at the end of the month, but we're going to run Sizzerbill's for Slim the rest of the season. He needs to find a manager and people to make the pies. Slim's a busy man. He's got a lot of irons in the fire. It'll be nice to sit in here with the rest of you and get served without cleaning the table," said a smiling Dottie while she filled Mac's and Elvis's cups with fresh coffee.

"I know this sounds silly, but have either of you seen a UFO or Bigfoot around Sizzerbill's in the last couple weeks?" asked Mac.

"UFOs? Bigfoot? I don't believe in any of that nonsense, Mac. You'll have to ask, Harry. He believes. What about it, fearless helicopter pilot? Have you seen any UFOs or Bigfoot with your new drone?" asked Dottie laughing at the thought.

Mac did a double-take looking between Dottie and Harry. Harry felt uneasy at the mention of his drone. "When did you get a drone, Harry? You never mentioned it before. What're you using it for?"

"Oh, he's had it a few weeks, Mac. He loves flying it at night after we close. Don't you, Harry? I guess he's already found a new hobby for his retirement. I might have to buy a drone so we have a hobby we can do together," laughed Dottie as she left to get the order from another table.

Harry and Mac sat thinking. Harry spoke first. "I didn't think to mention it, Mac. It's a hobby, like Dottie said."

"Why do you fly it at night?"

"Tell me when I have time to fly it in the daytime, Hero? What's the difference? I like flying it. It reminds me of flying helicopters in Nam. You ought to give it a try. It's fun."

"I'll bet it is fun, Harry. I'll bet it is. How can you fly it at night, though? How can you see where it is when you're on the ground, and it's in the sky?" asked Mac wondering if he might have a lead in his investigation.

Wary, Harry said, "Oh yeah, I can see pretty good. The drone's got a camera so I can see on the video screen of my controller. I don't try anything difficult. I keep it pretty simple. Up and down as they say. That's pretty much the extent of my flying."

Harry's chuckle sounded a little forced to Mac.

After finishing his coffee and ham sandwich, Elvis burped and looked for a place to lay down. He was drawn to an area at the bay window with a chair looking over the busy dock. Elvis got to the chair, and took a big whiff followed by several smaller sniffs. He was sure. There was no mistake. The chair had a piquant aroma made up of an assortment of odors no older than a few hours. The game's afoot, thought Elvis. 'How good am I?' He was ready to show off, but Mac was too busy talking.

'Okay, first I smell nine, no 11, different fox hounds, four males and seven females between the ages of one and 12. Oh, I am good,' chuckled Elvis. 'Oh, here it comes. The man who owns the pocketknife makes corn moonshine. Wait a minute, it's organic corn. Nice touch,' he thought with a raised brow. There was no doubt. His nose was sure. He looked over at Mac to see if he was paying attention to a real detective looking for actual clues. Perturbed, Elvis howled a bass yowl to tell Mac to get over to the chair and take a whiff.

Embarrassed by seeing Elvis' front paws on the chair, Mac said, "Get off that chair, Elvis. What's the matter with you? Get down and get over here! What have you seen at night with your drone, Harry? Did you see Bigfoot when it came through your place?"

"Sizzerbill's? How do you know Bigfoot came through here, Mac? I didn't see it. Did you?"

"No, Harry, I didn't see him. Elvis picked up his scent at the radio tower and tracked him down to your parking lot."

"Elvis?"

Elvis shook his massive head, yes, and howled out to Mac again, 'Get over here to this chair and take a whiff. Are you a pretend-detective? Are you off duty, officer? I need help over here, Mac.'

"What is wrong with you, Elvis? I said get off that chair, and get over here. I'm sorry, Harry, he knows better," said an embarrassed Mac.

'If you ignore me one more time, I'm coming over there and biting you on the butt to get your attention,' thought an impatient Elvis as he howled again.

"Mac, Bigfoot hasn't been here for a long time, but I believe there is a Bigfoot."

"Yeah, I know you do," said Mac gauging Harry to be telling what he thought was the truth. Agitated he stood up and strode over to grab Elvis by the collar and pull him back to his table. "I'm not sure I believe in Bigfoot, Harry. Count me skeptical."

"Then you agree with Bubba, Mac. He was sitting in Elvis' chair a few hours ago telling me the same thing. He doesn't believe in Bigfoot either."

'Bingo, that's Bubba's smell,' thought Elvis, 'At last, somebody's paying attention. At least Harry is listening. We need to find Bubba and return his pocketknife. Case solved.'

"You're saying Bubba doesn't believe, and he was sitting in the same chair, right there, a few hours ago?" said Mac pointing at the chair.

"Yeah," said Harry scratching his neck.

"Hey, Harry, didn't Bubba used to play Bigfoot at the Opry years ago for their Christmas show?" asked Mac. "No wonder he doesn't believe. He is Bigfoot," laughed Mac thinking about the double-entendre.

Harry joined the laugh and said, "Yeah, I think he wears a size 22 shoe. Bubba's Bigfoot alright."

Elvis nodded agreement, feeling superior. He knew how useless a human nose was. 'The only thing a human's nose does is stop them from going cross-eyed,' thought Elvis shaking his head as he climbed off the chair smiling at this joke.

●　●　●

It was a surprise when Mac drove up the lane to Bubba's farm. July heat was so unbearable Bubba's foxhounds were walking to chase the cats. They met Mac and Elvis at the front of the house.

'Eleven,' thought Elvis counting the hounds, knowing he was correct. Mac and Elvis climbed out of the Sheriff's SUV as Hortense came out on the porch and howdied to Mac. "Is this official business, Mac or is it sociable?"

"Hello, Hortense, no, this isn't official. It's sociable. I'm here to see Bubba and return his pocketknife. I borrowed it," said Mac.

"Well, if it's sociable Bubba's out back at the pot still," said Hortense with an inviting smile.

"Thanks, Hortense, I'll meander on back and give it to him," said Mac as he went through the white swinging gate holding it for Elvis and all of the hounds which followed them. Elvis was irritated by their yapping. He kept a low growl to warn the young foxhounds to hush up and stay away.

"Howdy!" said Mac sticking his hand out with the pocketknife in it. "Is this yours, Bubba?"

"Howdy, Mac. Yep, it's mine," said Bubba looking at it. "You know, don't you, Mac?" Bubba had felt guilty ever since he had pretended to be Bigfoot that night and was relieved to see his pocketknife. His daddy had given it to him when he was a young boy. He was sad that he'd lost it.

"I think I do, Bubba, but why don't you fill in the facts while we take a pull on your jug. I hear you're using organic corn for the mash," said Mac motioning to a jug sitting next to the still.

'Bingo, it's organic,' thought Elvis, not wanting a sip because he was still on duty.

Mac knew loose lips sunk ships, and he wanted to get the whole story from Bubba. He passed the jug to Bubba after faking a long pull himself. Elvis stretched out on the cool grass next to Mac as he woofed at Bubba's hounds so they'd settle down and keep away. He was ready to listen to Mac's interrogation.

"You don't miss much, do you, Mac?" It didn't take long for Bubba to spill the beans.

"Slim came to me with the idea of acting like Bigfoot for one of his shows at the KORN tower. He offered to pay me a pretty penny. Slim said it wasn't any different than when I played Bigfoot at the Hillbilly Opry for the Christmas shows. We were the only ones that knew about his plan. He told me not to tell anybody. Even Hortense. I parked in Sizzerbill's a couple of hours before the helicopters arrived and walked up to the station through the woods. I felt silly sitting in the woods waiting in my Bigfoot costume. It was a pleasant evening with lots of beautiful stars. I was nervous and kept re-playing in my mind what I was supposed to do. Bored and lying-in wait, I pulled out my knife to clean the dirt from under my fingernails. I dropped my knife when the helicopters came. It was dark though, and I couldn't find it. When the helicopter's spotlight hit the exploding tower, I ran out of the trees into the field to make sure I, I mean Bigfoot, was seen. I ran in a big circle to give everybody enough time to get a video of Bigfoot before I ran back into the woods. Once I got into the woods, and out of the spotlights, I took off my mask and hot-footed it down the hill to find my pickup. I had to get home without getting caught. With the talking heads going crazy, I was too nervous about going back for my knife. I didn't know this thing would blow up like it did, Mac. I'm sorry."

As Bubba caught his breath, Mac stayed quiet and listened.

'You've got him now, boy, let him sweat,' thought Elvis with a satisfied grunt.

"When things got so out of hand, I went straight to Slim and told him we should tell the truth about what happened.

He said we'd probably go to jail. So, I stayed quiet. I can't leave Hortense and the kids. I'm sorry I did it, and I promise I'll never do it again if you don't arrest me."

"Did you put the footprint at Sizzerbill's years ago for the first sighting, Bubba?"

"No, Mac, I don't know anything about it. I promise," said Bubba looking downcast.

Mac took a small swig of moonshine to clear his mind and think about his real challenge. Since everybody was claiming to see UFOs and Bigfoot all of the time now, who'd believe Bubba's story? Who'd hear it? The media wouldn't tell it. His story would be shunned because it contradicted the adle-brained Oracle's epistles. Mac stayed quiet while he processed his thoughts and took another small sip of moonshine. Mac passed the jug back to Bubba, who looked pitiful.

'Keep him blubbering, Mac,' thought Elvis. 'There's more to his story,' as he inched towards Mac. He was ready for a sip of moonshine too.

The next bombshell came after a couple more pulls on the jug. Bubba was talking about his hounds which led to his story about his trip to Chicago. They both laughed until they had tears in their eyes when Bubba told the story about Harry turning on his spotlight which caused Bubba to flip the boat into the pond. The story hit Mac like an 18-wheeler on the highway.

"You say your trip to Chicago was a couple of weeks before Memorial Day, Bubba? Are you sure?"

"Oh yeah, Mac, I'm sure. It was right after I opened the new cask on the full moon. Harry was here for it," said Bubba. Fact number two of the investigation slipped into place like a key into the lock.

Bubba passed his stoneware jug to Mac. He poured a sip in his hand for a grateful Elvis, who took the slurp. 'Case solved. Don't mind if I do. Thanks, ol' buddy,' thought a satisfied Elvis.

Forgetting, then abruptly remembering Faith, Mac checked the time on his phone. He realized he was over an hour late to pick her up. He felt a little frantic knowing it was a thirty-minute drive to her house. He planned to tell her about his meeting with Abner and ask her to marry him.

"Thanks for your help, Bubba. I appreciate it. I'll need your help to get all of this cleaned up. In the meantime, don't tell anybody about our little talk tonight. Keep it between the two of us. Okay?"

"You bet, Mac. I'm not proud of what I did. I'll do anything to help. Sorry for all of the pandemonium I've stirred up."

● ● ●

"Hello, Faith, I'm sorry I'm running a little late. I'm on my way over right now," said Mac sounding mournful and anxious on the phone.

"A little late, Mac? You were supposed to be here over an hour ago. That's more than a little late. You didn't even call to say you were running late. Do I mean so little to you?" Faith was hurt.

"You told me it didn't bother you that I was sheriff. My job is different. A lot of my work isn't on a regular schedule. Has anything changed, Faith?"

"You're clueless, Mac. This isn't about your job. It's about your regard for me. You've got a dangerous job. Did you ever wonder if I was worried about you? You should've called me to let me know you were going to be late. Well, you're too late, Mac. I don't want you coming over tonight. You don't have enough time for me—for us. Good night." Crying, she hung up before he could even answer.

Mac tried calling back a couple of times, but Faith wouldn't answer.

Letting out a controlled primal scream of anguish, Mac restrained himself from throwing his phone out the window. He slammed it on the seat, and drove home to Ironwood.

Enjoying his moonshine haze, Elvis felt smug at the thought of getting Faith out of their lives. 'Oh, she's sweet and easy to look at, but she's changed things. I don't feel comfortable in my own home. Mac cleans the house and puts me out on the porch whenever she's coming over. I'm expected to sit in the back seat like a common criminal when she's in the car. She doesn't fit our lives. We don't need her. She's the fly in my beer and just as unwelcome,' thought Elvis. 'She's all drama, Mac. Get your head screwed on right. You'll forget her soon enough. Then, it'll be the two amigos again. Things will be fine in the morning after a good night's sleep. Quit your crying, Mac. You're a grown man,' thought a disgusted Elvis as he moved to the back seat, stretched out, and didn't feel embarrassed when he passed gas. After all, Faith wasn't in the car.

Faith was a hot mess, and she was surprised Abner didn't abide her drama.

"What's wrong, Faith?" said Abner.

"What's wrong, Daddy? said Faith through her tears. "I'll tell you what's wrong. I'm in love with a selfish, stubborn man who will never put me first in his life. He's the wrong man for me, and I still love him. He's what's wrong in my life, Daddy."

"I don't think you're being fair to Mac, sweetheart. You knew who Mac was when you fell in love with him. Didn't you? Wasn't he sheriff then? Didn't you know how much he cared about the people who live here and visit the Lake? Didn't you know how responsible he felt about everyone's safety when you fell in love with him?"

"You've sure changed your tune, Daddy. Yesterday, you told me to forget Mac and move on with my life so I could find a better man. What changed your mind? He sure hasn't changed."

"I had coffee with Mac today. Although we'd howdied, we never really shook. I started to get to know him, and I like him. Mac would be a great husband. Every relationship comes with challenges, dear. When your mom and I first got married, I had to travel a lot for my job. Although I always felt guilty about being away, your mom didn't complain.

She didn't lay any guilt on me about being away. She told me we'd have to enjoy each other's company twice as much when we were together. We made a pact not to argue about anything whenever we were together. Those are the memories of Mom I hold most dear, Faith. You need to make up your mind. It's not my decision. It's yours. Good night, Dear. Try and get a good night's sleep."

Although she was beside herself with heartache, Faith didn't see how a marriage with Mac could ever work. She couldn't see a path to their happiness. She didn't think it would bother her if he was sheriff, but she didn't want to be taken for granted. 'Am I being selfish because I'm not his wife yet? Would things be different if we had children and I had a home to keep me busy when he's away? Suppose Mac quit being sheriff to give them a normal life. In that case, he'd never be happy with his job again. Mac likes the responsibility for keeping the peace. He likes helping people. He's a hero.' She sobbed herself to sleep, wondering if she could be the wife of a hero.

## CHAPTER 23
# Put Another Log on the Fire

Mac always did his best conjuring looking deep into the orange-red coals of a burning campfire. He'd built a good-size fire pit in his backyard, and loved watching the dancing flames and smelling the seasoned burning hardwoods. His fire pit was lined with red granite stones forming a circle. The stones had been hauled from around Ironwood over the past hundred years.

Mac had cut stump sections from oak trees for stools and made wooden benches with backs and arms so 20 people could sit around the fire pit. There was an area for grilling, but he could also barbecue a whole hog or cow on the spit if he had a hankering. The morning was already warming up as the sun rose in the blue sky. Every day was a good day to sit around a fire.

Elvis was lying on the cool ground with his back to the fire warming up. Content, he looked up at Mac, who was deep in contemplation. 'What are you cogitating about so early, ol' buddy? Don't fret. This is living! Ahh,' thought Elvis,

'I love the flavor of cowboy coffee in the morning.' Elvis sighed as he tumbled back into another nap.

Mac woke up long before dawn, which explained why he was sitting at the fire so early. He had two significant concerns on his mind. Faith and the chaos at the Lake. He had scheduled a confabulation with Slim, Bubba, and Harry this morning at eight. No one knew the others were invited. Impatient, Mac refilled his mug from the navy-blue enamelware coffee pot hanging on the metal hook over the fire.

"Good morning, Mac," said a curious Harry as he walked up, shook hands, grabbed a mug, and filled it. He sat next to Mac on a stump. "How're things going with you and Faith? Are there any wedding plans yet? We're expecting a big shindig."

"Yeah, well, we'll have to see, Harry. She's not too happy with me right now. Faith doesn't think my priorities are right when it comes to us. Things have been challenging this summer with all these UFO and Bigfoot happenings. I'm sure happy for you and Dottie. It's great you're going to retire."

"Oh, we're counting our lucky stars, Mac."

"I'm sure you are, Harry. Hello, Slim. Grab yourself a mug of coffee," said Mac nodding to the mugs and hanging coffee pot.

"Thanks, Sheriff. Nothing's better than a hunting fire in the morning and a cup of hot java. I smelled it as soon as I got out of my Caddy." Slim sipped, smacked his lips, and let out a loud "Howdy-do and good morning, boys! Why aren't you helping your bride serve the breakfast crowd, young man?" chuckled Slim blowing across his coffee and finding a stump to sit down.

"When the Sheriff calls, you better answer, Slim, or you're liable to end up in the hoosegow. Right, Mac?"

"Holy bovine, this must be a moonshine tasting, even Bubba's joining us," phony-laughed Slim. He wondered what in Sam Hill was going on and who else was going to attend this parley.

"Morning, Mac, Slim, Harry," said a reserved Bubba as he sat down on a bench. All of the stumps were too short. He didn't grab a mug of coffee. He had a miserable night's sleep, and he knew he had as much of a chance as a grasshopper in a hen house this morning.

Sensing all of the discomfort around the fire, Elvis opened his tired eyes and looked around. 'Man, even Slim's expensive musk cologne can't mask everybody's sweat. They must all be scared of something,' smiled Elvis. 'Hmm, Harry had Sizzerbill's eggs and bacon for breakfast. I'm hungry,' thought Elvis as he licked his chops and looked over at Mac.

'Good,' thought Mac. 'You scoundrels have cost me a summer of good sleep and turmoil. I'll let you stew in your own juices for a while.'

'I'm not sure what my boy's thinking, but it's a good time to nap,' thought Elvis.

"Well, boys, thanks for coming over this morning. I know you're all busy as bees making honey. How're things going? Any outer-world news for your sheriff? How about you, Slim?

Have you seen Bigfoot on any of your properties? I expect him to show up on your hillbilly farm tour or at the Opry for your Christmas show," said Mac in a mocking accusatory fashion. "It sure was fortuitous to have a bona fide Bigfoot sighting at your KORN radio station on the night you had a complete TV crew. Don't that beat all, Slim? You're the luckiest guy in the world. You've had a UFO attack your radio station, and a Bigfoot run across the same property during the same summer. What are the odds? You've made out like a bandit, haven't you? You're making a small fortune every day. Ka-ching!" said Mac as he smiled broadly and sipped his coffee.

"Uhh, yeah, I guess I have been fortunate, Sheriff. I guess I have," said Slim keeping his eyes down to the ground.

"I'm enjoying listening to KORN radio again. It's my favorite station," said Mac.

"Yeah, well, those boys really busted their backsides to get us back on the air, Sheriff. I didn't think we'd be on the air until after Labor Day. It's a miracle. We're planning to have a grand-reopening party as soon as possible. You're all invited," said Slim, wary of what Mac had in mind.

"I guess the second luckiest guy at the Lake is you, Harry. Who would've imagined you'd be able to retire with such grand style this year? Things couldn't have worked out any better for you and Dottie. I mean, here we are, boys. Just a few miles away from here, we've had the only two Bigfoot sightings at the Lake and the only actual UFO attack in the history of the world. Now, that's lottery-winning luck! We're sitting between the two luckiest businessmen in the world, Bubba. It's true. The two luckiest businessmen at the Lake. How does that make you feel, Bubba? Compared to these two pots of gold at the end of the rainbow, I feel like the unluckiest guy in the world. What about you, Bubba? Do you feel jinxed compared to these two lucky horseshoes?"

"Oh, I don't know, Mac. I feel blessed. I don't need any more money than I've got. I've got Hortense, the boys, the farm, the hounds, and my moonshine. What else do I need? I'm blessed for sure," said Bubba studying his size 22 shoes.

"Well, boys, you've taught me a life lesson this summer," said Mac as he put down his mug, slapped the tops of his thighs, and stood up ramrod straight to his full height.

"Yeah, what did we teach you, Sheriff?" asked Slim as he sipped his hot coffee and peered up from under his Stetson.

"Well, Slim, you've taught me if I'm not lucky enough to win the lottery, I should learn to make my luck. You know, be industrious. Be a visionary."

"You're already lucky, Hero," said Harry. "I mean, everybody likes you and respects you. You've got the most gorgeous woman at the Lake who loves you, and every guy at the Lake knows you can kick his butt. I'd say you're lucky, Mac. Everybody wishes they were you."

"Thanks, Harry, your kindhearted words mean a lot. Folks who wish they were me haven't been running around the Lake all summer chasing down every report of a UFO or Bigfoot running across someone's yard. It's making my deputies and me nutty as a bunch of squirrels. Things are going to change though, Harry."

"I'm enjoying my coffee and the fire this morning, Sheriff. It reminds me of a fox hunt out on the ridges listening to Bubba's hounds, but we've all got lots to do today. Is there a reason, other than enjoying each other's camaraderie, you've called us together?" Slim was relieved to pull the bandage off the wound with one quick pull.

"Thanks for getting me to the point, Slim. I wax philosophically when I'm searching for meaning in life, just like a good country-western song. I started doing it in the military before a mission. It was my way to get comfortable with the idea of dying in the field without ever seeing my family again. It's a habit. Here's how I interpret the facts, boys. Tell me where I'm wrong. First, Harry bought a drone and created, albeit accidentally, our first UFO attack in the history of the world. Then, with forethought, he created the second UFO sighting, which made Bumsteer tell us we had to believe he was the alien oracle. Taking advantage of the first UFO attack in the history of the world, Slim, being an entrepreneur extraordinaire, hired Bubba to create the first Bigfoot sighting at the Lake in 20 years. Now, what did I get wrong in my reckoning?"

"Well, Sheriff, it sounds like you're accusing us of nefarious and underhanded activities. I appreciate that you've been doing excellent investigative work, but you're a paladin of the court. We all know you need evidence to convict a person of a crime. I haven't heard any evidence just speculation. The main question I have is, what's the crime we're supposed to have committed? Your allegations are wild and extreme. For the sake of argument, let's say your assertions, however preposterous, are 100% correct. Is it against the law to fly a drone at night? I don't think so. Is it against the law to dress up in a costume? If it is, there are hundreds of costumed crusaders down at the dam right now. Are you going to arrest all of them? If you do, your jail is going to be pretty darn full. As the new owner of Sizzerbill's, I'd like the contract to feed all of those prisoners," said Slim. Then, he took his last sip of coffee, set down his mug, and stood up. Looking malnourished compared to Mac, he sat back down feeling sheepish.

"You sound like an officer of the court, Slim. You must have legal experience. Maybe you should be the sheriff. I'm not accusing you, gentlemen, of any illegal activities. I'm just speculating as any person might, unless, you're an incurious reporter holding make-believe conversations with aliens and Bigfoot."

"Let's say you're right, Mac," said Harry looking repentant. "What could be done if we wanted to undo things we might've done? What can we do to change the outcome? I don't see any way out. Do you?"

"I agree with Harry, Mac. Lots of people are superstitious. They want to believe in ghosts, Bigfoot, UFOs, and monsters under their beds. We're not going to change their minds no matter what we say or do. I don't see any way out. Do you?" asked Slim sincerely. Bubba nodded agreement with Harry, and Slim. He felt sorry for what he had done but didn't know how to fix it.

"Hmm, well, boys, I do have a plan to fix things at the Lake, but I'll need your help with it. Why don't we refill our mugs, and I'll tell you my plan," said Mac as he threw another log on the fire. Elvis was startled when the log hit the coals, but nodded off again, knowing Mac had things under control and breakfast wasn't ready.

## CHAPTER 24
# The Big Rock Candy Mountain

The sunset was getting pinker and prettier by the moment as the large red disc slid down the sky. Sunset was a spiritual time in Hollywood Hills. Everybody got high on the vibe of being in the powerful Hollywood dream world of blockbuster movies among the stardust.

"Where's the pipe? Let's do a hit before the sun sets," said Destiny.

"Here it is. I've got it," said Grunge putting a match over the bowl while he inhaled. After coughing out a cloud of stinking smoke as big as an exercise ball, Grunge passed the Fumo Pipe to Destiny. He reloaded it with a pinch of Acapulco Gold and put a match to it for Destiny.

"Holy shit, man, this stuff is killer." His eyes were watering like a garden hose as she inhaled with the same lung rattling result. Their hearts were beating as fast as a bunny's, but their brains were as slow as cold molasses. Although their speech was slurred, their appreciation for the colorful sunset was profound.

"Whoa, man, the sunset is gorgeous! Where do you get this amazing weed?" she said through her raspy throat.

"Yeah, man, it's beautiful," he agreed. "It's medicinal pot for my sore feet. It's easy to get. I've got a friend to help you if you want to get a prescription. Let's grab a chocolate sundae after the sun sets, Destiny."

"Awesome, Grunge. I'm getting the munchies."

"Yeah, me too."

Carloads of high schoolers and tourists started jamming the parking lot in anticipation of the glorious sunset. Destiny and Grunge were lucky to have secured their front row positions against the fence at the premier overlook along Mulholland Drive. It was a stunning vision of the wooded California valleys and the Santa Monica Mountains. Gawkers spied on the mysterious mansions while driving through Hollywood Hills.

Everyone played the imaginary guessing game of which celebrity owned each house. Truth was many of the houses belonged to plastic and reconstructive surgeons who provided breast, lip, and butt augmentation implants along with eyelid and nose jobs. Hair plugs were also popular. Lawyers and agents owned many of the rest. Only a few actors, like Brad Pitt, who was a hillbilly from Kickapoo High School in Missourah, made it to the top of Hollywood Hills. Angelina's surgeon did too. Below the observation area, onlookers could see downtown Los Angeles' neon lights. It was an awesome experience and view.

Everyone's phones were flashing simultaneously to provide the fill-in light on their faces and still catch the 45-foot-tall white letters in the background spelling 'Hollywood.' Every evening at the same time and the exact same spot, Instagram and Twitter lit up like movie lights from everyone's' posts. Onlookers had entered Hollywood—the adult Disneyland. They felt like players in the movie world. Maybe they had bit parts, but they were where the stars were. They were sharing a place and time with their cultural icons.

Everyone felt like they were a part of Hollywood itself. They traded stories about Tom Hanks buying Starbucks for a group of hot young female fans, and Bruce Willis giving someone the finger. Many fans wore their favorite players' Lakers jerseys and baseball team caps. They were all fans of someone and had dreams of meeting them.

As the sun was setting, a serious-looking professional photographer stepped forward with his extra-large 500/1000-millimeter f8 telephoto lens. He grabbed a spot by the front fence. He was wearing cowboy boots, a Stetson, and dark sunglasses. He acted like he wanted to get a photo of Madonna's house out towards the giant white letters. At least he heard; it was Madonna's. He told people around him he wanted a photograph to show his friends on *Facebook*. The light was about perfect. The clouds were still radiant, and the sky was indigo.

It had been a challenge to drive to Mount Lee Drive to put Harry and Bubba in position. Both had found a shady spot in the scrubby trees, but Bubba was sweating like a boar dressed in a three-piece suit. Tonight's whole scheme depended on him playing his part. He wasn't sure why he let himself get talked into this gambit. He'd spent the last three hours talking to himself while he waited. He heard in his earpiece, "Are you ready to rumble, MoMo?"

Mac had given each of them an assigned code name for the mission. The mission's code name was 'Tinsel Town.'

"Keep your earpiece in, and make sure you're smiling for the big show! Oh, and don't get caught or fall down the mountain, MoMo," said Harry trying to keep the moment light but feeling the world's weight on his shoulders.

"Don't get caught? Hortense will kill me if she finds out. I don't know, Harry-err, ALF. I'm not sure this is going to work. Let's try it tomorrow night after we do more planning and work through the rough spots. Things don't feel quite right to me. I've got a bad feeling about tonight."

"You aren't chickening out, again, MoMo. Tonight's the night. We can't afford more hotel rooms. We're driving out tonight. Pull your big-boy pants up and get ready. The show starts in five minutes," whispered Slim, whose codename was Hillbilly, into his mouthpiece.

"Darn, guys. What if we get caught?" mumbled Bubba. Neither ALF nor Hillbilly were listening. They were scanning the environment for hostiles like Mac reminded them to do.

"All you have to do is keep moving, MoMo. That's all. Let the Ghost do its job. It'll all be over in a few minutes.

Everyone needs to relax. Let's go into radio silence until the 30-second countdown. Over and out," said ALF.

Minutes passed like hours. Sweat was pouring down Bubba's face and down his arms and legs. He couldn't muster one positive thought to comfort himself except the jug of moonshine in the hotel room. The thought of it warmed him and bolstered his confidence a little.

The whole summer had been difficult. Bubba was sick and tired of the commotion. He was relieved to think it could all be over in a few minutes if he did his part.

Then he heard, "Mark, 30-seconds, and counting." He sighed, pulled on his mask, put on his gloves, and stood up, taking care where he placed his size 22s. He didn't want to step on a groundhog by accident.

· · ·

Patches, whose real name was Albert Moore, was used to being in the middle of chaos like explosions, burning buildings, and falling out of airplanes. He was a Hollywood stuntman. He got his nickname because his body had been patched up so often due to stunt-related injuries. Patches performed breathtaking stunts pretty-face actors were afraid to do. When Patches wasn't putting himself in teeth-drying situations, he took B and C-list actors on trail rides to scenic points around Hollywood on horseback. It was a great way to meet women who came to Hollywood to become red-carpet starlets. Tonight, the focus of his lustful attention was Tempest. Her real name was Mary Ann.

Tempest was born and raised in a small town outside of Cincinnati. At 16, when her parents divorced, she rebelled, quit high school, and ran away to Hollywood. It was unfortunate for her. She was a long-stem American rose. As a young girl in Hollywood, she was recruited to a booming career as a masseuse for old men and women claiming to be movie producers, directors, and actors. Many of her clandestine clients were politicians. She claimed to have massaged two presidents. After aging out of her masseuse career at 18, she strapped on a pair of double-F gummy bear silicone breast implants to become a movie star. Her adult film career exploded onto big-screen TVs. The money was fast, the action was furious, and the people were fun.

After pouring Tempest a glass of Napa Chardonnay, Patches, stupefied by her beauty, said, "You enjoy the sunset while I load the horses into the trailer." After loading the horses, he came back and tried to look Tempest in the eyes. His eyes kept dripping down to her mostly exposed breasts bulging out of her denim western-cut shirt. Her breasts had the exact effect she wanted when she picked them out at her surgeon's office. They created lustful desire.

Putting her forefinger under Patches' chin, she forced him to look into her eyes, "I'm up here, cowboy," she smiled.

"Sure, you are, but you're down there too," said Patches thinking her red-colored hair created an almost satanic-like halo with its spikes. "I can't help thinking we've met before.

Do you work in the movie business? I don't get on the main sets. I do the special effect stunts. I'm not around for the close-up scenes, and you don't look like you're on the camera crew."

"I'm between movies right now, cowboy. My agent's looking for the right role," she purred.

"You look so familiar. I thought we might've met around town." He could feel his lust for her grow by the moment. He wanted her right then. It was animal magnetism.

"Familiar? I'm crushed if we've met and you don't remember me. You might've seen me in my Bigfoot movies," teased Tempest. Her Bigfoot porn movies had drawn huge audiences for fraternity and bachelor parties. She'd even won an AVN for Female Performer of the Year before her movie career crested.

"Bigfoot? I knew I'd seen you. Weren't you Sheena in the Bigfoot erotica movies?" he smiled, knowing he'd pegged her. How had he forgotten her? Her Sheena Bigfoot movies were all the rage at his friends' bachelor parties. She was a bonafide star, and she was hot. He wanted her, and she thought he was attractive in a manly way. He looked like a model in a Levi's commercial.

● ● ●

"Ten, nine, eight, seven, six, five, four, three, two, one, lift-off," said ALF as the Ghost silently rose off the ground and quickly flew above the trees into the sky. The reflection of the last bit of sunlight on the enormous letters made the Hollywood sign luminescent on the horizon for just a moment.

Sitting among the dark scrubby trees, Bubba couldn't see his jutting size 22s through the eye-holes in his mask. He said a quick prayer as he walked into the clearing in front of the giant letter H and waited to be flooded by 100,000 lumens from the Hercules spotlight.

It only took a few seconds for Bubba to remember why he shouldn't look up at the light. He had forgotten how bright the spotlight was at Red's pond. He was bathed in the spotlight. It was so bright he had to squint to keep from going blind. He had wanted to wear sunglasses, but the guys nixed his idea. He couldn't afford to go blind—again. As MoMo, he was supposed to stroll along the bottom of the HOLLYWOOD letters and then descend Mount Lee without tripping and falling down the mountainside to Mulholland Highway.

Bubba's most important responsibility was to not get caught. Hillbilly was picking him up in the van. They were supposed to grab ALF and the Ghost further up Mulholland Highway where it intersected with Mulholland Trail. The way Mac had drawn up the plan, it looked like a piece of cake, but nothing goes according to plan. Tinsel Town was no exception.

"I can't see anything. I'm blind. Turn it off, Harry-er-ALF. Turn it off, ALF!" said Bubba as he stumbled trying to run away from the light. Bubba's scurrying from the light created a life-like scene.

Hillbilly was photographing everything from the scenic overlook as he exclaimed to the group, "Look, look over there at the sign. It's a UFO and a Bigfoot! Look!" said Slim as he feigned excitement.

"Holy crap," said Grunge, "It is! Look, Destiny. Get a photo for Twitter, quick!"

"Oh, my gawd, let's get a selfie."

"Forget the selfie, Destiny. Get a close-up photo with your phone. A frigging UFO is tele-transporting a Sasquatch. It'll be worth millions. Take some photos. Hurry!"

Hillbilly smiled as he shot photos and listened to them talking about what they would do with the money they would get paid.

"Stay cool, MoMo. Don't move around so much. I have a hard time keeping you in my view. Relax," said Harry. Hillbilly could hear the whole conversation.

"I can't relax, ALF. I can't see a dang thing!" To escape the spotlight, Bubba started loping away. Harry momentarily lost sight of Bubba who was trudging up the hillside behind the sign. Bubba crossed the road where Tempest and Patches were enraptured in a full embrace.

When the Ghost's stark white light found them observing each other, Patches, Tempest, and Bubba were disoriented and confused. They looked to and from each other, trying to make sense of the moment. Bubba felt like he did when

Hortense threw him a surprise birthday party. He thought, "Where am I? Who are these people? What's happening?'

When people took walks in the California hills, they knew it was possible to see a scrawny coyote or fox cross their path. Heck, there were even reports of bears. Californians knew they needed to be wary of wild animals and politicians when they were on the trails. However, very few people expected to come face-to-face with Sasquatch except for members of the Bigfoot Field Researchers Organization. This was the BFRO's righteous moment. Their moment of truth. This proved there were real-life Sasquatch, Bigfoot, Yeti, Wood Ape, and even MoMo lifeforms.

It hadn't occurred to Tempest or Patches that there was a spotlight as bright as the sun overhead making it seem like daylight. They were stunned to be staring eyeball to eyeball with a Sasquatch standing right before their very eyes.

Patches was a man steeped in the expectations of gallantry and loss of life and limb for imprudent purposes. He felt responsible for protecting the fair, Tempest, and rushed to step between her and the savage Sasquatch.

"What are you doing, Patches?" Tempest had other ideas. She'd taken acting classes with Roberto DeGnarly and learned the Stanislavski Method for acting. She didn't play a character in a movie; she became the character. Tempest was confident she could handle a wild Bigfoot, having starred in six Bigfoot porn movies with thousands of rehearsals. Aroused and protective, Tempest stepped in front of Patches to shield him. "Get back. It senses your fear."

The sight of an overpowering Bigfoot towering over her sent hot chills to every part of her body, which was on fire. Tempest couldn't tell if it was a male Bigfoot or female, but it didn't matter. She was ready to tame the beast as she did in countless movie scenes. Acting on instinct, Sheena grabbed the front of her shirt and ripped it open, exposing her voluptuous breasts to the beast. She extended her arms to soothe the beast in a beckoning fashion. Bubba was stupefied by Sheena and stood gawking at her body. He hadn't ever seen enhanced body parts like Sheena's. Drawn to her uncontrollably, Bubba started walking Boris Karloff-like towards Sheena with his arms outstretched.

Watching the scene from the drone above, Harry screamed into Bubba's earpiece, "Move, MoMo. You've got to get out of there, now!" Bubba didn't hear Harry.

"I'm not afraid," said Tempest to Patches. "Bigfoot isn't violent. They're vegetarians. Let me handle it," she said as she slid off her skintight jeans while smiling at Bubba, coaxing him.

"Not violent? Are you crazy? It's gigantic. How do you know it's not going to kill us? Would you walk towards a grizzly bear? We need to step back in a non-threatening way, Sheena. We don't want to frighten it."

"Stand back, Patches, let me handle it. Bigfoot sees men as aggressive hunters. We need to be submissive to soothe the beast," said an amorous Tempest. She seductively massaged her breasts and slunk towards a dazed Bubba who was unsure how to respond. Overcome and almost in a catatonic state, Bubba stopped walking. He was bewitched.

Sensing Bigfoot's indecision, Sheena adjusted her tactics to be more alluring. "Quick, Patches, strip off your clothes and stand here next to me."

"What? Are you out of your mind? Why should I take off my clothes? We need to get the hell out of here. Come back so we can get away before we're killed, Tempest."

"I'm sensing its indecision, Patches. It might be gay, or maybe it wants a menage-a-trois. I don't know its sexual orientation. We need to experiment and give it options."

"Sexual orientation? I don't give a damn about its orientation. I don't want to get killed. That's my orientation."

"My gawd, Patches. I thought you were an actor. Think of this as a role. Don't be such a tight ass. Strip and get up here next to me. Don't act like it's your first time."

"I'm a stunt man, Sheena, not a damn actor. I'm not stripping naked for one of your cockamamie ideas. I'm going back to the horse trailer and getting out of here. Are you coming?"

Anyone who has driven in Los Angeles hates the horrendous traffic. Every hour is rush hour. That's why La La Land has traffic helicopter 'personalities' for the radio and TV stations. Personalities are supposed to entertain the drivers while they're stuck in traffic. Dirk Conrads, or as Roxie his co-pilot personality called him, Connie, was the pilot for SASS radio. Roxie's nickname was the "asSASSin."

As comedienne du jour, Roxie's job was to entertain the poor schlubs stuck in traffic by insulting Connie, her hapless male pilot. She chided him as an in-the-closet transgender.

Dirk smiled at her insults and flew the helicopter, quietly wishing Roxie would fall out and splat on the ground. Dirk was an Air Force pilot in Desert Storm and claimed to have seen several UFOs during his illustrious military career. Roxie was an obnoxious personality who cussed and drank like a sailor on leave when they were flying around La La Land. Dirk only worked at SASS because he still loved flying helicopters. He could hardly wait for Roxie to be fired, as many before her were, when the audience ratings got released.

"What's that bright light over there by the Hollywood sign, Roxie?" asked Dirk, the straight man.

"It seems like somebody's searching for a conservative with a brain, Connie. Is there a movie promotion or a grand opening tonight? I didn't get an invitation because I'm with you," she sneered, laughing at her own joke.

"Let's take a quick look-see before our quarter on the hour traffic report," said Dirk as he swayed the stick and took a sharp veer toward the Hollywood icon at cruising speed.

It was an old combat habit for Harry to continuously scan the sky whether he was on a mission or not. Tonight, he was scanning the sky at the same time he was watching the Ghost's display. When Dirk was about a mile out, Harry's ears tuned in to the all-too-familiar sound of helicopter's rotors. Then, almost too late, Harry saw the blinking lights of the incoming bogie. It was time for evasive actions.

"MoMo, we've got an incoming bogie helicopter. Get ready. I'm turning off Hercules and taking cover on the count of three. 3-2-1-out." Bubba was so entranced by Sheena that he couldn't form a coherent thought until the spotlight was turned off. Everyone was left standing in the dark. When Bubba couldn't see Sheena, he gained consciousness and came to his senses.

"Hey, what the hell happened to that bright light, Sheena? Seeing Bigfoot, it didn't dawn on me that we had a searchlight over our heads. I thought it was still daylight. Who was watching us?" asked Patches.

"It must be a UFO like the one they saw out in the sticks," cried Sheena as she raced toward Bigfoot, pounced, and put him into a bear hug. She tightly wrapped her legs around his legs, almost knocking him over. "Take me, big boy, now," she demanded, humping his leg with her arms wrapped around his waist and her face in his crotch. Bubba was afire with the feel of Sheena smooshed against his body, even with the hairy Bigfoot costume between them. Bubba's eyelids fluttered as he waxed and waned in and out of consciousness.

Arriving at the spot, Dirk threw the switch to his emergency spotlight on the undercarriage of his helicopter. Even by Hollywood standards, Sheena's and Bigfoot's amorous embrace was an unexpected and bizarre scene. What made things even more bizarre was that the helicopter's video camera was automatically fed to the SASS website when the emergency landing spotlight was turned on.

"Geez, Connie, those two need a producer's couch in the casting room," laughed Roxie. "I'm pretty sure that's a Bigfoot having sex with a naked woman. This must be a

PETA commercial. This isn't a family-rated movie. We know why they call him Bigfoot now," cackled Roxie.

Bubba sobered up with ALF yelling in his earpiece and the helicopter's light shining from above. He knew he had to escape, but he didn't know how. In his earpiece, he heard, "I'm hovering over the helicopter, MoMo. When I turn on Hercules, use the diversion. Shake the bitch-in-heat off your leg and run like the devil's chasing you. On the count of three. 3-2-1-on."

The Hercules switch was pushed, and 100 thousand lumens rained down from above the SASS helicopter. "What the hell is that bright light? Where's it coming from, Connie?" squealed Roxie.

"I'm not sure. We might be in a UFO's transporter beam. Buckle up. I'm going to try evasive military maneuvers. I don't want aliens to abduct us and take us prisoner."

"Hell no, Connie! Don't let them take us. Unlike you, I've got fans," cried Roxie as Dirk turned off his running lights and jetted off in a reverse zig-zag pattern with a few loops making Roxie nauseous enough to vomit. Dirk wanted to shake the UFO from his tail, so they could head back to the station's landing pad. Dirk never considered flying back to the Hollywood sign. After the helicopter escaped, Harry dropped his altitude to hover above Bubba and follow him down the mountainside to his pick-up point.

"Get the hell out of there, MoMo! Get rid of the alley cat, and get down the hill as fast as possible. Hillbilly, drive to the pick-up point. Everybody needs to be moving now," commanded ALF.

Bubba drug Tempest as she clung to his leg begging him to take her with him. She was desperate for attention and affection. *Beauty and the Beast* had always been her favorite movie. She tried to make Bigfoot understand she'd love him forever between her sobs. Dragging her made Bubba run stiff-legged until she bounced off his leg into a hysterical heap. Harry turned off the Hercules, and Bigfoot vanished into the night. Bawling and momentarily blind, Sheena was left wondering why Bigfoot rejected her for the role she always wanted to play.

Watching and listening to the mayhem on the hillside left Slim speechless. He gathered his camera equipment and headed to their van for his drive down Mulholland Drive, "I copy, ALF. I'm on my way."

Big feet are never an advantage unless you're swimming or walking on a street filled with potholes. Bubba knew his ginormous clodhoppers weren't any help running down the sage-covered rocky mountainside in the dark with a hot mask over his head. He was so warm; his sweat was leaking through his Bigfoot costume. Still stupefied by the vision of the pleading naked hellcat, he came face-to-mask with a couple of the notorious LA coyotes.

Coyotes are known to steal children, dogs, and barbe-cued meat right off your grill in LA. At the Lake, hillbillies shot them. Shaken but not stirred, Bubba was used to track-ing coyotes with his hounds, so he tried to stare them down.

When that didn't work, Bubba let out a roar so loud it echoed throughout the mountain. Unfazed, the coyotes cocked their heads and started stalking him. Either they didn't know they were supposed to be afraid of Bigfoot, or they knew Bigfoot was a vegetarian. The coyotes only scattered when they heard what they thought was a she-wolf's mournful howl.

Startled that Sheena was still tracking him, Bubba broke radio silence. "What should I do, ALF? She's tracking me."

"Copy, MoMo. Don't break radio silence. ALF is overhead now and sees your heat image. If you walk straight ahead about 200 yards you will get to the pick-up point. Hellcat is about 50 yards behind you and moving up fast. Take evasive action now; we don't want her following you to the pick-up point. Wait, I've got an idea. Take a sharp right turn and walk about 50 yards."

Bubba clumsily scrambled over the rocks as fast as possible. He tried not to trip over his own feet and fall off the cliff. He heard her eerie screeches every few seconds.

Sheena was in love and didn't plan to give up the hunt. Deep in her primal being, she knew her kindred love spirit was in the animal world not the human. Raised on a farm, Sheena understood animals. She knew people would think she was crazy tracking a Bigfoot naked on a mountain. As she tracked Bigfoot, she was inspired to write a new movie. She was gaining on her prey and tried to activate her primal sense of smell to track Bigfoot's scent.

Bubba could hear the wild woman on his heels. He secretly wondered if he wanted to get caught. He knew

Hortense would push him into the barn for the rest of the summer if she found out.

"Keep moving, MoMo. She's gaining!" urged ALF. "I need you to climb on top of the rock outcropping in about 25 yards. Wave your arms if you see it? Good. I can see you waving your arms. When you get on top of the rock, stop and face her. She's hot on your tail. Once you see her, hold your arms up in the air. Then, shut your eyes tight. Over and out."

Bubba was standing on the rock with his arms outstretched to the sky in seconds. "On three. 3-2-1-On." Harry threw the Hercules switch, which covered Sheena and Bubba in enough light to fill the Hollywood Bowl. Blinded from the drone's light, Sheena screamed at the top of her lungs, "No, don't take him. Please leave him with me or take me with you. I believe. I love Bigfoot!" She didn't dare remove her hands from her eyes even though she could see the bones in her hands. Her panicked screams and loud sobs made it difficult for Bubba to hear ALF's instructions.

"Turn left, walk slowly down the rock outcropping, MoMo. Take another left and keep walking down the hill. Hillbilly's waiting. Don't look up. I'll keep the light on her until you get to the van. When I turn the light off, it'll take a few minutes for her eyes to adjust and figure out what she thinks happened to Bigfoot."

As Bubba clambered into the van, he could still hear Sheena's wretched wailing into the night sky.

"I can't believe we did it. I thought she'd catch me, and we'd get caught."

"You're sweating like a lawn sprinkler, Bubba. Better get your costume off before you pass out."

Sheena had seen all of the Oracle's YouTube videos from the Lake. She knew Bigfoot was an interdimensional being, a star traveler, an ancient astronaut, an ET. She was heartbroken she had lost her chance to mate with it. Her Bigfoot movies were right all along. Bigfoot wasn't an animal. It was a vegetarian and as human as she was. Maybe more so. She was heartbroken because she loved an extraterrestrial being, and their love would never be consummated in the biblical sense. As if struck by a star, she understood her mission. The Ancients wanted her to produce a new series of movies, including a prequel and a sequel, and a Nutflux TV series to tell Bigfoot's ET story.

Each man released an adrenalin-laced primal scream of relief once they were all in the van. The men were lucky to escape and couldn't wait to tell Mac what happened.

"Let's get to Las Vegas as fast as we can drive, boys! You know what they say, Bubba. Unlucky at love, lucky at cards," laughed Slim as he drove hell-bent on hitting Caesar's Palace while his luck was hot.

Mac told them not to call him on his sheriff's phone because his calls and texts could be claimed through the Freedom of Information Act. Big Tech and Government agencies were constantly scanning the digital world for everything said on phones. They needed to stay dark, which wasn't easy for country boys who grew up saying what was on their minds. City kids were taught to whisper so they didn't bother people bunched up right next to them. Country kids spoke loudly because they had to yell across a pasture to say hello.

As the men drove to Vegas, they watched the media shaggery on their phones. Mac didn't want to leave a direct trail between Hollywood Hills and the Lake. Dark government intelligence agencies were already combing Hollywood Hills for witnesses, aliens, and Bigfoot. They were clueless, but Mac didn't want an agent tripping over an incidental oversight.

Mac spit beer all over his wooden floor when he saw the helicopter footage of Sheena humping Bubba's leg. Fortunately, Elvis stayed dry and never flinched an ear in defense.

Looking up at the screen, Elvis screeched his disgust at the California leg-humper. 'Tsk tsk,' he thought. 'Now, I understand this whole Californication thing.'

Mac had been as nervous as a sinner in church ever since he dreamed up the Tinsel Town mission. He hated putting the guys in jeopardy, but they deserved it. They had made everyone's life, except their own, miserable with their fantastical shenanigans. He was desperate and had to try a Hail Mary pass. Since he couldn't change believers' minds, he offered them an opportunity to chase their nightmares someplace else.

He checked his watch and sighed, knowing it was too late to call Faith. He was willing to do anything in his power to get her back into his life. He went to bed knowing he had a lot of work to do in the morning.

## CHAPTER 25
# Drink Up and Go Home

Talking heads created a furious whipsaw of news stories with UFO and Bigfoot experts. Bumsteer was bingeing on Moon Pies while he watched and re-watched the media feeds from the Hollywood traffic helicopter. He was forced to delay appearing on TV about the new sightings because he had wicked-bad indigestion. He burped whenever he talked because of all the pie and excitement. He felt blessed, but not in a religious way. The Ancients had spoken to him during the media chaos. He was desperate to spread their message and become the center of attention again. Staying relevant was the key to the news business. Drinking bottle after bottle of Pepto Bismol helped him as he called his limousine driver.

"Hello," carped the sleepy driver.

"Harlen, pick me up at the front door in 15 minutes. You need to drive me to the dam immediately. I must convey the Ancients' message to the multitudes."

"But, it's after midnight, boss, are you sure? Nobody is going to be awake. Aren't you tired? I know I am."

"You lazy bumbler, get out of bed and bring the limousine around, or you're fired. This will be the most important epistle I've ever spoken. BURP!"

"What'd you say, boss?"

"I said get the acolytes and be outside in 15 minutes!" 'Damn this indigestion,' thought Bumsteer. As oracle, Bumsteer felt a deep and abiding responsibility to deliver the Ancients' messages to his faithful followers, sleep deprivation and comfort be damned. He was a celebrity.

He had an obligation to his fans to teach them how to be virtuous and self-righteous. He was as happy as a hog in mud except for his severe acid reflux. It felt like a hole was being burned into his chest. He reasoned that working for the greater good of the universe was worth the insignificant personal sacrifices he made. The Ancients had spoken.

Bumsteer's believers had become clinically-depressed. They were in a constant state of rage. Listening to his daily epistles created a mass psychosis. Believers moved in lock-step with one another. They knew what the other person was thinking because they all had the same thoughts. They were mental and emotional clones. Spiritual twins.

After his social-media post, word about Bumsteer's surprise epistle spread like the wind. His believers rose from their cardboard box homes and U-Hauls to get as close as possible to the front of the stage. They were attracted like hogs to persimmons and could hardly wait to hear what the Ancients had to say about the recent Bigfoot and UFO sightings. They were entranced.

Believers charged with temple duties cleaned the stage, turned on the colored LED stage lights, and started the smoke machine in preparation of Bumsteer's appearance. The Oracle's believers felt frightened seeing his somber and subdued countenance, which was actually indigestion. He lumbered up the stage steps in his flowing robes. His sleepy-eyed acolytes followed.

His more advanced believers, known as disciples because they had studied directly under Bumsteer and his acolytes, were already wiping their tears with their newly approved robes. Acolytes and disciples had achieved mental and emotional networks with Bumsteer through telepathy. Everyone felt the Oracle's pain and seething rage. It was their gift from the Ancients. The audience could see Bumsteer was sweating more than usual. It showed through his white toga with the yellow backlighting and fog machine.

Bumsteer felt the weight of the world on his shoulders because it was. His experiences at the Lake were transformative. He believed he was connected with the Ancients and was thankful. His time spent at Sizzerbill's, a key landmark in the Ancients' power grid, had mutated him into a higher life form. He wasn't an Ancient yet but was on a higher plane than commoners destined to rot in ignorance. He likened himself to an archangel but not in a religious way. His potent all-knowing mental energy granted by the Ancients was exhilarating.

If plebeian Joe-the-Plumbers didn't believe and heed his message, Ancients assured him it would be Armageddon. Worthless non-believers didn't matter, but believers deserved a second chance to change Earth's grim future. Earth's death would create negative consequences for other lifeforms throughout the universe which needed its resources. Believers felt obliged to keep the galaxy and universe in balance. A solemn silence overtook the mystical brood as Bumsteer began his final Lake sermon.

"Children of the Ancients, the Ancients have summoned us to Hollywood Hills. We will reconvene on the west coast to rediscover our ancestral forebearer, Bigfoot. In Hollywood Hills, our dreadful past will metamorphous into our glorious resurrection as we nurture the universe and keep it alive! The Ancients have charged us to find every surviving Bigfoot. We need to support their breeding so they don't become extinct. Their extinction is our apocalypse. We must not fail in our duty. Bigfoot is nearly extinct due to thoughtless human acts of rampant overpopulation and senseless overuse of non-renewable resources like white Vaseline petroleum jelly and plastic straws. Humans need to become citizens of the universe, we can't wallow in immediate self-gratification.

True believers must leave the Lake as soon as possible and travel to Hollywood Hills to reverse these dire and existential threats. If we can preserve Panda bears and whales, we can preserve Bigfoot's reproduction too. The Ancients assure me we will see the end of Earth in 10 years if we can't find and support Bigfoot. We must be resolute in our commitment to the universe's very survival. The universe is counting on us. Now, I will take a few questions."

"Rachel Maddox, from the World Domination Network, Oracle. Blather reported that the Ancient's UFO first attacked the KORN radio station because of all the hate speech in country-western and bluegrass music. Bigfoot left the Lake because of the species-hate speech it heard here. Western country songs are about broken-hearted beer drinkers driving pickup trucks to watch women in short shorts. It's disgusting. We need to demand the government shut down all country, western, and bluegrass music stations and recording studios. Hillbillies should be put in jail for the way they hunt defenseless animals and make illegal moonshine. They're disgusting too."

"Uh, Rachel, do you have a question for me," asked the Oracle.

"Yes, I do. Don't you agree with me?"

"Yes, yes, I do, Rachel. I support putting hillbillies in jail, shutting down all country-western radio stations, and putting moonshiners in prison for life. As you know, hillbillies think they'll find truth in a glass of moonshine. It's a bold lie repeatedly told in the screechy sounds of country-western music. Ban it all! Let me take a question from my audience of believers. You're important to me also."

A disciple went into the audience and escorted a middle-aged woman dressed in a ratty Princess Leia costume toward the stage. Quickly, stormtroopers assembled to block Leia's path.

"Let her pass," ordered the Oracle. "We're all equal in the eyes of the Ancients." The stormtroopers stepped aside to let Leia pass begrudgingly.

"Thank you for this wonderful opportunity, great and powerful, Oracle! I'm shaking. I'm so nervous. It's truly an honor."

"Go ahead, ask me your question," said a queasy Bumsteer.

"Well, Oracle, I have one question many of us have discussed over the last month. Do we need to wear our costumes when we get to Hollywood Hills? Many of our costumes are worn out." Most people in the audience shook their masked Chewbacca heads in agreement.

"I wonder about your commitment to the universe, Leia. Is it all about your comfort? Can't you think about anyone else besides yourself? The universe is under attack. I don't want to publicly shame you, but," and the Oracle let his voice trail off as the audience turned their heads to shun her.

"Oh no, sir," Leia was stricken. "I'm not asking for any special concession. I want to help the universe get healthy again. I'm more than happy to wear my costume all of the time. I hope to change into a clean one before I arrive in Hollywood. Is that possible?"

With a benevolent smile, Bumsteer acknowledged Leia's question. "Whatever gave you the idea you were supposed to wear a dirty costume, Leia? Of course, you're supposed to keep your costume clean. In fact, you should clean it daily. You need more than one costume, but please stay in your same Leia costume as we're trying to rebalance the universe and don't want to confuse it."

Leia was relieved to bow her way back past the stormtroopers to the general audience with the other sweaty costumes as Bumsteer gave his final directions.

The end of Bumsteer's epistle, which was hopeful in a dark way, left believers dobbing tears from their eyes filled with a zealot's sparkle. They were reinvigorated and determined to stop the universe from collapsing into a giant black hole. They were going where no human had gone before. They were going to save Bigfoot.

Along with their newfound responsibility, they felt relieved. Truth be told, they were bored at the Lake. There wasn't anything to do if you didn't own a boat, or at least a WaveRunner or Jet Ski. They had been land-locked with just a couple of movie theaters for months. Believers were ready for a change of scenery and costumes. California had beaches and plentiful legal marijuana edibles and psychedelics. They wanted to save the universe and preferred to do it in California, where they could move into one of the new tent cities cropping everywhere.

If believers were relieved, reporters and fact-checkers were ecstatic. Most were already packed as they watched the news feeds of the UFO and Bigfoot sightings in Hollywood Hills. In the blink of an eye, everybody had booked flights and rented U-Hauls to get out of the Lake. They were ready to move back to civilization, where they could find a nice bottle of Napa Chardonnay.

## CHAPTER 26

# The Road Goes on Forever

Mac quietly knocked on Faith's front door at eight A.M. It was another beautiful sunny morning. It wasn't hot yet, but he was unsure of his plan. He hadn't called because he knew Faith and Abner would be awake, and he didn't want Faith to hang up on him. She was surprised to see him on her porch.

"Good morning, Faith. You're as beautiful as the morning itself."

"Hello, Mac, what a wonderful surprise. You're looking dashing today, Hero," she said with a big smile. "What're you doing here so early. What's on your mind?"

"I do."

"There you go again, Mac. You're always teasing me. Please don't. I can't take it anymore. It makes me sad."

"No, Faith, I mean it. I do. I want you to be my wife and the mother of our children. I'm going to resign as Sheriff. I want to spend every day of the rest of my life with you. It doesn't matter where life leads us. I want to be with you.

Will you marry me, please?" and then Mac went down on one knee and held out a beautiful diamond engagement ring he had picked out for her. He started to cry, but he wasn't sure why.

Elvis was laying on the porch and groaned about his buddy's display of emotions. 'Come on, old buddy,' he thought, 'Get yourself together, show a little self-control. Why are you promising you'll quit being Sheriff? What about me? What am I supposed to do? All I know is how to be a detective.'

"I can't, Mac. I'm sorry. I'm not going to marry a man without a job and who can't support a big family. We're not cows. We don't eat grass."

Mac was crest-fallen. "I'll find another job, Faith. I'm asking for you to give me a chance. That's all. I can make it work."

"You've got a good job now, Mac. Why would you quit being sheriff? The Lake needs you as its sheriff. Why would you let all of your neighbors down? They voted for you. They need you."

"It's not about them anymore, Faith. It's going to be about us. I won't let anything stand between us anymore. I will put us first from this day forward, and that's how it will be."

"Why, Rob MacGregor, I never knew you were so selfish. Who's going to take care of everyone?"

"I don't understand. You told me you wouldn't marry me if I was sheriff, Faith. You told me I needed to decide what was most important in my life. I've decided. You're the most important person in my life. I'm quitting as soon as I find a replacement. Maybe Snuffy or Barney will be sheriff."

"Do you mean to tell me Barney and Snuffy can keep us as safe as you do? I don't believe it. Are you telling me I'm so selfish I would make you stop being the sheriff of Lincoln County? You mustn't think much of me, Sheriff. If you quit, you'll wonder the rest of your life if you made the right decision, and you might blame me, Mac. I don't want you walking around grumpy blaming me because you're unhappy. It wouldn't work. I know you like being the sheriff. I can see it in your whole being. It's who you are. You love doing what you do."

"No, Faith, I love you. I like my job. I want to make you and our family the center of my world. I'd never second guess my decision if I quit."

"Maybe, Mac, but I couldn't live with myself if you quit because you think I want you to quit. I'd always feel like I made you be someone different than who you are. Besides, a girl has a right to change her mind. Doesn't she?"

"Why? What made you change your mind?"

"Because I realized I fell in love with you, Mac, and you're the Sheriff of Lincoln County. I don't want you to change who you are for me or anybody else. You need to be true to yourself, and then I know you'll be true to me too. If you quit being sheriff, who will stop the crazies from taking over the Lake? Don't you love me enough to protect me, our family, and our neighbors, Mac?"

Mac stood up, grabbed her into his arms for a full-body

embrace, and they kissed as they had never kissed before. Deeply and passionately. Their kiss made Abner blush, so he closed the window curtain and walked away smiling. Even Elvis covered his eyes with his paws.

"I do, and I will, Faith."

•   •   •

As Mac, Snuffy, and Barney surveyed the dam area, it looked like a tornado had blown through. Cardboard houses, trash, and painted graffiti of UFOs and Bigfoot covered every flat surface. Nobody even put their empty plastic water bottles and worn and filthy costumes into piles of trash. They just dropped their garbage where they stood. They had to save the universe, and it was somebody else's job to clean up their collateral trash. They had to spread the word about existential threats.

The best part about the mess was that the stormtroopers, Trekkies, and Chewbaccas had vanished with Spacey and Ducktail in the dark of the night. They were following the Oracle to Hollywood to commune with the UFOs and Bigfoot or whatever they called it in Hollywood. Media flacks couldn't have been happier. TV ratings would go through the roof with sightings in California. Nobody cared what happened in flyover country. The Lake didn't even have a *Planet Hollywood.*

"What the heck happened, Mac? Why'd everyone giddyap out of here so fast?" asked Barney.

"Well, like our good friend Dr. Carl Jung said, Barney, it doesn't matter whether there's UFOs or not, it only matters what the media says about them. Heck, boys, everybody's scared of something, and flying saucers and Bigfoot are pretty darn convenient for the media to use as boogeymen. I'm just glad they found UFOs and Bigfoot to chase in Hollywood. It's going to make our lives a lot easier. Hollywood's been scaring the bejeebers out of people for over a hundred years. Hollywood movies have killed more people than all of the wars put together," laughed Mac. "They'll probably find the Wolfman and Frankenstein hanging out in the Redwoods with Bigfoot and the UFOs."

# Epilogue

Standing in the center of the round stage under a bright spotlight, a beaming and gracious Moonbeam said, "Hello, dear readers. To revive a wonderful Shakespearean tradition, your author, Dennis Ganahl, has asked, moi, the ever-popular, Moonbeam, to deliver this epilogue for his political satire. As the male counterpoint to my theatrical interpretation, Dennis has asked the ever-droll Elvis to join me on stage."

With a gravelly harrumph, Elvis stood, raised his head, and said, "Political satire? It's more like the theatre of the absurd, Moonbeam. Ganahl asked us to do this epilogue because he's tired of writing. He didn't want to pay any more union wages for humans, cryptids, and alien actors. He knows animals get paid the cheapest wages, and we don't have our own union. He's as cheap as a Sears suit. And, don't act like you speak any French. You grew up on a hillbilly farm like me, and you speak hillbilly just like me. Who do you think you are, Miss Piggy? Let's get this over so I can get a cup of real coffee and take a nap."

Showing her disdain for Elvis's uncouth remarks, Moonbeam gave him her cold pork shoulder and continued with her always-in-place smile, knowing the show must go on.

"First things first, book fans. Slim, Harry, and Bubba escaped from southern California without getting caught after creating their dazzling Bigfoot and UFO sightings at the iconic Hollywood sign. They stopped in Las Vegas for a head-banging celebration at Caesar's Palace on the way back to the Lake in their white non-descript Ford van.

They watched the riotous and frenzied news stories from their hot tubs while they sipped Bubba's newest batch of organic bourbon-rye whiskey. Even though everyone had media fatigue, the networks and cable TV stations were afire with hyperbolic stories about the Bigfoot and UFO sighting in Hollywood Hills. Plenty of photos and video footage were verified by the media fact-checkers from the traffic helicopter and stoners on the overlook. You'll notice gentle readers people in California say Sasquatch, Wood Ape, or Skunk Ape interchangeably with Bigfoot. They never say MoMo as we say in hillbilly country."

"What you say may all be true, my porcine ingénue, but what about Sheena? Hubba-hubba! Anybody who has read up to this point wants to know what happened to her. I sure do. I've already found some of her old Bigfoot DVDs at a garage sale."

"Soon enough, my vulgar confrere. While in Las Vegas, Slim became mesmerized by the flashing-colored lights and undulating water fountains up and down The Strip. He went on a non-stop quest to every Vegas casino until he found the perfect home for our new 'Hillbilly, UFO, and Bigfoot Hoedown.' We're opening next month at the MGM, and guess who the star is? Moi! The show's finale features me singing and dancing a square dance number with Slim, Bigfoot, and a short green alien with a whopping-sized head," smiled Moonbeam. She was proud of her exploding fame.

"Now that you've told us about your shooting star, tell us about Mac. He's the real hero in this story. He saved the Lake from all of the crazies, Moonbeam."

"Fair enough, my doleful doggie. Tired of living a monastic life with his sluggish and grumpy bloodhound, Elvis, Mac married the love of his life, the stunning Faith. Her doting father, Abner, was joyful and is building a new home closer to Ironwood. He's dating a widow named, Daisy. She's the new church organist."

"Oh, come on, Moonbeam, don't agitate me, my over-rated co-star. You're telling us the family part of his story. To feel safe, people need to know Mac's still Sheriff of Lincoln County, and I'm still his loyal detective."

"True, but you'll soon be playing a more minor role in Mac's life."

"Oh, yeah, who says, you glorified hammock? Mac and I go way back. We were spotted pups together. Nothing can come between us. Nothing, my aspiring pork chop."

"Well, my petulant pooch, Dennis, our gracious author, has asked me to announce that Faith and Mac are expecting twins next spring, my gloomy sidekick. They're going to have a girl and a boy. After Faith's mother, the daughter will be named Hope, and the boy will be named Elvis." A huge smile grew on Elvis' face. Moonbeam sneered and said, "Just kidding hound dog. The boy will be named "Robert Roy, or Rob Roy for short."

"Twins? One is plenty of anything except for bones and coffee. I'm moving out to the barn. I'll never get any sleep in that house with two yapping pups."

"Sooner than you think, my mournful bow-wow. Now, let's see. Oh yes, Bumsteer has grown as big as Buddha, literally and figuratively. In mongrel speak, he's fatter than the town dog. He moved to Los Angeles and hosts a cable show called Bumsteer's Guide to the Galaxy for the Global News Network. His audience numbers are falling faster than red and orange leaves in the fall. He's also used his celebrity status to open a Bigfoot Pie Shop on Rodeo Drive near his gated Beverly Hills mansion."

"He's built a substantial cult of acolytes and disciples who are praying for aliens to take over Earth. Ducktail's 'Save Bigfoot' crusade is a smashing success based on the number of weekly Bigfoot sightings and adoptions by actresses and actors. Bigfoot has been removed from the endangered species list, but it is against the law to shoot or trap one. Spacey launched his own GoFundMe for his 'Adopt a Bigfoot' non-profit trust fund. Dan Blather never got the news traction he needed to become more than an acolyte. He's still working hard to be relevant and searching for a job as a reporter. Sheena, your love crush, gumshoe, is establishing a Bigfoot Museum with the profits from her new Bigfoot movie series."

"I'll tell everyone about Dottie and Harry. They're my friends. Well, at least Dottie is. Harry never showed me much attention one way or the other," lamented Elvis. Moonbeam showed restraint by not commenting.

"Harry and Dottie bought a luxury fifth-wheel RV and a dually pickup truck to pull it to every national park in the United States. They're traveling until they get tired and decide to go home to the Lake. Harry flies his drone to take vacation videos of the parks. He was posting them on Twitter and YouTube until they were declared incendiary patriotic content and banned. He's moved them to GETTR and Rumble, where they're very popular. Tell everyone about the mayor, the governor, and the senator, Moonbeam. You know the most about pork barrel. I don't have any use for politicians unless I've got them under investigation," laughed Elvis.

"I guess we should report on them, my cranky canine. Mayor Klaxton was re-elected because nobody else wanted the job. Most people figured he wouldn't do much harm because they knew where he lived, and they had Mac. Smugg and Moldy are a different story. Governor Smugg was convicted for stealing pennies off a dead man's eyes and spending campaign contributions on jewelry and vacations.

She hopes she won't be removed from office by the Ethics Committee, which hasn't met in a year. Senator Moldy died. He was so crooked they had to screw him into the ground to bury him. His son is under investigation for selling access to his father by selling his childish artwork to lobbyists for excessive amounts of money. Moldy died denying knowing his son," smirked Moonbeam. "We don't want to end on the political news, droopy. Why don't you tell everyone about Bubba's family?"

"Great idea, porky. Let's end with a huge fireworks display. Hortense doesn't get excited about much and wouldn't walk 10 feet to watch an ant eat a bale of hay, don'chya know. But, when she learned about Sheena humping Bubba's leg, she told him how the cow ate the cabbage. He slept with the hounds until he promised to never put on another Bigfoot costume," snorted Elvis.

"You're barking mad. That's certainly not a General Audience ending, my droll troll, but it will have to do since we're out of pages. We'd like to thank all of this book's real and imagined characters for their fine performances. A big thanks to you, our fine readers, for spending your money and taking your time to read this book.

This book closes with a toast of amber-colored moonshine while Obie Blevens and the Practical Jokers play Hank Williams, Jr.'s song *A Country Boy Can Survive*.

# The Story Behind My Book

I want my books to be life-like so I write about what I know. After I wrote my first novel, I got concerned. People asked me if I had written a memoir. When I re-read it, I understood why they asked. I wrote about people, places and traditions I knew growing up. Mickey, my protagonist, isn't completely me, but he's close enough for horse shoes. It's the same for my other characters too. Each one is an amalgamation of kids I knew and grew up with in St. Ann. No matter how hard a fiction author tries not to do it, they're going to relate their story to people, places and things they know even if it's another century.

*Don't Shoot. We come in Peace.* is my third fiction novel, but my first satire. It's about hillbillies, UFOs, Bigfoot, and journalism.

I know hillbillies. As I mentioned in my dedication, I've got a Hoosier bloodline. Thanks to my Irish/Scottish hillbilly blood, I know how to laugh. I also met hillbillies and worked with them throughout the Lake of the Ozarks and rural mid-Missouri when I was a publisher.

Like everyone else, I don't know diddly about UFOs except what I've seen in movies. I've never met an alien or seen a UFO, but I've seen lots of movies about space like *E.T.* I've also met believers who believe they've seen a UFO, and believe they know more than me.

I know something about Bigfoot, I've seen it and touched it. Bigfoot was the first famous monster truck. It was headquartered in Hazelwood, Missouri near where my mom lived. I don't know squat about a big, hairy Bigfoot or Sasquatch, although I did see *Harry and the Hendersons*. I've never met a Bigfoot, but I've met believers who believe they know a lot more than me.

After my research for this book, I don't claim to know any more about UFOs or Bigfoot than when I started writing this book. I do know a lot more about the people who believe they're experts on UFOs and Bigfoot.

I know a lot about journalism. I learned it from actual journalists not PhDs with little experience. My journalism professors made livings producing newspapers, radio stations, TV stations and magazines. They knew the difference between informing, entertaining and persuading. I've published my own newspapers, worked on others throughout the Midwest, and have three degrees from the world's first journalism school, the University of Missouri School of Journalism. I've taught in three different journalism programs. All of the professors who taught news classes were liberal or very liberal. I only remember a couple of conservatives. They usually taught journalism law.

Dr. John Calhoun Merrill, esteemed author, journalist, scholar, and philosopher was my personal friend and mentor. John taught me the difference between information and propaganda.

I also spent time talking with Ben Bradlee, friend of President John F. Kennedy, and famed executive editor of the *Washington Post* of Watergate and the Pentagon Papers fame. We talked about the future of journalism when he visited Drake University. I also spent a memorable evening on Mizzou's campus with Mike Royko famed columnist for the *Chicago Tribune*. Mike told it like it was. We talked about political corruption and drank beer.

Over the last 45 years as a faculty member, publisher, and student, I've seen a tsunami change in journalism. It ain't pretty, and it ain't journalism. It's propaganda. It's "yellow journalism."

The second most popular question I get asked is, "What inspired you to write this book?"

The core idea for this book, the corruption of the news media, has been germinating over two decades. It sprouted when I heard Carl Bernstein speak at Southern Illinois University-Carbondale, when I was a professor. Bernstein and Woodward became journalism icons, when their stories caught President Nixon in a political scandal. Nixon was hated by the media, and Watergate was blown up to be the worst political scandal in America's history. It's not.

I asked Bernstein a question in a public forum which angered him. My question was, "How do you think celebrity-journalists, like Dan Rather, will change journalism?" He blurted, "Journalists, like Dan Rather, deserve to be paid well." He didn't answer my question.

Bernstein was defensive. He was by definition a celebrity-journalist, which is why I asked my question using Dan Rather as my example. Bernstein was played by Dustin Hoffman in a popular movie, and he had written a book about Watergate. He was being paid to present that night, and was chauffeured to all of his contracted speaking engagements. Is Bernstein a journalist or a celebrity? Can they co-exist? Is his goal to inform, entertain or persuade?

Watergate created an entire generation of mostly liberal reporters planning to hold the powerful elite accountable. In 1979, 51% of the public trusted newspapers. Today, according to Gallup, 16% trust newspapers and just 11% trust television news.

Some claim it's not the media's fault. It's because of the plethora of choices a person has to get news. Others say it's because the media are only concerned about ratings. Many blame the 24/7 news cycle which requires more and more dramatic stories. No matter who or what's to blame, Gallop reports 84% of the public blame the news media for the political divide in America. I agree.

The demise of the Fourth Estate's credibility is an American tragedy.

# Special Request

After you read my book, please take the time to write a brief review on Amazon. You will also see other books I've written which may be of interest. If you want to reach out to me, please follow my author's page on Facebook: **www.facebook.com/dennisganahlauthor**. You can message me directly. Thanks for reading my book, reviewing it. Please tell your friends, and support my political satire on social media.

—Dennis

Buy your copies of my
books today on Amazon.

Made in the USA
Coppell, TX
03 November 2022